SHORT STORIES

OF THE

TRAGEDY AND COMEDY OF LIFE

BY

GUY DE MAUPASSANT

VOL. V

DESMOND PUBLISHING COMPANY

BOSTON   NEW YORK

TABLE OF CONTENTS*

———

———

* At the close of the last Volume will be found a complete list of the French Titles of De Maupassant's writings, with their English equivalents.

(ix)

ILLUSTRATIONS

———

A DUEL

THE war was over. The Germans occupied France. The country was panting like a wrestler lying under the knee of his successful opponent.

The first trains from Paris, after the city's long agony of famine and despair, were making their way to the new frontiers, slowly passing through the country districts and the villages. The passengers gazed through the windows at the ravaged fields and burned hamlets. Prussian soldiers, in their black helmets with brass spikes, were smoking their pipes on horseback or sitting on chairs in front of the houses which were still left standing. Others were working or talking just as if they were members of the families. As you passed through the different towns, you saw entire regiments drilling in the squares, and, in spite of the rumble of the carriage-wheels, you could, every moment, hear the hoarse words of command.

M. Dubuis, who during the entire siege had served as one of the National Guard in Paris, was going to join his wife and daughter, whom he had prudently sent away to Switzerland before the invasion.

Famine and hardship had not diminished the big paunch so characteristic of the rich, peace-loving merchant. He had gone through the terrible events of the past year with sorrowful resignation and bitter complaints at the savagery of men. Now that he was journeying to the frontier at the close of the war, he saw the Prussians for the first time, although he had done his duty at the ramparts, and staunchly mounted guard on cold nights.

He stared with mingled fear and anger at those bearded armed men installed all over French soil as if in their own homes, and he felt in his soul a kind of fever of impotent patriotism even while he yielded to that other instinct of discretion and self-preservation which never leaves us. In the same compartment, two Englishmen, who had come to the country as sight-seers, were gazing around with looks of stolid curiosity. They were both stout also, and kept chatting in their own language, sometimes referring to their guidebook, and reading in loud tones the names of the places indicated.

Suddenly, the train stopped at a little village station, and a Prussian officer jumped up with a great clatter of his saber on the double footboard of the railway-carriage. He was tall, wore a tight-fitting uniform, and his face had a very shaggy aspect. His red hair seemed to be on fire and his long mustache and beard, of a paler color, was stuck out on both sides of his face, which it seemed to cut in two.

The Englishmen at once began staring at him with smiles of newly-awakened interest, while M.

Dubuis made a show of reading a newspaper. He sat crouched in a corner, like a thief in the presence of a gendarme.

The train started again. The Englishmen went on chatting, and looking out for the exact scene of different battles; and, all of a sudden, as one of them stretched out his arm toward the horizon to indicate a village, the Prussian officer remarked in French, extending his long legs and lolling backward:

"We killed a dozen Frenchmen in that village, and took more than a hundred prisoners."

The Englishmen, quite interested, immediately asked:

"Ha! and what is the name of this village?"

The Prussian replied:

"Pharsbourg."

He added: "We caught these French blackguards by the ears."

And he glanced toward M. Dubuis, laughing into his mustache in an insulting fashion.

The train rolled on, always passing through hamlets occupied by the victorious army. German soldiers could be seen along the roads, on the edges of fields, standing in front of gates, or chatting outside *cafés*. They covered the soil like African locusts.

The officer said, with a wave of his hand:

"If I were in command, I'd take Paris, burn everything, and kill everybody. No more France!"

The Englishmen, through politeness, replied simply:

"Ah! yes."

He went on:

"In twenty years, all Europe, all of it, will belong to us. Prussia is more than a match for all of them."

The Englishmen, getting uneasy, said nothing in answer to this. Their faces, which had become impassive, seemed made of wax behind their long whiskers. Then the Prussian officer began to laugh. And then, lolling back, he began to sneer. He sneered at the downfall of France, insulted the prostrate enemy; he sneered at Austria which had been recently conquered; he sneered at the furious but fruitless defense of the departments; he sneered at the Garde Mobile and at the useless artillery. He announced that Bismarck was going to build a city of iron with the captured cannons. And suddenly he pushed his boots against the thigh of M. Dubuis, who turned his eyes away, reddening to the roots of his hair.

The Englishmen seemed to have assumed an air of complete indifference, as if they had found themselves all at once shut up in their own island, far from the din of the world.

The officer took out his pipe, and, looking fixedly at the Frenchman, said:

"You haven't got any tobacco — have you?"

M. Dubuis replied:

"No, Monsieur."

The German said:

"You might go and buy some for me when the train stops next."

And he began laughing afresh, as he added:

"I'll let you have the price of a drink."

The train whistled and slackened its pace. They had reached a station which had been burned down and here there was a regular stop.

The German opened the carriage door, and, catching M. Dubuis by the arm, said:

"Go, and do what I told you — quick, quick!"

A Prussian detachment occupied the station. Other soldiers were looking on from behind wooden gratings. The engine was already getting up steam in order to start off again. Then M. Dubuis hurriedly jumped on the platform, and, in spite of the warnings of the station-master, dashed into the adjoining compartment.

*   *   *   *   *   *   *

He was alone! He tore open his waistcoat, so rapidly did his heart beat, and, panting for breath, he wiped the perspiration off his forehead.

The train drew up at another station. And suddenly the officer appeared at the carriage door, and jumped in, followed close behind by the two Englishmen, who were impelled by curiosity. The German sat facing the Frenchman, and, laughing still, said:

"You did not want to do what I asked you."

M. Dubuis replied: "No, Monsieur."

The train had just left the station, when the officer said:

"I'll cut off your mustache to fill my pipe with." And he put out his hand toward the Frenchman's face.

The Englishmen kept staring in the same impassive fashion with fixed glances. Already the German had caught hold of the mustache and was tugging at it, when M. Dubuis, with a back-stroke of his hand threw back the officer's arm, and, seizing him by the collar, flung him down on the seat. Then, excited to a pitch of fury, with his temples swollen and his eyes glaring, he kept throttling the officer with one hand while with the other clenched, he began to strike him violent blows in the face. The Prussian struggled, tried to draw his saber, and to get a grip, while lying back, of his adversary. But M. Dubuis crushed him with the enormous weight of his stomach, and kept hitting him without taking breath or knowing where his blows fell. Blood flowed down the face of the German, who, choking and with a rattling in his throat, spat forth his broken teeth, and vainly strove to shake off this infuriated man who was killing him.

The Englishmen had got on their feet and came closer in order to see better. They remained standing, full of mirth and curiosity, ready to bet for or against each of the combatants.

And suddenly M. Dubuis, exhausted by his violent efforts, went and resumed his seat without uttering a word.

The Prussian did not attack him, for the savage assault had scared and terrified the officer. When he was able to breathe freely, he said:

"Unless you give me satisfaction with pistols, I will kill you."

M. Dubuis replied:

"Whenever you like. I'm quite ready."

The German said:

"Here is the town of Strasbourg. I'll get two officers to be my seconds, and there will be time before the train leaves the station."

M. Dubuis, who was puffing as much as the engine, said to the Englishmen:

"Will you be my seconds?" They both answered together:

"Oh! yes."

And the train stopped.

In a minute, the Prussian had found two comrades who carried pistols, and they made their way toward the ramparts.

The Englishmen were continually looking at their watches, shuffling their feet, and hurrying on with the preparations, uneasy lest they should be too late for the train.

M. Dubuis had never fired a pistol in his life. They made him stand twenty paces away from his enemy. He was asked:

"Are you ready?"

While he was answering "Yes, Monsieur," he noticed that one of the Englishmen had opened his umbrella in order to keep off the rays of the sun.

A voice gave the word of command.

"Fire!"

M. Dubuis fired at random without minding what he was doing, and he was amazed to see the Prussian staggering in front of him, lifting up his arms, and immediately afterward, falling straight on his face. He had killed the officer.

One of the Englishmen ejaculated "Ah!" quivering with delight, satisfied curiosity, and joyous impatience. The other who still kept his watch in his hand, seized M. Dubuis's arm, and hurried him in double-quick time toward the station, his fellow-countryman counting their steps, with his arms pressed close to his sides: "One! two! one! two!"

And all three marching abreast they rapidly made their way to the station like three grotesque figures in a comic newspaper.

The train was on the point of starting. They sprang into their carriage. Then the Englishmen, taking off their traveling-caps, waved them three times over their heads, exclaiming:

"Hip! hip! hip! hurrah!"

Then gravely, one after the other, they stretched out their right hands to M. Dubuis, and then went back and sat in their own corner.

THE LOVE OF LONG AGO

THE old-fashioned château was built on a wooded height. Tall trees surrounded it with dark greenery; and the vast park extended its vistas here over a deep forest and there over an open plain. Some little distance from the front of the mansion stood a huge stone basin in which marble nymphs were bathing. Other basins arranged in order succeeded each other down as far as the foot of the slope, and a hidden fountain sent cascades dancing from one to the other.

From the manor-house, which preserved the grace of a superannuated coquette, down to the grottos incrusted with shellwork, where slumbered the loves of a bygone age, everything in this antique demesne had retained the physiognomy of former days. Everything seemed to speak still of ancient customs, of the manners of long ago, of faded gallantries, and of the elegant trivialities so dear to our grandmothers.

In a parlor in the style of Louis XV., the walls of which were covered with shepherds courting shepherdesses, beautiful ladies in hoop petticoats, and gallant gentlemen in wigs, a very old woman, who seemed dead as soon as she ceased to move, was almost lying down in a large easy-chair while her thin, mummy-like hands hung down, one at each side of her.

Her eyes were gazing languidly toward the distant horizon as if they sought to follow through the park visions of her youth. Through the open window every now and then came a breath of air laden with the scent of grass and the perfume of flowers. It made her white locks flutter around her wrinkled forehead and old memories sweep through her brain.

Beside her on a tapestried stool, a young girl, with long, fair hair hanging in plaits over her neck, was embroidering an altar-cloth. There was a pensive expression in her eyes, and it was easy to see that, while her agile fingers worked, her brain was busy with thoughts.

But the old lady suddenly turned round her head.

"Berthe," she said, "read something out of the newspapers for me, so that I may still know sometimes what is happening in the world."

The young girl took up a newspaper, and cast a rapid glance over it.

"There is a great deal about politics, grandmamma; am I to pass it by?"

"Yes, yes, darling. Are there no accounts of love affairs? Is gallantry, then, dead in France that they no longer talk about abductions or adventures as they did formerly?"

The girl made a long search through the columns of the newspaper.

"Here is one," she said. "It is entitled, 'A Love-Drama.'"

The old woman smiled through her wrinkles. "Read that for me," she said.

And Berthe commenced. It was a case of vitriol-throwing. A wife, in order to avenge herself on her husband's mistress, had burned her face and eyes. She had left the Assize-Court acquitted, declared to be innocent, amid the applause of the crowd.

The grandmother moved about excitedly in her chair, and exclaimed:

"This is horrible — why, it is perfectly horrible! See whether you can find anything else to read for me, darling."

Berthe again made a search; and further down in the reports of criminal cases at which her attention was still directed. She read:

"'Gloomy Drama. — A shopgirl, no longer young, allowed herself to yield to the embraces of a young man. Then, to avenge herself on her lover, whose heart proved fickle, she shot him with a revolver. The unhappy man is maimed for life. The jury consisted of men of moral character, and took the part of the murderess — regarding her as the victim of illicit love. They honorably acquitted her.'"

This time, the old grandmother appeared quite shocked, and, in a trembling voice, said:

"Why, you are mad, then, nowadays. You are mad! The good God has given you love, the only allurement in life. Man has added to this gallantry, the only distraction of our dull hours, and here are you mixing up with it vitriol and revolvers, as if one were to put mud into a flagon of Spanish wine."

Berthe did not seem to understand her grandmother's indignation.

"But, grandmamma, this woman avenged herself. Remember, she was married, and her husband deceived her."

The grandmother gave a start.

"What ideas have they been putting into the heads of you young girls of to-day?"

Berthe replied:

"But marriage is sacred, grandmamma."

The grandmother's heart, which had its birth in the great age of gallantry, gave a sudden leap.

"It is love that is sacred," she said. "Listen, child, to an old woman who has seen three generations and who has had a long, long experience of men and women. Marriage and love have nothing in common. We marry to found a family, and we form families in order to constitute society. Society cannot dispense with marriage. If society is a chain, each family is a link in that chain. In order to weld those links, we always seek for metals of the same kind. When we marry, we must bring together suitable conditions; we must combine fortunes, unite similar races, and aim at the common interests, which are riches and children. We marry only once, my child, because the world requires us to do so, but we may love twenty times in one lifetime because nature has made us able to do this. Marriage, you see, is law, and love is an instinct, which impels us sometimes along a straight and sometimes along a crooked path. The world has made laws to combat our instincts— it was necessary to make them; but our instincts are always stronger, and we ought not to resist them too much, because they come from God, while the laws only come from men. If we did not perfume life with love, as much love as possible, darling, as we put sugar into drugs for children, nobody would care to take it just as it is."

Berthe opened her eyes widely in astonishment. She murmured:

"Oh! grandmamma, we can only love once."

The grandmother raised her trembling hands toward Heaven, as if again to invoke the defunct god of gallantries. She exclaimed indignantly:

"You have become a race of serfs, a race of common people. Since the Revolution, it is impossible any longer to recognize society. You have attached big words to every action, and wearisome duties to every corner of existence; you believe in equality and eternal passion. People have written verses telling you that people have died of love. In my time, verses were written to teach men to love every woman. And we!—when we liked a gentleman, my child, we sent him a page. And when a fresh caprice came into our hearts, we were not slow in getting rid of the last lover—unless we kept both of them."

The old woman smiled with a keen smile, and a gleam of roguery twinkled in her gray eye, the sprightly, sceptical roguery of those people who did not believe that they were made of the same clay as the others, and who lived as rulers for whom common restrictions were not made.

The young girl, turning very pale, faltered out:

"So, then, women have no honor."

The grandmother ceased to smile. If she had kept in her soul some of Voltaire's irony, she had also a little of Rousseau's glowing philosophy: "No honor! because we loved, and dared to say so, and even

boasted of it? But, my child, if one of us, among
the greatest ladies in France, were to live without a
lover, she would have the entire court laughing at
her. Those who wished to live differently had only
to enter a convent. And you imagine perhaps that
your husbands will love you alone all their lives. As
if, indeed, this could be the case. I tell you that
marriage is a thing necessary in order that society
should exist, but it is not in the nature of our race,
do you understand? There is only one good thing
in life, and that is love. And how you misunder-
stand it! how you spoil it! You treat it as something solemn, like a sacrament, or something to be
bought, like a dress."

The young girl caught the old woman's trembling
hands in her own.

"Hold your tongue, I beg of you, grandmamma!"

And, on her knees, with tears in her eyes, she
prayed to Heaven to bestow on her a great passion,
one eternal passion alone, in accordance with the
dream of modern poets, while the grandmother, kissing her on the forehead, still penetrated by that
charming, healthy logic by which the philosophers of
gallantry sprinkled salt upon the life of the eighteenth
century, murmured:

"Take care, my poor darling! If you believe in
such follies as this, you will be very unhappy."

THE FARMER'S WIFE

ONE day Baron René du Treilles said to me:

"Will you come and open the hunting season with me in my farmhouse at Marinville? By doing so, my dear fellow, you will give me the greatest pleasure. Besides, I am all alone. This will be a hard hunting-bout, to start with, and the house where I sleep is so primitive that I can only bring my most intimate friends there."

I accepted his invitation. So on Saturday we started by the railway-line running into Normandy, and alighted at the station of Alvimare. Baron René, pointing out to me a country jaunting-car drawn by a restive horse, driven by a big peasant with white hair, said to me:

"Here is our equipage, my dear boy."

The man extended his hand to his landlord, and the Baron pressed it warmly, asking:

"Well, Maître Lebrument, how are you?"

"Always the same, M'sieu l' Baron."

We jumped into this hencoop suspended and shaken on two immense wheels. The young horse, after a violent swerve, started into a gallop, flinging us into the air like balls. Every fall backward on to the wooden bench gave me the most dreadful pain.

The peasant kept repeating in his calm, monotonous voice:

"There, there! it's all right, all right, Moutard, all right!"

But Moutard scarcely heard and kept scampering along like a goat.

Our two dogs, behind us, in the empty part of the hencoop, stood erect and sniffed the air of the plains as if they could smell the game.

The Baron gazed into the distance, with a sad eye. The vast Norman landscape, undulating and melancholy as an immense English park, with farmyards surrounded by two or four rows of trees and full of dwarfed apple-trees which rendered the houses invisible, gave a vista, as far as the eye could see, of old forest-trees, tufts of wood and hedgerows, which artistic gardeners provide for when they are tracing the lines of princely estates.

And René de Treilles suddenly exclaimed:

"I love this soil; I have my very roots in it."

A pure Norman, tall and strong, with the more or less projecting paunch of the old race of adventurers who went to found kingdoms on the shores of every ocean, he was about fifty years of age, ten years less perhaps than the farmer who was driving us. The latter was a lean peasant, all skin and bone, one of those men who live a hundred years.

After two hours' traveling over stony roads, across that green and monotonous plain, the vehicle entered one of those fruit-gardens which adorn the fronts of farmhouses, and drew up before an old structure falling into decay, where an old maid-servant stood waiting at the side of a young fellow who seized the horse's bridle.

We entered the farmhouse. The smoky kitchen was high and spacious. The copper utensils and the earthenware glistened under the reflection of the big fire. A cat lay asleep under the table. Within, you inhaled the odor of milk, of apples, of smoke, that indescribable smell peculiar to old houses where peasants have lived — the odor of the soil, of the walls, of furniture, of stale soup, of washing, and of the old inhabitants, the smell of animals and human beings intermingled, of things and of persons, the odor of time and of things that have passed away.

I went out to have a look at the farmyard. It was big, full of old apple-trees dwarfed and crooked, and laden with fruit which fell on the grass around them. In this farmyard the smell of apples was as strong as that of the orange-trees which blossom on the banks of southern rivers.

Four rows of beeches surrounded this inclosure. They were so tall that they seemed to touch the clouds, at this hour of nightfall, and their summits, through which the night winds passed, shook and sang a sad, interminable song.

I re-entered the house. The Baron was warming his feet at the fire, and was listening to the farmer's talk about country matters. He talked about marriages, births, and deaths, then about the fall in the price of corn and the latest news about the selling value of cattle. The "Veularde" (as he called a cow that had been bought at the fair of Veules) had calved in the middle of June. The cider had not been first-class last year. The apricot-apples were almost disappearing from the country.

Then we had dinner. It was a good rustic meal, simple and abundant, long and tranquil. And while we were dining, I noticed the special kind of friendly familiarity between the Baron and the peasant which had struck me from the start.

Without, the beeches continued sobbing in the nightwind, and our two dogs, shut up in a shed, were whining and howling in uncanny fashion. The fire was dying out in the big grate. The maid-servant had gone to bed. Maître Lebrument said in his turn:

"If you don't mind, M'sieu l' Baron, I'm going to bed. I am not used to staying up late."

The Baron extended his hand toward him and said: "Go, my friend," in so cordial a tone that I said, as soon as the man had disappeared:

"He is devoted to you, this farmer?"

"Better than that, my dear fellow! It is a drama, an old drama, simple and very sad, that attaches him to me. Here is the story:

"You know that my father was a colonel in a cavalry regiment. His orderly was this young fellow, now an old man, the son of a farmer. Then, when my father retired from the army, he took this retired soldier, then about forty, as his servant. I was at that time about thirty. We lived then in our old château of Valrenne, near Caudebec-in-Caux.

"At this period, my mother's chambermaid was one of the prettiest girls you could see, fair-haired, slender, and sprightly in manner, a genuine specimen of the fascinating Abigail, such as we scarcely ever find nowadays. To-day these creatures spring up into hussies before their time. Paris, with the aid of the railways, attracts them, calls them, takes hold of them, as soon as they are bursting into woman-hood — these little wenches who, in old times, re-mained simple maid-servants. Every man passing by, as long ago recruiting sergeants did with conscripts, entices and debauches them — foolish lassies — till now we have only the scum of the female sex for servant-maids, all that is dull, nasty, common, and ill-formed, too ugly even for gallantry.

"Well, this girl was charming, and I often gave her a kiss in dark corners — nothing more, I swear to you! She was virtuous, besides; and I had some respect for my mother's house, which is more than can be said of the blackguards of the present day.

"Now it happened that my father's man-servant, the ex-soldier, the old farmer you have just seen, fell in love with this girl, but in an unusual sort of way. The first thing we noticed was that his memory was affected; he did not pay attention to anything.

"My father was incessantly saying: 'Look here, Jean! What's the matter with you? Are you un-well?'

"'No, no, M'sieu l' Baron. There's nothing the matter with me.'

"Jean got thin. Then, when serving at table, he broke glasses and let plates fall. We thought he must have been attacked by some nervous malady, and we sent for the doctor, who thought he could detect symptoms of spinal disease. Then my father, full of anxiety about his faithful man-servant, decided to place him in a private hospital. When the poor fellow heard of my father's intentions, he made a clean breast of it.

"'M'sieu l' Baron—'

"'Well, my boy?'

"'You see, the thing I want is not physic.'

"'Ha! what is it, then?'

"'It's marriage!'

"My father turned round and stared at him in astonishment.

"'What's that you say—eh?'

"'It's marriage.'

"'Marriage? So then, you donkey, you're in love.'

"'That's how it is, M'sieu l' Baron.'

"And my father began to laugh in such an immoderate fashion that my mother called out through the wall of the next room:

"'What in the name of goodness is the matter with you, Gontran?'

"My father replied:

"'Come here, Catherine.'

"And, when she came in, he told, with tears in his eyes from sheer laughter, that his idiot of a servant-man was love-sick.

"But my mother, instead of laughing, was deeply affected.

"'Who is it that you have fallen in love with, my poor fellow?' she asked.

"He answered, without hesitation:

"'With Louise, Madame la Baronne.'

"My mother said, with the utmost gravity: 'We must try to arrange the matter the best way we can.'

"So Louise was sent for, and questioned by my mother. She said in reply that she knew all about Jean's liking for her, that in fact Jean had spoken to her about it several times, but that she did not want him. She refused to say why.

"And two months elapsed during which my father and mother never ceased to urge this girl to marry Jean. As she declared she was not in love with any other man, she could not give any serious reason for her refusal. My father, at last, overcame her resistance by means of a big present of money, and started the pair of them on a farm on the estate—this very farm. At the end of three years, I learned that Louise had died of consumption. But my father and my mother died, too, in their turn, and it was two years more before I found myself face to face with Jean.

"At last, one autumn day, about the end of October, the idea came into my head to go hunting on this part of my estate, which my tenant had told me was full of game.

"So, one evening, one wet evening, I arrived at this house. I was shocked to find the old soldier who had been my father's servant perfectly white-haired, though he was not more than forty-five or forty-six years of age. I made him dine with me, at the very table where we're now sitting. It was raining hard. We could hear the rain battering at the roof, the walls, and the windows, flowing in a perfect deluge into the farmyard; and my dog was howling in the shed where the other dogs are howling to-night.

"All of a sudden, when the servant-maid had gone to bed, the man said in a timid voice:

"'M'sieu l' Baron.'

"'What is it, my dear Jean?'

"'I have something to tell you.'

"'Tell it, my dear Jean.'

"'You remember Louise, my wife?'

"'Certainly, I do remember her.'

"'Well, she left me a message for you.'

"'What was it?'

"'A—a—well, it was what you might call a confession.'

"'Ha! And what was it about?'

"'It was—it was—I'd rather, all the same, tell you nothing about it—but I must—I must. Well, it's this—it wasn't consumption she died of at all. It was grief—well, that's the long and the short of it. As soon as she came to live here, after we were married, she grew thin; she changed so that you wouldn't know her at the end of six months—no, you wouldn't know her, M'sieu l' Baron. It was all just as before I married her, but it was different, too, quite another sort of thing.

"'I sent for the doctor. He said it was her liver that was affected—he said it was what he called a "hepatic" complaint—I don't know these big words M'sieu l' Baron. Then I bought medicine for her, heaps on heaps of bottles, that cost about three hundred francs. But she'd take none of them; she wouldn't have them; she said: "It's no use, my poor Jean; it wouldn't do me any good." I saw well that she had some hidden trouble; and then I found her one time crying, and I didn't know what to do

— no, I didn't know what to do. I bought caps and
dresses and hair-oil and earrings for her. No good!
And I saw that she was going to die. And so one
night in the end of November, one snowy night,
after remaining the whole day without stirring out of
the bed, she told me to send for the curé. So I went
for him. As soon as he had come, she saw him.
Then, she asked him to let me come into the room,
and she said to me: "Jean, I'm going to make a
confession to you. I owe it to you, Jean. I have
never been false to you, never!—never, before or
after you married me. M'sieu le Curé is there, and
can tell it is so, and he knows my soul. Well, listen,
Jean. If I am dying, it is because I was not able to
console myself for leaving the château—because—I
was too—too fond of the young Baron, Monsieur
René—too fond of him, mind you, Jean,—there was
no harm in it! This is the thing that's killing me.
When I could see him no more, I felt that I should
die. If I could only have seen him, I might have
lived; only seen him, nothing more. I wish you'd
tell it to him some day, by-and-by, when I am no
longer there. You will tell him—swear you will,
Jean—swear it in the presence of M'sieu le Curé! It
will console me to know that he will know it one
day—that this was the cause of my death! Swear it!"

"'Well, I gave her my promise, M'sieu l' Baron! and,
on the faith of an honest man, I have kept my word.'

"And then he ceased speaking, his eyes filling
with tears.

*   *   *   *   *   *   *

"Upon my soul, my dear boy, you can't form any
idea of the emotion that filled me when I heard this

poor devil, whose wife I had caused the death of without knowing it, telling me this story on that wet night in this very kitchen.

"I exclaimed: 'Ah! my poor Jean! my poor Jean!'

"He murmured: 'Well, that's all, M'sieu l' Baron. I could do nothing, one way or another — and now it's all over!'

"I caught his hand across the table, and I began to cry.

"He asked: 'Will you come and see her grave?' I nodded by way of assent, for I couldn't speak. He rose up, lighted a lantern, and we walked through the blinding rain which, in the light of the lamp, looked like falling arrows.

"He opened a gate, and I saw some crosses of blackwood.

"Suddenly, he said: 'There it is, in front of a marble slab,' and he flashed the lantern close to it so that I could read the inscription:

> "'To Louise-Hortense Marinet,
> Wife of *Jean-François Lebrument, farmer*.
> She was a faithful Wife! God rest her Soul!'

"We fell on our knees in the damp grass, he and I, with the lantern between us, and I saw the rain beating on the white marble slab. And I thought of the heart of her sleeping there in her grave. Ah! poor heart! poor heart!

* * * * * * *

"Since then, I have been coming here every year. And I don't know why, but I feel as if I were guilty of some crime in the presence of this man who always shows that he forgives me!"

BESIDE A DEAD MAN

HE WAS slowly dying, as consumptives die. I saw him sitting down every day at two o'clock under the windows of the hotel, facing the tranquil sea, on an open-air bench. He remained for some time without moving, in the heat of the sun, gazing mournfully at the Mediterranean. Every now and then he cast a glance at the lofty mountain with vaporous summits which shuts in Mentone; then, with a very slow movement, he crossed his long legs, so thin that they seemed two bones, around which fluttered the cloth of his trousers, and opened a book, which was always the same. And then he did not stir any more, but read on, read on with his eye and with his mind; all his poor expiring body seemed to read, all his soul plunged, lost itself, disappeared, in this book, up to the hour when the cool air made him cough a little. Then he got up and re-entered the hotel.

He was a tall German, with a fair beard, who breakfasted and dined in his own room, and spoke to nobody.

A vague curiosity attracted me to him. One day, I sat down by his side, having taken up a book, too, to keep up appearances, a volume of Musset's poems.

And I began to run through "Rolla."

Suddenly, my neighbor said to me, in good French:

"Do you know German, Monsieur?"

"Not at all, Monsieur."

"I am sorry for that. Since chance has thrown us side by side, I could have lent you, I could have shown you, an inestimable thing — this book which I hold in my hand."

"What is it, pray?"

"It is a copy of my master, Schopenhauer, annotated with his own hand. All the margins, as you may see, are covered with his handwriting."

I took the book from him reverently, and I gazed at those forms incomprehensible to me, but which revealed the immortal thoughts of the greatest shatterer of dreams who had ever dwelt on earth.

And Musset's verses arose in my memory:

"Hast thou found out, Voltaire, that it is bliss to die,
  Or does thy hideous smile over thy bleached bones fly?"

And involuntarily I compared the childish sarcasm, the religious sarcasm, of Voltaire with the irresistible irony of the German philosopher whose influence is henceforth ineffaceable.

Let us protest and let us be angry, let us be indignant or let us be enthusiastic. Schopenhauer has marked humanity with the seal of his disdain and of his disenchantment. A disabused pleasure-seeker, he overthrew beliefs, hopes, poetic ideals, and chimeras, destroyed the aspirations, ravaged the confidence of souls, killed love, dragged down the chivalrous worship of woman, crushed the illusions of hearts, and accomplished the most gigantic task ever attempted by scepticism. He passed over everything with his mocking spirit, and left everything empty. And even to-day those who execrate him seem to carry portions of his thought, in spite of themselves, in their own souls.

"So, then, you were intimately acquainted with Schopenhauer?" I said to the German.

He smiled sadly.

"Up to the time of his death, Monsieur."

And he spoke to me about the philosopher, and told me about the almost supernatural impression which this strange being made on all who came near him.

He gave me an account of the interview of the old iconoclast with a French politician, a *doctrinaire* Republican, who wanted to get a glimpse of this man, and found him in a noisy tavern, seated in the midst of his disciples, dry, wrinkled, laughing with an unforgettable laugh, eating and tearing ideas and beliefs with a single word, as a dog tears with one bite of his teeth the tissues with which he plays.

He repeated for me the comment of this Frenchman as he went away, scared and terrified: "I thought that I had spent an hour with the devil."

Then he added:

"He had, indeed, Monsieur, a frightful smile, which terrified us even after his death. I can tell you an anecdote about it not generally known, if it has any interest for you."

And he began, in a tired voice, interrupted by frequent fits of coughing:

"Schopenhauer had just died, and it was arranged that we should watch, in turn, two by two, till morning.

"He was lying in a large apartment, very simple, vast, and gloomy. Two wax-candles were burning on the bedside stand.

"It was midnight when I took up my task of watching along with one of our comrades. The two friends whom we replaced had left the apartment, and we came and sat down at the foot of the bed.

"The face was not changed. It was laughing. That pucker which we knew so well lingered still around the corners of the lips, and it seemed to us that he was about to open his eyes, to move, and to speak. His thought, or rather his thoughts, enveloped us. We felt ourselves more than ever in the atmosphere of his genius, absorbed, possessed by him. His domination seemed to us even more sovereign now that he was dead. A sense of mystery was blended with the power of this incomparable spirit.

"The bodies of these men disappear, but they remain themselves; and in the night which follows the stoppage of their heart's beating, I assure you, Monsieur, they are terrifying.

"And in hushed tones we talked about him, recalling to mind certain sayings, certain formulas of his, those startling maxims which are like jets of flame flung, by means of some words, into the darkness of the Unknown Life.

"'It seems to me that he is going to speak,' said my comrade. And we stared with uneasiness bordering on fear at the motionless face with its eternal laugh. Gradually, we began to feel ill at ease, oppressed, on the point of fainting. I faltered:

"'I don't know what is the matter with me, but, I assure you I am not well.'

"And at that moment we noticed that there was an unpleasant odor from the corpse.

"Then, my comrade suggested that we should go into the adjoining room, and leave the door open; and I assented to this proposal.

"I took one of the wax-candles which burned on the bedside stand, and I left the second behind. Then we went and sat down at the other end of the adjoining apartment, so as to be able to see from where we were the bed and the corpse clearly revealed by the light.

"But he still held possession of us. One would have said that his immaterial essence, liberated, free, all-powerful, and dominating, was flitting around us. And sometimes, too, the dreadful smell of the decomposing body came toward us and penetrated us, sickening and indefinable.

"Suddenly a shiver passed through our bones: a sound, a slight sound, came from the death-chamber. Immediately we fixed our glances on him, and we saw, yes, Monsieur, we saw distinctly, both of us, something white flying over the bed, falling on the carpet, and vanishing under an armchair.

"We were on our feet before we had time to think of anything, distracted by stupefying terror, ready to run away. Then we stared at each other. We were horribly pale. Our hearts throbbed so fiercely that our clothes swelled over our chests. I was the first to speak.

" 'You saw?'

" 'Yes, I saw.'

" 'Can it be that he is not dead?'

" 'Why not, when the body is putrefying?'

" 'What are we to do?'

"My companion said in a hesitating tone:

" 'We must go and look.'

"I took our wax-candle and I entered first, searching with my eye through all the large apartment with its dark corners. There was not the least movement now, and I approached the bed. But I stood transfixed with stupor and fright: Schopenhauer was no longer laughing! He was grinning in a horrible fashion, with his lips pressed together and deep hollows in his cheeks. I stammered out:

" 'He is not dead!'

"But the terrible odor rose up to my nose and stifled me. And I no longer moved, but kept staring fixedly at him, scared as if in the presence of an apparition. Then my companion, having seized the other wax-candle, bent forward. Then, he touched my arm without uttering a word. I followed his glance, and I saw on the floor, under the arm-chair by the side of the bed, all white on the dark carpet, open as if to bite, Schopenhauer's set of artificial teeth.

"The work of decomposition, loosening the jaws, had made it jump out of the mouth.

"I was really frightened that day, Monsieur."

And as the sun was sinking toward the glittering sea, the consumptive German rose from his seat, gave me a parting bow, and retired into the hotel.

A QUEER NIGHT IN PARIS

Maître Saval, notary at Vernon, was passionately fond of music. Still young, though already bald, always carefully shaved, a little corpulent, as was fitting, wearing a gold *pince-nez* instead of old-fashioned spectacles, active, gallant, and joyous, he passed in Vernon for an artist. He thrummed on the piano and played on the violin, and gave musical evenings where interpretations were given of new operas.

He had even what is called a bit of a voice; nothing but a bit, a very little bit of a voice; but he managed it with so much taste that cries of "Bravo!" "Exquisite!" "Surprising!" "Adorable!" issued from every throat as soon as he had murmured the last note.

He was a subscriber to a music publisher in Paris, who sent all new pieces to him. From time to time to the high society of the town he sent little notes something in this style:

"You are invited to be present on Monday evening at the house of M. Saval, notary, Vernon, at the first production of 'Sais.'"

A few officers, gifted with good voices, formed the chorus. Two or three of the vinedressers' families also sang. The notary filled the part of leader of the orchestra with so much skill that the band-master of the 190th regiment of the line said one day, at the Café de l'Europe:

"Oh! M. Saval is a master. It is a great pity that he did not adopt the career of an artist."

When his name was mentioned in a drawing-room, there was always somebody found to declare: "He is not an amateur; he is an artist, a genuine artist." And two or three persons would repeat, in a tone of profound conviction: "Oh! yes, a genuine artist," laying particular stress on the word "genuine."

Every time that a new work was interpreted at a big Parisian theater, M. Saval paid a visit to the capital. Last year, according to his custom, he went to hear "Henry VIII." He then took the express which arrives in Paris at 4:30 P. M., intending to return by the 12:35 A. M. train so as not to have to sleep at a hotel. He had put on evening dress, a black coat and white tie, which he concealed under his overcoat with the collar turned up.

As soon as he had planted his foot on the Rue d' Amsterdam, he felt in quite a jovial mood, and said to himself:

"Decidedly the air of Paris does not resemble any other air. It has in it something indescribably stimulating, exciting, intoxicating, which fills you with a strange longing to gambol and to do many other things. As soon as I arrive here, it seems to me, all of a sudden, that I have taken a bottle of champagne. What a life one can lead in this city in the midst of artists! Happy are the elect, the great men who enjoy renown in such a city! What an existence is theirs!"

And he made plans; he would have liked to know some of those celebrated men, to talk about them in Vernon, and to spend an evening with them from time to time in Paris.

But suddenly an idea struck him. He had heard allusions to little *cafés* in the outer boulevards at which well-known painters, men of letters, and even musicians gathered, and he proceeded to go up toward Montmartre at a slow pace.

He had two hours before him. He wanted to have a look round. He passed in front of taverns frequented by belated Bohemians, gazing at the different faces, seeking to discover the artists. Finally, he came to the sign of "The Dead Rat," and, allured by the name, he entered.

Five or six women, with their elbows resting on the marble tables, were talking in low tones about their love affairs, the quarrels of Lucie with Hortense, and the scoundrelism of Octave. They were no longer young, but were fat or thin, tired out, used up. You could see that they were almost bald; and they drank bocks like men.

M. Saval sat down at some distance from them, and waited, for the hour for taking absinthe was at hand.

A tall young man soon came in and took a seat beside him. The landlady called him "M. Romantin."

5 G. de M.—3

The notary quivered. Was this the Romantin who had taken a medal at the last Salon?

The young man made a sign to the waiter:

"You will bring up my dinner at once, and then carry to my new studio, 15, Boulevard de Clichy, thirty bottles of beer and the ham I ordered this morning. We are going to have a housewarming."

M. Saval immediately ordered dinner. Then he took off his overcoat, so that his dress coat and his white tie could be seen. His neighbor did not seem to notice him. He had taken up a newspaper, and was reading it. M. Saval glanced sideways at him, burning with the desire to speak to him.

Two young men entered, in red velvet, and peaked beards in the fashion of Henry III. They sat down opposite Romantin.

The first of the pair said:

"It is for this evening?"

Romantin pressed his hand.

"I believe you, old chap, and everyone will be there. I have Bonnat, Guillemet, Gervex, Béraud, Hébert, Duez, Clairin, and Jean-Paul Laurens. It will be a glorious blowout! And women, too! Wait till you see! Every actress without exception — of course I mean, you know, all those who have nothing to do this evening."

The landlord of the establishment came across.

"Do you often have this housewarming?"

The painter replied:

"Certainly — every three months, each quarter."

M. Saval could not restrain himself any longer, and in a hesitating voice said:

"I beg your pardon for intruding on you, Monsieur, but I heard your name pronounced, and I would be very glad to know if you really are M. Romantin whose work in the last Salon I have so much admired."

The painter answered:

"I am the very person, Monsieur."

The notary then paid the artist a very well-turned compliment, showing that he was a man of culture. The painter, gratified, thanked him politely in reply. Then they chatted. Romantin returned to the subject of his housewarming, going into details as to the magnificence of the forthcoming entertainment.

M. Saval questioned him as to all the men he was going to receive, adding:

"It would be an extraordinary piece of good fortune for a stranger, to meet at one time, so many celebrities assembled in the studio of an artist of your rank."

Romantin, overcome, answered: "If it would be agreeable to you, come."

M. Saval accepted the invitation with enthusiasm, reflecting:

"I'll always have time enough to see 'Henry VIII.'"

Both of them had finished their meal. The notary insisted on paying the two bills, wishing to repay his neighbor's civilities. He also paid for the drinks of the young fellows in red velvet; then he left the establishment with the painter.

They stopped in front of a very long house, by no means high, the first story of which had the appearance of an interminable conservatory. Six studios stood in a row with their fronts facing the boulevards.

Romantin was the first to enter. Ascending the stairs, he opened a door, and lighted a match and then a candle.

They found themselves in an immense apartment, the furniture of which consisted of three chairs, two easels, and a few sketches lying on the floor along the walls. M. Saval remained standing at the door in a stupefied state of mind.

The painter remarked:

"Here you are! We've got to the spot; but everything has yet to be done."

Then, examining the high, bare apartment, whose ceiling was veiled in shadows he said:

"We might make a great deal out of this studio."

He walked round it, surveying it with the utmost attention, then went on:

"I have a mistress who might easily give us a helping hand. Women are incomparable for hanging drapery. But I sent her to the country for to-day in order to get her off my hands this evening. It is not that she bores me, but she is too much lacking in the ways of good society. It would be embarrassing to my guests."

He reflected for a few seconds, and then added:

"She is a good girl, but not easy to deal with. If she knew that I was holding a reception, she would tear out my eyes."

M. Saval had not even moved; he did not understand.

The artist came over to him.

"Since I have invited you, you are going to give me some help."

The notary said emphatically:

"Make any use of me you please. I am at your disposal."

Romantin took off his jacket.

"Well, citizen, to work! We are first going to clean up."

He went to the back of the easel, on which there was a canvas representing a cat, and seized a very worn-out broom.

"I say! Just brush up while I look after the lighting."

M. Saval took the broom, inspected it, and then began to sweep the floor very awkwardly, raising a whirlwind of dust.

Romantin, disgusted, stopped him: "Deuce take it! you don't know how to sweep the floor! Look at me!"

And he began to roll before him a heap of grayish sweepings, as if he had done nothing else all his life. Then he gave back the broom to the notary, who imitated him.

In five minutes, such a cloud of dust filled the studio that Romantin asked:

"Where are you? I can't see you any longer."

M. Saval, who was coughing, came nearer to him. The painter said to him:

"How are you going to manage to get up a chandelier."

The other, stunned, asked:

"What chandelier?"

"Why, a chandelier to light—a chandelier with wax-candles."

The notary did not understand.

He answered: "I don't know."

The painter began to jump about, cracking his fingers.

"Well, Monseigneur, I have found out a way."

Then he went more calmly:

"Have you got five francs about you?"

M. Saval replied:

"Why, yes."

The artist said:

"Well! you'll go and buy for me five francs' worth of wax-candles while I go and see the cooper."

And he pushed the notary in his evening coat into the street. At the end of five minutes, they had returned, one of them with the wax-candles, and the other with the hoop of a cask. Then Romantin plunged his hand into a cupboard, and drew forth twenty empty bottles, which he fixed in the form of a crown around the hoop. He then came down, and went to borrow a ladder from the doorkeeper, after having explained that he had obtained the favors of the old woman by painting the portrait of her cat exhibited on the easel.

When he mounted the ladder, he said to M. Saval:

"Are you active?"

The other, without understanding answered:

"Why, yes."

"Well, you just climb up there, and fasten this chandelier for me to the ring of the ceiling. Then you must put a wax-candle in each bottle, and light it. I tell you I have a genius for lighting up. But off with your coat, damn it! you are just like a Jeames."

The door was opened violently. A woman appeared, with her eyes flashing, and remained standing on the threshold. Romantin gazed at her with a look of terror. She waited some seconds, crossed her arms over her breast, and then in a shrill, vibrating, exasperated voice said:

"Ha! you villain, is this the way you leave me?"

Romantin made no reply. She went on:

"Ha! you scoundrel! You are again doing the swell, while you pack me off to the country. You'll soon see the way I'll settle your jollification. Yes, I'm going to receive your friends."

She grew warmer:

"I'm going to slap their faces with the bottles and the wax-candles."

Romantin uttered one soft word:

"Mathilde."

But she did not pay any attention to him; she went on:

"Wait a little, my fine fellow! wait a little!"

Romantin went over to her, and tried to take her by the hands:

"Mathilde."

But she was now fairly under way; and on she went, emptying the vials of her wrath with strong words and reproaches. They flowed out of her mouth, like a stream sweeping a heap of filth along with it. The words hurled out seemed struggling for exit. She stuttered, stammered, yelled, suddenly recovering her voice to cast forth an insult or a curse.

He seized her hands without her having even noticed it. She did not seem to see anything, so much occupied was she in holding forth and relieving her heart. And suddenly she began to weep. The tears flowed from her eyes without making her stem the tide of her complaints. But her words had taken a howling, shrieking tone; they were a continuous cry interrupted by sobbings. She commenced afresh twice or three times, till she stopped as if something were choking her, and at last she ceased with a regular flood of tears.

Then he clasped her in his arms and kissed her hair, himself affected.

"Mathilde, my little Mathilde, listen. You must be reasonable. You know, if I give a supper party to my friends, it is to thank these gentlemen for the medal I got at the Salon. I cannot receive women. You ought to understand that. It is not the same with artists as with other people."

She stammered in the midst of her tears:

"Why didn't you tell me this?"

He replied:

"It was in order not to annoy you, not to give you pain. Listen, I'm going to see you home. You will be very sensible, very nice; you will remain quietly waiting for me in bed, and I'll come back as soon as it's over."

She murmured:

"Yes, but you will not begin over again?"

"No, I swear to you!"

He turned toward M. Saval, who had at last hooked on the chandelier:

"My dear friend, I am coming back in five minutes. If anyone arrives in my absence, do the honors for me, will you not?"

And he carried off Mathilde, who kept drying her eyes with her handkerchief as she went along.

Left to himself, M. Saval succeeded in putting everything around him in order. Then he lighted the wax-candles and waited.

He waited for a quarter of an hour, half an hour, an hour. Romantin did not return. Then, suddenly, there was a dreadful noise on the stairs, a song shouted out in chorus by twenty mouths and a regular march like that of a Prussian regiment. The whole house was shaken by the steady tramp of feet. The door flew open, and a motley throng appeared — men and women in a row, holding one another arm in arm, in pairs, and kicking their heels on the floor, in proper time — advancing into the studio like a snake uncoiling itself. They howled:

> "Come, let us all be merry,
> Pretty maids and soldiers gay!"

M. Saval, thunderstruck, remained standing in evening dress under the chandelier. The procession of revellers caught sight of him, and uttered a shout:

"À Jeames! À Jeames!"

And they began whirling round him, surrounding him with a circle of vociferation. Then they took each other by the hand and went dancing about madly.

He attempted to explain:

"Messieurs — Messieurs — Mesdames —"

But they did not listen to him. They whirled about, they jumped, they brawled.

At last the dancing ceased. M. Saval uttered the word:

"Messieurs —"

A tall young fellow, fair-haired and bearded to the nose, interrupted him:

"What's your name, my friend?"

The notary, quite scared, said:

"I am M. Saval."

A voice exclaimed:

"You mean Baptiste."

A woman said:

"Let the poor waiter alone! You'll end by making him get angry. He's paid to attend on us, and not to be laughed at by us."

Then, M. Saval noticed that each guest had brought his own provisions. One held a bottle of wine, another a pie. This one had a loaf of bread, that one a ham.

The tall, fair, young fellow placed in his hands an enormous sausage, and gave him orders:

"Go and settle up the sideboard in the corner over there. You are to put the bottles at the left and the provisions at the right."

Saval, getting quite distracted, exclaimed:

"But, Messieurs, I am a notary!"

There was a moment's silence and then a wild outburst of laughter. One suspicious gentleman asked:

"How are you here?"

He explained, telling about his project of going to the opera, his departure from Vernon, his arrival in Paris, and the way in which he had spent the evening.

They sat around him to listen to him; they greeted him with words of applause, and called him Scheherazade.

Romantin did not come back.   Other guests arrived.
M. Saval was presented to them so that he might begin
his story over again.   He declined; they forced him
to relate it.   They fixed him on one of three chairs
between two women who kept constantly filling his
glass.   He drank; he laughed; he talked; he sang, too.
He tried to waltz with his chair, and fell on the floor.

From that moment, he forgot everything.   It
seemed to him, however, that they undressed him,
put him to bed, and that his stomach got sick.

When he awoke, it was broad daylight, and he
lay stretched with his feet against a cupboard, in a
strange bed.

An old woman with a broom in her hand was
glaring angrily at him.   At last, she said:

"Clear out, you blackguard!   Clear out!   What
right has anyone to get drunk like this?"

He sat up in the bed, feeling very ill at ease.   He
asked:

"Where am I?"

"Where are you, you dirty scamp?   You are
drunk.   Take your rotten carcass out of here as quick
as you can,—and lose no time about it!"

He wanted to get up.   He found that he was
naked in the bed.   His clothes had disappeared.   He
blurted out:

"Madame, I—"

Then he remembered.   What was he to do?   He
asked:

"Did Monsieur Romantin come back?"

The doorkeeper shouted:

"Will you take your dirty carcass out of this so
that he at any rate may not catch you here?"

M. Saval said, in a state of confusion:

"I haven't got my clothes; they have been taken away from me."

He had to wait, to explain his situation, give notice to his friends, and borrow some money to buy clothes. He did not leave Paris till evening.

And, when people talk about music to him in his beautiful drawing-room in Vernon, he declares with an air of authority that painting is a very inferior art.

THE PEDDLER

How many trifling occurrences — things which have left only a passing impression on our minds, humble dramas of which we have got a mere glimpse, so that we have to guess at or suspect their real nature — are, while we are still young and inexperienced, guiding us, step by step, toward a knowledge of the painful truth!

Every now and then, when I am retracing my steps during the long wandering reveries which distract my thoughts along the path through which I saunter at random, my soul takes wing, and suddenly I recall little incidents of a gay or sinister character which, emerging from the shades of the past, flit before my memory as the birds flit through the bushes before my eyes.

This summer, I wandered along a road in Savoy which commands a view of the right bank of the Lake of Bourget, and, while my glance floated over that mass of water, mirror-like, and blue with a unique blue, tinted with glittering beams by the setting sun, I felt my heart stirred by that attachment which I have had since my childhood for the surface of lakes, for rivers, and for the sea. On the opposite bank of the vast liquid plate, so long that you did not see the ends of it, one vanishing in the Rhône, and the other in the Bourget, rose the high mountain, jagged like a crest up to the topmost peak of the "Cat's Tooth." On either side of the road, vines, trailing from tree to tree, massed under their leaves their slender supporting branches, and extended in garlands through the fields, green, yellow, and red garlands, festooning from one trunk to the other, and spotted with clusters of dark grapes.

The road was deserted, white, and dusty. All of a sudden a man emerged out of the thicket of large trees which shuts in the village of Saint-Innocent, and, bending under a load, came toward me, leaning on a stick.

When he had come closer to me, I discovered that he was a peddler, one of those itinerant dealers who go about the country from door to door selling paltry objects cheaply, and thereupon a reminiscence of long ago arose up in my mind, a mere nothing almost, the recollection simply of an accidental meeting I had one night between Argenteuil and Paris when I was twenty-one.

All the happiness of my life, at that period, was derived from boating. I had taken a room in an obscure inn at Argenteuil, and every evening I took the Government clerks' train, that long, slow train which, in its course, sets down at different stations a crowd of men with little parcels, men fat and heavy, for they scarcely walk at all, with trousers that are always baggy owing to their constant occupation of the office-stool. This train, in which it seemed to me I could even sniff the odor of the writing-desk, of official documents and boxes, deposited me at Argenteuil. My boat was waiting for me, ready to glide over the water. And I rapidly plied my oar so that I might get out and dine at Bezons or Chatou or Epinay or Saint-Ouen. Then I came back, put up my boat, and made my way back on foot to Paris with the moon shining down on me.

Well, one night on the white road I perceived just in front of me a man walking. Oh! I was constantly meeting those night travelers of the Parisian suburbs so much dreaded by belated citizens. This man went on slowly before me with a heavy load on his shoulders.

I came right up to him, quickening my pace so much that my footsteps rang on the road. He stopped, and turned round; then, as I kept approaching nearer and nearer, he crossed to the opposite side of the road.

As I rapidly passed him, he called out to me:

"Hallo! good evening, Monsieur."

I responded:

"Good evening, comrade."

He went on:

"Are you going far?"

"I am going to Paris."

"You won't be long getting there; you're going at a good pace. As for me, I have too big a load on my shoulders to walk so quickly."

I slackened my pace. Why had this man spoken to me? What was he carrying in this big pack?

Vague suspicions of crime sprang up in my mind, and rendered me curious. The columns of the newspapers every morning contain so many accounts of crimes committed in this place, the peninsula of Gennevilliers, that some of them must be true. Such things are not invented merely to amuse readers — all this catalogue of arrests and varied misdeeds with which the reports of the law-courts are filled.

However, this man's voice seemed more timid than bold, and up to the present his manner had been more discreet than aggressive.

In my turn I began to question him:

"And you — are you going far?"

"Not farther than Asnières."

"Is Asnières your place of abode?"

"Yes, Monsieur, I am a peddler by occupation, and I live at Asnières."

He had quitted the sidewalk, where pedestrians move along in the daytime under the shadows of the trees, and was soon in the middle of the road. I followed his example. We kept staring at each other suspiciously, each of us holding his stick in his hand. When I was sufficiently close to him, I felt less distrustful. He evidently was disposed to assume the same attitude toward me, for he asked:

"Would you mind going a little more slowly?"

"Why do you say this?"

"Because I don't care for this road by night. I have goods on my back, and two are always better than one. When two men are together, people don't attack them."

I felt that he was speaking truly, and that he was afraid. So I yielded to his wishes, and the pair of us walked on side by side, this stranger and I, at one o'clock in the morning, along the road leading from Argenteuil to Asnières.

"Why are you going home so late when it is so dangerous?" I asked my companion.

He told me his history. He had not intended to return home this evening, as he had brought with him that very morning a stock of goods to last him three or four days. But he had been so fortunate in disposing of them that he found it necessary to get back to his abode without delay in order to deliver next day a number of things which had been bought on credit.

He explained to me with genuine satisfaction that he had managed the business very well, having a tendency to talk confidentially, and that the knick-knacks he displayed were useful to him in getting rid, while gossiping, of other things which he could not easily sell.

He added:

"I have a shop in Asnières. 'Tis my wife keeps it."

"Ah! So you're married?"

"Yes, M'sieu, for the last fifteen months. I have got a very nice wife. She'll get a surprise when she sees me coming home to-night."

He then gave me an account of his marriage. He had been after this young girl for two years, but she had taken time to make up her mind.

She had since her childhood kept a little shop at the corner of a street, where she sold all sorts of things—ribbons, flowers in summer, and principally pretty little shoe-buckles, and many other gewgaws, in which, owing to the favor of a manufacturer, she

enjoyed a monopoly. She was well known in Asnières as "La Bluette." This name was given to her
because she often dressed in blue. And she made
money, as she was very skillful in everything she did.
His impression was that she was not very well at the
present moment; but he was not quite sure. Their
business was prospering; and he traveled about exhibiting samples to all the small traders in the adjoining districts. He had become a sort of traveling
commission-agent for some of the manufacturers,
working at the same time for them and for himself.

"And you—what are you?" he said.

I answered him with an air of embarrassment. I
explained that I had a sailing-boat and two yawls in
Argenteuil, that I came for a row every evening,
and that, as I was fond of exercise, I sometimes
walked back to Paris, where I had a profession,
which—I led him to infer—was a lucrative one.

He remarked:

"Faith, if I had money like you, I wouldn't amuse
myself by trudging that way along the roads at night.
'Tisn't safe along here."

He gave me a sidelong glance, and I asked myself
whether he might not, all the same, be a criminal of
the sneaking type who did not want to run any
fruitless risk.

Then he restored my confidence, when he murmured:

"A little less quickly, if you please. This pack of
mine is heavy."

The sight of a group of houses showed that we
had reached Asnières.

"I am nearly at home," he said. "We don't sleep

in the shop; it is watched at night by a dog, but a dog who is worth four men. And then it costs too much to live in the center of the town. But listen to me, Monsieur! You have rendered me a precious service, for I don't feel my mind at ease when I'm traveling with my pack along the roads. Well, now you must come in with me, and drink a glass of mulled wine with my wife if she hasn't gone to bed, for she is a sound sleeper and doesn't like to be waked up. Besides, I'm not a bit afraid without my pack, and so I'll see you to the gates of the city with a cudgel in my hand."

I declined the invitation; he insisted on my coming in; I still held back; he pressed me with so much eagerness, with such an air of real disappointment, such expressions of deep regret—for he had the art of expressing himself very forcibly—asking me in the tone of one who felt wounded "whether I objected to have a drink with a man like him," that I finally gave way and followed him up a lonely road toward one of those big dilapidated houses which are to be found on the outskirts of suburbs.

In front of this dwelling I hesitated. This high barrack of plaster looked like a den for vagabonds, a hiding-place for suburban brigands. But he pushed open a door which had not been locked, and made me go in before him. He led me forward by the shoulders, through profound darkness, toward a staircase where I had to feel my way with my hands and feet, with a well-grounded apprehension of tumbling into some gaping cellar.

When I had reached the first landing, he said to me: "Go on up! 'Tis the sixth story."

I searched my pockets, and, finding there a box of vestas, I lighted the way up the ascent. He followed me, puffing under his pack, repeating:

"'Tis high! 'tis high!"

When we were at the top of the house, he drew forth from one of his inside pockets a key attached to a thread, and unlocking his door, he made me enter.

It was a little whitewashed room, with a table in the center, six chairs, and a kitchen-cupboard close to the wall.

"I am going to wake up my wife," he said; "then I am going down to the cellar to fetch some wine; it doesn't keep here."

He approached one of the two doors which opened out of this apartment, and exclaimed:

"Bluette! Bluette!" Bluette did not reply. He called out in a louder tone: "Bluette! Bluette!"

Then knocking at the partition with his fist, he growled: "Will you wake up in God's name?"

He waited, glued his ear to the keyhole, and muttered, in a calmer tone: "Pooh! if she is asleep, she must be let sleep! I'll go and get the wine: wait a couple of minutes for me."

He disappeared. I sat down and made the best of it.

What had I come to this place for? All of a sudden, I gave a start, for I heard people talking in low tones, and moving about quietly, almost noiselessly, in the room where the wife slept.

Deuce take it! Had I fallen into some cursed trap? Why had this woman — this Bluette — not been awakened by the loud knocking of her husband at the doorway leading into her room? Could it have been merely a signal conveying to accomplices: "There's a mouse in the trap! I'm going to look out to prevent him escaping. 'Tis for you to do the rest!"

Certainly there was more stir than before now in the inner room; I heard the door opening from within. My heart throbbed. I retreated toward the further end of the apartment, saying to myself, "I must make a fight of it!" and, catching hold of the back of a chair with both hands, I prepared for a desperate struggle.

The door was half-opened; a hand appeared which kept it ajar; then a head, a man's head covered with a billycock hat, slipped through the folding-doors, and I saw two eyes staring hard at me. Then, so quickly that I had not time to make a single movement by way of defense, the individual, the supposed criminal, a tall young fellow in his bare feet with his shoes in his hands, a good-looking chap, I must admit,— half a gentleman, in fact,— made a dash for the outer door, and rushed down the stairs.

I resumed my seat. The adventure was assuming a humorous aspect, and I waited for the husband, who took a long time fetching the wine. At last, I heard him coming up the stairs, and the sound of his footsteps made me laugh, with one of those solitary laughs which it is hard to restrain.

He entered with two bottles in his hands. Then he asked me:

"Is my wife still asleep? You didn't hear her stirring, did you?"

I knew instinctively that there was an ear pasted

against the other side of the partition-door, and I said: "No, not at all."

And now he again called out:

"Pauline!"

She made no reply, and did not even move.

He came back to me, and explained:

"You see, she doesn't like me to come home at night, and take a drop with a friend."

"So then you believe she was not asleep?"

He wore an air of dissatisfaction.

"Well, at any rate," he said, "let us have a drink together."

And immediately he showed a disposition to empty the two bottles one after the other without more ado.

This time, I did display some energy. When I had swallowed one glass, I rose up to leave. He no longer spoke of accompanying me, and with a sullen scowl, the scowl of a common man in an angry mood, the scowl of a brute whose violence is only slumbering, in the direction of his wife's sleeping apartment, he muttered:

"She'll have to open that door when you've gone."

I stared at this poltroon, who had worked himself into a fit of rage without knowing why, perhaps owing to an obscure presentiment, the instinct of the deceived male who does not like closed doors. He had talked about her to me in a tender strain; now assuredly he was going to beat her.

He exclaimed, as he shook the lock once more:

"Pauline!"

A voice, like that of a woman waking out of her sleep, replied from behind the partition:

"Eh! what?"

"Didn't you hear me coming in?"

"No, I was asleep! Let me rest!"

"Open the door!"

"Yes, when you're alone. I don't like you to be bringing home fellows at night to drink with you."

Then I took myself off, stumbling down the stairs, as the other man, of whom I had been the accomplice, had done. And, as I resumed my journey toward Paris, I realized that I had just witnessed in this wretched abode a scene of the eternal drama which is being acted every day under every form and among every class.

THE UMBRELLA

Mme. Oreille was a very economical woman; she thoroughly knew the value of a half-penny, and possessed a whole storehouse of strict principles with regard to the multiplication of money, so that her cook found the greatest difficulty in making what the servants call their "market-penny," while her husband was hardly allowed any pocket-money at all. They were, however, very comfortably off, and had no children. It really pained Mme. Oreille to see any money spent; it was like tearing at her heartstrings when she had to take any of those nice crownpieces out of her pocket; and whenever she had to spend anything, no matter how necessary it was, she slept badly the next night.

Oreille was continually saying to his wife:

"You really might be more liberal, as we have no children and never spend our income."

"You don't know what may happen," she used to reply. "It is better to have too much than too little."

She was a little woman of about forty, very active, rather hasty, wrinkled, very neat and tidy, and with a very short temper. Her husband very often used to complain of all the privations she made him endure; some of them were particularly painful to him, as they touched his vanity.

He was one of the upper clerks in the War Office, and only stayed there in obedience to his wife's wish, so as to increase their income, which they did not nearly spend.

For two years he had always come to the office with the same old patched umbrella, to the great amusement of his fellow-clerks. At last he got tired of their jokes, and insisted upon his wife buying him a new one. She bought one for eight francs and a-half, one of those cheap things which large houses sell as an advertisement. When the others in the office saw the article, which was being sold in Paris by the thousand, they began their jokes again, and Oreille had a dreadful time of it with them. They even made a song about it, which he heard from morning till night all over the immense building.

Oreille was very angry, and peremptorily told his wife to get him a new one, a good silk one, for twenty francs, and to bring him the bill, so that he might see that it was all right.

She bought him one for eighteen francs, and said, getting red with anger as she gave it to her husband:

"This will last you for five years at least."

Oreille felt quite triumphant, and obtained a small ovation at the office with his new acquisition. When he went home in the evening, his wife said to him, looking at the umbrella uneasily:

"You should not leave it fastened up with the elastic; it will very likely cut the silk. You must take care of it, for I shall not buy you a new one in a hurry."

She took it, unfastened it, and then remained dumfounded with astonishment and rage. In the middle of the silk there was a hole as big as a six-penny-piece, as if made with the end of a cigar.

"What is that?" she screamed.

Her husband replied quietly, without looking at it:

"What is it? What do you mean?"

She was choking with rage and could hardly get out a word.

"You—you—have burned—your umbrella! Why —you must be—mad! Do you wish to ruin us out-right?"

He turned round hastily, as if frightened.

"What are you talking about?"

"I say that you have burned your umbrella. Just look here—"

And rushing at him, as if she were going to beat him, she violently thrust the little circular burned hole under his nose.

He was so utterly struck dumb at the sight of it that he could only stammer out:

"What—what is it? How should I know? I have done nothing, I will swear. I don't know what is the matter with the umbrella."

"You have been playing tricks with it at the office; you have been playing the fool and opening it, to show it off!" she screamed.

"I only opened it once, to let them see what a nice one it was, that is all, I declare."

But she shook with rage, and got up one of those conjugal scenes which make a peaceable man dread the domestic hearth more than a battlefield where bullets are raining.

She mended it with a piece of silk cut out of the old umbrella, which was of a different color, and the next day Oreille went off very humbly with the mended article in his hand. He put it into a cupboard, and thought no more of it than of some unpleasant recollection.

But he had scarcely got home that evening when his wife took the umbrella from him, opened it, and nearly had a fit when she saw what had befallen it, for the disaster was now irreparable. It was covered with small holes, which evidently, proceeded from burns, just as if some one had emptied the ashes from a lighted pipe on to it. It was done for utterly, irreparably.

She looked at it without a word, in too great a passion to be able to say anything. He also, when he saw the damage, remained almost dumb, in a state of frightened consternation.

They looked at each other; then he looked on to the floor. The next moment she threw the useless article at his head, screaming out in a transport of the most violent rage, for she had now recovered her voice:

"Oh! you brute! you brute! You did it on purpose, but I will pay you out for it. You shall not have another."

And then the scene began again. After the storm had raged for an hour, he, at last, was enabled to explain himself. He declared that he could not understand it at all, and that it could only proceed from malice or from vengeance.

A ring at the bell saved him; it was a friend whom they were expecting to dinner.

Mme. Oreille submitted the case to him. As for buying a new umbrella, that was out of the question; her husband should not have another. The friend very sensibly said that in that case his clothes would be spoiled, and they were certainly worth more than the umbrella. But the little woman, who was still in a rage, replied:

"Very well, then, when it rains he may have the kitchen umbrella, for I will not give him a new silk one."

Oreille utterly rebelled at such an idea.

"All right," he said; "then I shall resign my post. I am not going to the office with the kitchen umbrella."

The friend interposed:

"Have this one recovered; it will not cost much."

But Mme. Oreille, being in the temper that she was, said:

"It will cost at least eight francs to recover it. Eight and eighteen are twenty-six. Just fancy, twenty-six francs for an umbrella! It is utter madness!"

The friend, who was only a poor man of the middle classes, had an inspiration:

"Make your fire insurance pay for it. The companies pay for all articles that are burned, as long as the damage has been done in your own house."

On hearing this advice the little woman calmed down immediately, and then, after a moment's reflection, she said to her husband:

"To-morrow, before going to your office, you will go to the Maternelle Insurance Company, show them the state your umbrella is in, and make them pay for the damage."

M. Oreille fairly jumped, he was so startled at the proposal.

"I would not do it for my life! It is eighteen francs lost, that is all. It will not ruin us."

The next morning he took a walking-stick when he went out, for, luckily, it was a fine day.

Left at home alone, Mme. Oreille could not get over the loss of her eighteen francs by any means. She had put the umbrella on the dining-room table, and she looked at it without being able to come to any determination.

Every moment she thought of the insurance company, but she did not dare to encounter the quizzical looks of the gentlemen who might receive her, for she was very timid before people, and grew red at a mere nothing, feeling embarrassed when she had to speak to strangers.

But regret at the loss of the eighteen francs pained her as if she had been wounded. She tried not to think of it any more, and yet every moment the recollection of the loss struck her painfully. What was she to do, however? Time went on, and she could not decide; but suddenly, like all cowards, she made up her mind.

"I will go, and we will see what will happen."

But first of all she was obliged to prepare the umbrella so that the disaster might be complete, and the reason of it quite evident. She took a match from the mantelpiece, and between the ribs she burned a hole as big as the palm of her hand. Then she rolled it up carefully, fastened it with the elastic band, put on her bonnet and shawl, and went quickly toward the Rue de Rivoli, where the insurance office was.

But the nearer she got the slower she walked. What was she going to say, and what reply would she get?

She looked at the numbers of the houses; there were still twenty-eight. That was all right, she had time to consider, and she walked slower and slower. Suddenly she saw a door on which was a large brass plate with "La Maternelle Fire Insurance Office" engraved on it. Already! She waited for a moment, for she felt nervous and almost ashamed; then she went past, came back, went past again, and came back again.

At last she said to herself:

"I must go in, however, so I may as well do it now as later."

She could not help noticing, however, how her heart beat as she entered. She went into an enormous room with grated wicket openings all round, and a man behind each of them, and as a gentleman, carrying a number of papers, passed her, she stopped him and said, timidly:

"I beg your pardon, Monsieur, but can you tell me where I must apply for payment for anything that has been accidentally burned?"

He replied in a sonorous voice:

"The first door on the left; that is the department you want."

This frightened her still more, and she felt inclined to run away, to make no claim, to sacrifice her eighteen francs. But the idea of that sum revived her courage, and she went upstairs, out of breath, stopping at almost every other step.

She knocked at a door which she saw on the first landing, and a clear voice said, in answer:

"Come in!"

She obeyed mechanically, and found herself in a large room where three solemn gentlemen, each with a decoration in his buttonhole, were standing talking.

One of them asked her: "What do you want, Madame?"

She could hardly get out her words, but stammered: "I have come—I have come on account of an accident, something—"

He very politely pointed out a seat to her.

"If you will kindly sit down I will attend to you in a moment."

And, returning to the other two, he went on with the conversation.

"The company, gentlemen, does not consider that it is under any obligation to you for more than four hundred thousand francs, and we can pay no attention to your claim to the further sum of a hundred thousand, which you wish to make us pay. Besides that, the surveyor's valuation—"

One of the others interrupted him:

"That is quite enough, Monsieur; the law-courts will decide between us, and we have nothing further to do than to take our leave." And they went out after mutual ceremonious bows.

Oh! if she could only have gone away with them, how gladly she would have done it; she would have run away and given up everything. But it was too late, for the gentleman came back, and said, bowing:

"What can I do for you, Madame?"

She could scarcely speak, but at last she managed to say:

"I have come — for this."

The manager looked at the object which she held out to him in mute astonishment. With trembling fingers she tried to undo the elastic, and succeeded, after several attempts, and hastily opened the damaged remains of the umbrella.

"It looks to me to be in a very bad state of health," he said, compassionately.

"It cost me twenty francs," she said, with some hesitation.

He seemed astonished. "Really! As much as that?"

"Yes, it was a capital article, and I wanted you to see the state it is in."

"Very well, I see; very well. But I really do not understand what it can have to do with me."

She began to feel uncomfortable; perhaps this company did not pay for such small articles, and she said:

"But — it is burned."

He could not deny it.

"I see that very well," he replied.

She remained open-mouthed, not knowing what to say next; then suddenly forgetting that she had left out the main thing, she said hastily:

"I am Mme. Oreille; we are assured in La Maternelle, and I have come to claim the value of this damage. I only want you to have it recovered," she added quickly, fearing a positive refusal.

The manager was rather embarrassed, and said:

"But, really, Madame, we do not sell umbrellas; we cannot undertake such kinds of repairs."

The little woman felt her courage reviving; she was not going to give up without a struggle; she was not even afraid now, so she said:

"I only want you to pay me the cost of repairing it; I can quite well get it done myself."

The gentleman seemed rather confused.

"Really, Madame, it is such a very small matter! We are never asked to give compensation for such trivial losses. You must allow that we cannot make good pocket-handkerchiefs, gloves, brooms, slippers, all the small articles which are every day exposed to the chances of being burned."

She got red, and felt inclined to fly into a rage.

"But, Monsieur, last December one of our chimneys caught fire, and caused at least five hundred francs' damage. M. Oreille made no claim on the company, and so it is only just that it should pay for my umbrella now."

The manager, guessing that she was telling a lie, said, with a smile:

"You must acknowledge, Madame, that it is very surprising that M. Oreille should have asked no compensation for damages amounting to five hundred francs, and should now claim five or six francs for mending an umbrella."

She was not the least put out, and replied:

"I beg your pardon, Monsieur, the five hundred francs affected M. Oreille's pocket, whereas this damage, amounting to eighteen francs, concerns Mme. Oreille's pocket only. which is a totally different matter."

As he saw that he had no chance of getting rid of her, and that he would only be wasting his time, he said, resignedly:

"Will you kindly tell me how the damage was done?"

She felt that she had won the victory, and said:

"This is how it happened, Monsieur: In our hall there is a bronze stick- and umbrella-stand, and the other day, when I came in, I put my umbrella into it. I must tell you that just above there is a shelf for the candlesticks and matches. I put out my hand, took three or four matches, and struck one, but it missed fire, so I struck another, which ig-nited, but went out immediately, and a third did the same."

The manager interrupted her, to make a joke.

"I suppose they were Government matches, then?"

She did not understand him, and went on:

"Very likely. At any rate, the fourth caught fire, and I lit my candle, and went into my room to go to bed; but in a quarter-of-an-hour I fancied that I smelled something burning, and I have always been terribly afraid of fire. If ever we have an accident it will not be my fault, I assure you. I am terribly nervous since our chimney was on fire, as I told you; so I got up, and hunted about everywhere, sniffing like a dog after game, and at last I noticed that my umbrella was burning. Most likely a match had fallen between the folds and burned it. You can see how it has damaged it."

The manager had taken his clue, and asked her:

"What do you estimate the damage at?"

She did not know what to say, as she was not certain what amount to put on it, but at last she replied:

"Perhaps you had better get it done yourself. I will leave it to you."

He, however, naturally refused.

"No, Madame, I cannot do that. Tell me the amount of your claim, that is all I want to know."

"Well!—I think that— Look here, Monsieur, I do not want to make any money out of you, so I will tell you what we will do. I will take my umbrella to the maker, who will recover it in good, durable silk, and I will bring the bill to you. Will that suit you, Monsieur?"

"Perfectly, Madame; we will settle it on that basis. Here is a note for the cashier, who will repay you whatever it costs you."

He gave Mme. Oreille a slip of paper. She took it, got up, and went out, thanking him, for she was in a hurry to escape lest he should change his mind.

She went briskly through the streets, looking out for a really good umbrella-maker, and when she found a shop which appeared to be a first-class one, she went in, and said, confidently:

"I want this umbrella recovered in silk, good silk. Use the very best and strongest you have; I don't mind what it costs."

THE QUESTION OF LATIN

THIS question of Latin, with which we were so much bothered some time since, recalls to my mind a story — a story of my youth.

I was finishing my studies with a teacher, in a big central town, at the Institution Robineau, celebrated through the entire province owing to the special attention paid there to Latin studies.

For the past ten years, the Institution Robineau beat at every competitive examination the Imperial "lycée" of the town, and all the colleges of the Subprefecture; and these constant successes were due, they said, to an usher, a simple usher, M. Piquedent, or rather Père Piquedent.

He was one of those middle-aged men, quite gray, whose real age it is impossible to know, and whose history we can guess at a first glance. Having entered as an usher at twenty into the first institution that presented itself so that he could proceed to take out his degree of Master of Arts first, and afterward the degree of Doctor of Laws, he found himself so much enmeshed in this sinister life that he remained an usher all his life. But his love for Latin did not leave him, but harassed him like an unhealthy passion. He continued to read the poets, the prose-writers, the historians, to interpret them, to study their meaning, to comment on them with a perseverance bordering on madness.

One day, the idea came into his head to force all the students of his class to answer him in Latin only; and he persisted in this resolution until at last they were capable of sustaining an entire conversation with him just as they would in their mother-tongue. He listened to them, as a leader of an orchestra listens to his musicians rehearsing, and, striking his desk every moment with his ruler, he exclaimed:

"Monsieur Lefrère, Monsieur Lefrère, you are committing a solecism! You are not recalling the rule to mind.

"Monsieur Plantel, your turn of phrase is altogether French and in no way Latin. You must understand the genius of a language. Look here, listen to me."

Now it came to pass that the pupils of the Institution Robineau carried off, at the end of the year, all the prizes for composition, translation, and Latin conversation.

Next year, the principal, a little man, as cunning as an ape, and with the same grinning and grotesque physique, got printed on his programmes, on his advertisements, and painted on the door of his institution:

"Latin Studies a Speciality. Five first prizes carried off in the five classes of the lycée.

"Two prizes of honor at the general Competitive
Examinations with all the lycées and colleges of
France."

For ten years the Institution Robineau triumphed
in the same fashion. Now, my father, allured by
these successes, sent me as a day-pupil to Robineau's
—or, as we called it, Robinetto or Robinettino—and
made me take special private lessons from Père
Piquedent at the rate of five francs per hour, out of
which the usher got two francs and the principal
three francs. I was at the time in my eighteenth
year, and was in the philosophy class.

These private lessons were given in a little room
looking out on the street. It so happened that Père
Piquedent, instead of talking Latin to me, as he did
when teaching publicly in the Institution, kept telling
about his troubles in French. Without relations,
without friends, the poor man conceived an attachment for me, and poured out into my heart his own
misery.

He had never for the last ten or fifteen years
chatted confidentially with anyone.

"I am like an oak in a desert," he said—"*sicut
quercus in solitudine.*"

The other ushers disgusted him. He knew nobody
in the town since he had no liberty for the purpose
of making acquaintances.

"Not even the nights, my friend, and that is the
hardest thing on me. The dream of my life is to
have a room of my own with furniture, my own
books, little things that belonged to myself and which
others could not touch. And I have nothing of my
own, nothing except my shirt and my frock-coat,

nothing, not even my mattress and my pillow! I have not four walls to shut myself up in, except when I come to give a lesson in this room. Do you see what this means — a man forced to spend his life without ever having the right, without ever finding the time to shut himself up all alone, no matter where, to think, to reflect, to work, to dream? Ah! my dear boy, a key, the key of a door which one can open — this is happiness, mark you, the only happiness!

"Here, all day long, the study with all those dirty brats jumping about in it, and during the night the dormitory with the same dirty brats snoring. And I have to sleep in the public bed at the end of two rows of beds occupied by these brats whom I must look after. I can never be alone, never! If I go out, I find the street full of people, and, when I am tired of walking, I go into some *café* crowded with smokers and billiard players. I tell you that it is a regular prison."

I asked him:

"Why did you not take up some other line, Monsieur Piquedent?"

He exclaimed:

"What, my little friend? I am not a bootmaker or a joiner or a hatter or a baker or a hairdresser. I only know Latin, and I have not the diploma which would enable me to sell my knowledge at a high price. If I were a doctor, I would sell for a hundred francs what I now sell for a hundred sous; and I would supply it probably of an inferior quality, for my academic rank would be enough to sustain my reputation."

Sometimes, he would say to me:

"I have no rest in life except in the hours spent with you. Don't be afraid! you'll lose nothing by that. I'll make it up to you in the study by teaching you to speak twice as much Latin as the others."

One day, I grew bolder and offered him a cigarette. He stared at me with astonishment at first, then he gave a glance toward the door:

"If anyone were to come in, my dear boy!"

"Well, let us smoke at the window," said I.

And we went and leaned with our elbows on the window-sill facing the street, keeping our hands over the little rolls of tobacco wrapped up in tissue-paper so that they concealed them from view like a shell. Just opposite to us was a laundry. Four women in white bodices were passing over the linen spread out before them the heavy and hot irons, letting a damp fume escape from them.

Suddenly, another, a fifth carrying on her arm a large basket which made her back stoop, came out to bring the customers their shirts and chemises, their handkerchiefs and their sheets. She stopped on the threshold as if she were already fatigued; then, she raised her eyes, smiled when she saw us smoking, flung at us, with her left hand, which was free, the sly kiss characteristic of a free-and-easy working-woman; and she went away at a slow pace dragging her shoes after her.

She was a damsel of about twenty, small, rather thin, pale, rather pretty, with the manners of a street-wench, and eyes laughing under her ill-combed fair hair.

Père Piquedent, affected, began murmuring:

"What an occupation for a woman.   Really a trade only fit for a horse."

And he spoke with emotion about the misery of the people. He had a heart which swelled with lofty democratic sentiment, and he referred to the fatiguing pursuits of the working class with phrases borrowed from Jean-Jacques Rousseau and with sobs in his throat.

Next day, as we were resting our elbows at the same window, the same workwoman perceived us, and cried out to us:

"Good day, my scholars!" in a comical sort of tone, while she made a contemptuous gesture with her hands.

I flung her a cigarette, which she immediately began to smoke. And the four other ironers rushed out to the door with outstretched hands to get cigarettes also.

And, each day, a friendly relationship was being formed between the working-women of the pavement and the idlers of the boarding-school.

Père Piquedent was really a comic sight to look at. He trembled at being noticed, for he might have lost his place; and he made timid and ridiculous gestures, quite a theatrical display of amorousness, to which the women responded with a regular fusillade of kisses.

A perfidious idea sprang up in my head. One day, on entering our room, I said to the old usher in a low tone:

"You would not believe it, Monsieur Piquedent, I met the little washerwoman! You know the one — the woman who had the basket — and I spoke to her!"

He asked, rather excited by the tone I had taken:
"What did she say to you?"

"She said to me — goodness gracious! — she said she thought you were very nice. The fact of the matter is, I believe — I believe — that she is a little in love with you." I saw that he was growing pale. He exclaimed:

"She is laughing at me, of course. These things don't happen at my age."

I said gravely:

"How is that? You are very nice."

As I felt that my trick had produced its effect on him, I did not press the matter.

But every day I pretended that I had met the little laundress and that I had spoken to her about him, so that in the end he believed me, and sent her ardent and earnest kisses.

Now, it happened that, one morning, on my way to the boarding-school, I really came across her. I accosted her without hesitation, as if I had known her for the last ten years.

"Good day, Mademoiselle. Are you quite well?"

"Very well, Monsieur, thank you."

"Will you have a cigarette?"

"Oh! not in the street."

"You can smoke it at home."

"In that case, I will."

"Let me tell you, Mademoiselle, there's something you don't know."

"What is that, Monsieur?"

"The old gentleman — my old professor, I mean —"

"Père Piquedent."

"Yes, Père Piquedent. So you know his name?"

"Faith, I do! What of that?"

"Well, he is in love with you!"

She burst out laughing like a crazy woman and exclaimed:

"This is only humbug!"

"Oh! no, 'tis no humbug! He keeps talking of you all the time he is giving lessons. I bet that he'll marry you!"

She ceased laughing. The idea of marriage makes every girl serious. Then, she repeated, with an incredulous air:

"This is humbug!"

"I swear to you 'tis true.'

She picked up her basket which she had laid down at her feet.

"Well, we'll see," she said. And she went away.

Presently, when I had reached the boarding-school, I took Père Piquedent aside, and said:

"You must write to her: she is mad about you."

And he wrote a long letter of a soft and affectionate character full of phrases and circumlocutions, metaphors and similes, philosophy and academic gallantry; and I took on myself the responsibility of delivering it to the young woman.

She read it with gravity, with emotion; then, she murmured:

"How well he writes! It is easy to see he has got education! Does he really mean to marry me?"

I replied intrepidly: "Faith, he has lost his head about you!"

"Then he must invite me to dinner on Sunday at the Île des Fleurs."

I promised that she would be invited.

Père Piquedent was much touched by everything I told him about her.

I added:

"She loves you, Monsieur Piquedent, and I believe her to be a decent girl. It is not right to seduce her and then abandon her."

He replied in a firm tone:

"I hope I, too, am a decent man, my friend."

I confess I had at the time no plan. I was playing a practical joke, a schoolboy's practical joke, nothing more. I had been aware of the simplicity of the old usher, his innocence, and his weakness. I amused myself without asking myself how it would turn out. I was eighteen, and had been for a long time looked upon· at the lycée as a knowing practical joker.

So, it was agreed that Père Piquedent and I should set out in a hackney-coach for the ferry of Queue de Vache, that we should there pick up Angèle, and that I should get them to come into my boat, for at this time I was fond of boating. I would then bring them to the Île de Fleurs, where the three of us would dine. I had made it my business to be present, in order the better to enjoy my triumph, and the usher, consenting to my arrangement, proved clearly, in fact, that he had lost his head by thus risking his post.

When we arrived at the ferry where my boat had been moored since morning, I saw in the grass, or rather above the tall weeds of the bank, an enormous red parasol, resembling a monstrous wild poppy. Under the parasol waited the little laundress in her

Sunday clothes. I was surprised. She was really nice-looking, though pale, and graceful, though with a suburban gracefulness.

Père Piquedent raised his hat and bowed. She put out her hand toward him and they stared at one another without uttering a word. Then they stepped into my boat and I took the oars.

They were seated side by side on the seat near the stern. The usher was the first to speak:

"This is nice weather for a row in a boat."

She murmured: "Oh! yes."

She drew her hand through the current, skimming the water with her fingers, which raised up a thin transparent little stream like a sheet of glass. It made a light sound, a gentle ripple, as the boat moved along.

When they were in the restaurant, she took it on herself to speak, and ordered dinner—fried fish, a chicken, and salad; then, she led us on toward the isle, which she knew perfectly.

After this, she was gay, romping, and even rather mocking.

Up to the dessert, no question of love arose. I had treated them to champagne and Père Piquedent was tipsy. Herself slightly elevated, she called out to him:

"Monsieur Piquenez."

He said all of a sudden:

"Mademoiselle, Monsieur Raoul has communicated my sentiments to you."

She became as serious as a judge:

"Yes, Monsieur."

"Are you going to give any answer?"

"We never reply to these questions!"

He panted with emotion, and went on:

"After all, a day will come when I may make you like me."

She smiled: "You big fool! You are very nice."

"In short, Mademoiselle, do you think that, later on, we might—"

She hesitated a second; then in a trembling voice she said:

"Is it in order to marry me you say that? For never otherwise, you know."

"Yes, Mademoiselle!"

"Well, that's all right, Monsieur Piquedent!"

It is thus that these two silly creatures promised marriage to each other through the wiles of a reckless schoolboy. But I did not believe that it was serious, nor indeed did they themselves, perhaps.

On her part there was a certain feeling of hesitation:

"You know, I have nothing—not four sous."

He stammered, for he was as drunk as Silenus:

"I have saved five thousand francs."

She exclaimed triumphantly:

"Then we can set up in business!"

He became restless: "In what business?"

"What do I know about that? We shall see. With five thousand francs, we could do many things. You don't want me to go and live in your boarding-school, do you?"

He had not looked forward so far as this, and he stammered in great perplexity:

"What business could we set up in? It is not convenient, for all I know is Latin!"

She reflected in her turn, passing in review all the professions which she had longed for.

"You could not be a doctor?"

"No, I have not the diploma."

"Or a chemist?"

"No more than the other."

She uttered a cry, a cry of joy. She had discovered it.

"Then we'll buy a grocer's shop! Oh! what luck! we'll buy a grocer's shop! Not on a big scale, all the same; with five thousand francs one cannot go far."

He was shocked at the suggestion:

"No, I can't be a grocer. I am — I am — too well known. I only know Latin — that's all I know."

But she poured a glass of champagne down his throat. He drank it and was silent.

We got back into the boat. The night was dark, very dark. I saw clearly, however, that he had caught her by the waist, and that they were hugging each other again and again.

It was a frightful catastrophe. Our escapade was discovered with the result that Père Piquedent was dismissed. And my father, in a fit of anger, sent me to finish my course of philosophy at Ribaudet's School.

Six months later I passed for my degree of Bachelor of Arts. Then I went to study law in Paris, and I did not return to my native town till ten years after.

At the corner of the Rue de Serpent, a shop caught my eye. Over the door were the words: "Colonial products — Piquedent"; then underneath so as to enlighten the most ignorant: "Grocery."

I exclaimed: *"Quantum mutatus ab illo!"*

He raised his head, left his female customer, and rushed toward me with outstretched hands.

"Ah! my young friend, my young friend, here you are! What luck! What luck!"

A beautiful woman, very plump, abruptly left the counter and flung herself on my breast. I had some difficulty in recognizing her, so fat had she grown.

I asked: "So then you're going on well?"

Piquedent had gone back to weigh the groceries:

"Oh! very well, very well, very well. I have made three thousand francs clear this year!"

"And what about the Latin, Monsieur Piquedent?"

"Oh! goodness gracious! the Latin — the Latin — the Latin. Well, you see, it does not keep the pot boiling!"

MOTHER AND SON!!!

WE WERE chatting in the smoking-room after a dinner at which only men were present. We talked about unexpected legacies, strange inheritances. Then M. le Brument, who was sometimes called "the illustrious master" and at other times the "illustrious advocate," came and stood with his back to the fire.

"I have," he said, "just now to search for an heir who disappeared under peculiarly terrible circumstances. It is one of those simple and ferocious dramas of ordinary life, a thing which possibly happens every day, and which is nevertheless one of the most dreadful things I know. Here are the facts:

"Nearly six months ago I got a message to come to the side of a dying woman. She said to me:

"'Monsieur, I want to intrust to you the most delicate, the most difficult, and the most wearisome mission than can be conceived. Be good enough to take cognizance of my will, which is there on the table. A sum of five thousand francs is left to you as a fee if you do not succeed and of a hundred thousand francs if you do succeed. I want to have my son found after my death.'

"She asked me to assist her to sit up in the bed, in order that she might be able to speak with greater ease, for her voice, broken and gasping, was gurgling in her throat.

"I saw that I was in the house of a very rich person. The luxurious apartment, with a certain simplicity in its luxury, was upholstered with materials solid as the walls, and their soft surfaces imparted a caressing sensation, so that every word uttered seemed to penetrate their silent depths and to disappear and die there.

"The dying woman went on:

"'You are the first to hear my horrible story. I will try to have strength enough to go on to the end of it. You must know everything so that you, whom I know to be a kind-hearted man as well as a man of the world should have a sincere desire to aid me with all your power.

"'Listen to me.

"'Before my marriage, I loved a young man, whose suit was rejected by my family because he was not rich enough. Not long afterward, I married a man of great wealth. I married him through ignorance, through obedience, through indifference, as young girls do marry.

"'I had a child, a boy. My husband died in the course of a few years.

"'He whom I had loved had got married, in his

turn. When he saw that I was a widow, he was crushed by horrible grief at knowing that he was not free. He came to see me; he wept and sobbed so bitterly before my eyes that it was enough to break my heart. He at first came to see me as a friend. Perhaps I ought not to have seen him. What could I do? I was alone, so sad, so solitary, so hopeless! And I loved him still. What sufferings we women have sometimes to endure!

"'I had only him in the world, my parents also being dead. He came frequently; he spent whole evenings with me. I should not have let him come so often, seeing that he was married. But I had not enough will-power to prevent him from coming.

"'How am I to tell you what next happened? He became my lover. How did this come about? Can I explain it? Can anyone explain such things? Do you think it could be otherwise when two human beings are drawn toward each other by the irresistible force of a passion by which each of them is possessed? Do you believe, Monsieur, that it is always in our power to resist, that we can keep up the struggle forever, and refuse to yield to the prayers, the supplications, the tears, the frenzied words, the appeals on bended knees, the transports of passion, with which we are pursued by the man we adore, whom we want to gratify even in his slightest wishes, whom we desire to crown with every possible happiness, and whom, if we are to be guided by a worldly code of honor, we must drive to despair. What strength would it not require? What a renunciation of happiness? what self-denial? and even what virtuous selfishness?

" 'In short, Monsieur, I was his mistress; and I was happy. For twelve years, I was happy. I became — and this was my greatest weakness and my greatest piece of cowardice — I became his wife's friend.

" 'We brought up my son together; we made a man of him, a thorough man, intelligent, full of sense and resolution, of large and generous ideas. The boy reached the age of seventeen.

" 'He, the young man, was fond of my — my lover, almost as fond of him as I was myself, for he had been equally cherished and cared for by both of us. He used to call him his "dear friend," and respected him immensely, having never received from him anything but wise counsels and a good example of rectitude, honor, and probity. He looked upon him as an old, loyal, and devoted comrade of his mother, as a sort of moral father, tutor, protector — how am I to describe it?

" 'Perhaps the reason why he never asked any questions was that he had been accustomed from his earliest years to see this man in the house, by his side, and by my side, always concerned about us both.

" 'One evening the three of us were to dine together (these were my principal festive occasions), and I waited for the two of them, asking myself which of them would be the first to arrive. The door opened; it was my old friend. I went toward him with outstretched arms; and he drew his lips toward mine in a long, delicious kiss.

" 'All of a sudden, a sound, a rustling which was barely audible, that mysterious sensation which indicates the presence of another person, made us start

and turn round with a quick movement. Jean, my son, stood there, livid, staring at us.

"'There was a moment of atrocious confusion. I drew back, holding out my hands toward my son as if in supplication; but I could see him no longer. He had gone.

"'We remained facing each other—my lover and I—crushed, unable to utter a word. I sank down on an armchair, and I felt a desire, a vague, powerful desire to fly, to go out into the night, and to disappear forever. Then, convulsive sobs rose up in my throat, and I wept, shaken with spasms, with my heart torn asunder, all my nerves writhing with the horrible sensation of an irremediable misfortune, and with that dreadful sense of shame which, in such moments as this, falls on a mother's heart.

"'He looked at me in a scared fashion, not venturing to approach me or to speak to me or to touch me, for fear of the boy's return. At last he said:

"'"I am going to follow him—to talk to him—to explain matters to him. In short, I must see him and let him know—"

"'And he hurried away.

"'I waited—I waited in a distracted frame of mind, trembling at the least sound, convulsed with terror, and filled with some unutterably strange and intolerable emotion by every slight crackling of the fire in the grate.

"'I waited for an hour, for two hours, feeling my heart swell with a dread I had never before experienced, with such an anguish as I would not wish the greatest of criminals to experience. Where was my son? What was he doing?

"'About midnight, a messenger brought me a note from my lover. I still know its contents by heart:

"'"Has your son returned? I did not find him. I am down here. I do not want to go up at this hour."

"'I wrote in pencil on the same slip of paper:

"'"Jean has not returned. You must go and find him."

"'And I remained all night in the armchair, waiting for him.

"'I felt as if I were going mad. I longed to run wildly about, to roll myself on the floor. And yet I did not even stir, but kept waiting hour after hour. What was going to happen? I tried to imagine, to guess. But I could form no conception, in spite of my efforts, in spite of the tortures of my soul!

"'And now my apprehension was lest they might meet. What would they do in that case? What would my son do? My mind was lacerated by fearful doubts, by terrible suppositions.

"'You understand what I mean, do you not, Monsieur?

"'My chambermaid, who knew nothing, who understood nothing, was coming in every moment, believing, naturally, that I had lost my reason. I sent her away with a word or a movement of the hand. She went for the doctor, who found me in the throes of a nervous fit.

"'I was put to bed. Then came an attack of brain-fever. When I regained consciousness, after a long illness, I saw beside my bed my—lover—alone. I exclaimed:

"'"My son? Where is my son?"

" 'He replied :

" ' "I assure you every effort has been made by me to find him, but I have failed!"

" 'Then, becoming suddenly exasperated and even indignant,—for women are subject to such outbursts of unaccountable and unreasoning anger,—I said:

" ' "I forbid you to come near me or to see me again unless you find him. Go away!"

" 'He did go away.

" 'I have never seen one or the other of them since, Monsieur, and thus I have lived for the last twenty years.

" 'Can you imagine what all this meant to me? Can you understand this monstrous punishment, this slow perpetual laceration of a mother's heart, this abominable, endless waiting? Endless, did I say? No: it is about to end, for I am dying. I am dying without ever again seeing either of them—either one or the other!

" 'He—the man I loved—has written to me every day for the last twenty years; and I—I have never consented to see him, even for one second; for I had a strange feeling that if he came back here, it would be at that very moment my son would again make his appearance! Ah! my son! my son! Is he dead? Is he living? Where is he hiding? Over there perhaps, at the other side of the ocean, in some country so far away that even its very name is unknown to me! Does he ever think of me? Ah! if he only knew! How cruel children are! Did he understand to what frightful suffering he condemned me, into what depths of despair, into what tortures, he cast me while I was still in the prime of life, leaving me to suffer like this even to this moment when I am going to die—me, his mother, who loved him with all the violence of a mother's love! Oh! isn't it cruel, cruel?

"'You will tell him all this, Monsieur—will you not? You will repeat for him my last words:

"'"My child, my dear, dear child, be less harsh toward poor women! Life is already brutal and savage enough in its dealings with them. My dear son, think of what the existence of your poor mother has been ever since the day when you left her. My dear child, forgive her, and love her, now that she is dead, for she has had to endure the most frightful penance ever inflicted on a woman."'

"She gasped for breath, shuddering, as if she had addressed the last words to her son and as if he stood by her bedside.

"Then she added:

"'You will tell him also, Monsieur, that I never again saw—the other.'

"Once more she ceased speaking, then, in a broken voice she said:

"'Leave me now, I beg of you. I want to die all alone, since they are not with me.'"

Maître le Brument added:

"I left the house, Messieurs, crying like a fool, so vehemently, indeed, that my coachman turned round to stare at me.

"And to think that every day heaps of dramas like this are being enacted all around us!

"I have not found the son—that son—well, say what you like about him, but I call him that criminal son!"

HE ?*

M Y DEAR friend, you cannot understand it by any possible means, you say, and I perfectly believe you. You think I am going mad? It may be so, but not for the reasons which you suppose.

Yes, I am going to get married, and I will tell you what has led me to take that step.

My ideas and my convictions have not changed at all. I look upon all legalized cohabitation as utterly stupid, for I am certain that nine husbands out of ten are cuckolds; and they get no more than their deserts for having been idiotic enough to fetter their lives and renounce their freedom in love, the only happy and good thing in the world, and for having clipped the wings of fancy which continually drives us on toward all women. You know what I mean. More than ever I feel that I am incapable of loving one woman alone, because

---

*It was in this story that the first gleams of De Maupassant's approaching madness became apparent. Thenceforward he began to revel in the strange and terrible, until his malady had seized him wholly. "The Diary of a Madman," is in a similar vein.

I shall always adore all the others too much. I should like to have a thousand arms, a thousand mouths, and a thousand — *temperaments,* to be able to strain an army of these charming creatures in my embrace at the same moment.

And yet I am going to get married!

I may add that I know very little of the girl who is going to become my wife to-morrow; I have only seen her four or five times. I know that there is nothing unpleasing about her, and that is enough for my purpose. She is small, fair, and stout; so of course the day after to-morrow I shall ardently wish for a tall, dark, thin woman.

She is not rich, and belongs to the middle classes. She is a girl such as you may find by the gross, well adapted for matrimony, without any apparent faults, and with no particularly striking qualities. People say of her: "Mlle. Lajolle is a very nice girl," and to-morrow they will say: "What a very nice woman Madame Raymon is." She belongs, in a word, to that immense number of girls who make very good wives for us till the moment comes when we discover that we happen to prefer all other women to that particular woman we have married.

"Well," you will say to me, "what on earth do you get married for?"

I hardly like to tell you the strange and seemingly improbable reason that urged me on to this senseless act; the fact, however, is that I am frightened of being alone!

I don't know how to tell you or to make you understand me, but my state of mind is so wretched that you will pity me and despise me.

I do not want to be alone any longer at night; I want to feel that there is some one close to me touching me, a being who can speak and say something, no matter what it be.

I wish to be able to awaken somebody by my side, so that I may be able to ask some sudden question, a stupid question even, if I feel inclined, so that I may hear a human voice, and feel that there is some waking soul close to me, some one whose reason is at work — so that when I hastily light the candle I may see some human face by my side — because — because — I am ashamed to confess it — because I am afraid of being alone.

Oh! you don't understand me yet.

I am not afraid of any danger; if a man were to come into the room I should kill him without trembling. I am not afraid of ghosts, nor do I believe in the supernatural. I am not afraid of dead people, for I believe in the total annihilation of every being that disappears from the face of this earth.

Well, — yes, well, it must be told; I am afraid of myself, afraid of that horrible sensation of incomprehensible fear.

You may laugh, if you like. It is terrible and I cannot get over it. I am afraid of the walls, of the furniture, of the familiar objects, which are animated, as far as I am concerned, by a kind of animal life. Above all, I am afraid of my own dreadful thoughts, of my reason, which seems as if it were about to leave me, driven away by a mysterious and invisible agony.

At first I feel a vague uneasiness in my mind which causes a cold shiver to run all over me. I look round, and of course nothing is to be seen, and I wish there were something there, no matter what, as long as it were something tangible: I am frightened, merely because I cannot understand my own terror.

If I speak, I am afraid of my own voice. If I walk, I am afraid of I know not what, behind the door, behind the curtains, in the cupboard, or under my bed, and yet all the time I know there is nothing anywhere, and I turn round suddenly because I am afraid of what is behind me, although there is nothing there, and I know it.

I get agitated; I feel that my fear increases, and so I shut myself up in my own room, get into bed, and hide under the clothes, and there, cowering down rolled into a ball, I close my eyes in despair and remain thus for an indefinite time, remembering that my candle is alight on the table by my bedside, and that I ought to put it out, and yet—I dare not do it!

It is very terrible, is it not, to be like that?

Formerly I felt nothing of all that; I came home quite comfortably, and went up and down in my rooms without anything disturbing my calmness of mind. Had anyone told me that I should be attacked by a malady—for I can call it nothing else—of most improbable fear, such a stupid and terrible malady as it is, I should have laughed outright. I was certainly never afraid of opening the door in the dark; I used to go to bed slowly without locking it, and never got up in the middle of the night to make sure that everything was firmly closed.

It began last year in a very strange manner, on a damp autumn evening. When my servant had left the room, after I had dined, I asked myself what I was going to do. I walked up and down my room for some time, feeling tired without any reason for it, unable to work, and without enough energy to read. A fine rain was falling, and I felt unhappy, a prey to one of those fits of casual despondency which make us feel inclined to cry, or to talk, no matter to whom, so as to shake off our depressing thoughts.

I felt that I was alone and that my rooms seemed to me to be more empty that they had ever been before. I was surrounded by a sensation of infinite and overwhelming solitude. What was I to do? I sat down, but then a kind of nervous impatience agitated my legs, so that I got up and began to walk about again. I was feverish, for my hands, which I had clasped behind me, as one often does when walking slowly, almost seemed to burn one another. Then suddenly a cold shiver ran down my back, and I thought the damp air might have penetrated into my room, so I lit the fire for the first time that year, and sat down again and looked at the flames. But soon I felt that I could not possibly remain quiet. So I got up again and determined to go out, to pull myself together, and to seek a friend to bear me company.

I could not find anyone, so I went on to the boulevards to try and meet some acquaintance or other there.

I was wretched everywhere, and the wet pavement glistened in the gaslight, while the oppressive mist of the almost impalpable rain lay heavily over the streets and seemed to obscure the light from the lamps.

I went on slowly, saying to myself, "I shall not find a soul to talk to."

I glanced into several *cafés*, from the Madeleine as far as the Faubourg Poissonière, and saw many unhappy-looking individuals sitting at the tables, who did not seem even to have enough energy left to finish the refreshments they had ordered.

For a long time I wandered aimlessly up and down, and about midnight I started off for home; I was very calm and very tired. My *concierge** opened the door at once, which was quite unusual for him, and I thought that another lodger had no doubt just come in.

When I go out I always double-lock the door of my room. Now I found it merely closed, which surprised me; but I supposed that some letters had been brought up for me in the course of the evening.

I went in, and found my fire still burning so that it lighted up the room a little. In the act of taking up a candle, I noticed somebody sitting in my arm-chair by the fire, warming his feet, with his back toward me.

I was not in the slightest degree frightened. I thought very naturally that some friend or other had come to see me. No doubt the porter, whom I had told when I went out, had lent him his own key. In a moment I remembered all the circumstances of my return, how the street door had been opened immediately, and that my own door was only latched, and not locked.

---

* Hall-porter.

I could see nothing of my friend but his head. He had evidently gone to sleep while waiting for me, so I went up to him to rouse him. I saw him quite clearly; his right arm was hanging down and his legs were crossed, while his head, which was somewhat inclined to the left of the armchair, seemed to indicate that he was asleep. "Who can it be?" I asked myself. I could not see clearly, as the room was rather dark, so I put out my hand to touch him on the shoulder, and it came in contact with the back of the chair. There was nobody there; the seat was empty.

I fairly jumped with fright. For a moment I drew back as if some terrible danger had suddenly appeared in my way; then I turned round again, impelled by some imperious desire to look at the armchair again. I remained standing upright, panting with fear, so upset that I could not collect my thoughts, and ready to drop.

But I am naturally a cool man, and soon recovered myself. I thought: "It is a mere hallucination, that is all," and I immediately began to reflect about this phenomenon. Thoughts fly very quickly at such moments.

I had been suffering from a hallucination, that was an incontestable fact. My mind had been perfectly lucid and had acted regularly and logically, so there was nothing the matter with the brain. It was only my eyes that had been deceived; they had had a vision, one of those visions which lead simple folk to believe in miracles. It was a nervous accident to the optical apparatus, nothing more; the eyes were rather overwrought, perhaps.

I lit my candle, and when I stooped down to the fire in so doing, I noticed that I was trembling, and I raised myself up with a jump, as if somebody had touched me from behind.

I was certainly not by any means reassured.

I walked up and down a little, and hummed a tune or two. Then I double-locked my door, and felt rather reassured; now, at any rate, nobody could come in.

I sat down again, and thought over my adventure for a long time; then I went to bed, and put out my light.

For some minutes all went well; I lay quietly on my back. Then an irresistible desire seized me to look round the room, and I turned on to my side.

My fire was nearly out and the few glowing embers threw a faint light on to the floor by the chair, where I fancied I saw the man sitting again.

I quickly struck a match, but I had been mistaken, for there was nothing there; I got up, however, and hid the chair behind my bed, and tried to get to sleep as the room was now dark. But I had not forgotten myself for more than five minutes when in my dream I saw all the scene which I had witnessed as clearly as if it were reality. I woke up with a start, and, having lit the candle, sat up in bed, without venturing even to try and go to sleep again.

Twice, however, sleep overcame me for a few moments in spite of myself, and twice I saw the same thing again, till I fancied I was going mad. When day broke, however, I thought that I was cured, and slept peacefully till noon.

It was all past and over. I had been feverish, had had the nightmare; I don't know what. I had been ill, in a word, but yet I thought that I was a great fool.

I enjoyed myself thoroughly that evening; I went and dined at a restaurant; afterward I went to the theater, and then started home. But as I got near the house I was seized by a strange feeling of uneasiness once more; I was afraid of *seeing* him again. I was not afraid of him, not afraid of his presence, in which I did not believe; but I was afraid of being deceived again; I was afraid of some fresh hallucination, afraid lest fear should take possession of me.

For more than an hour I wandered up and down the pavement; then I thought that I was really too foolish, and returned home. I panted so that I could scarcely get upstairs, and remained standing outside my door for more than ten minutes; then suddenly I took courage and pulled myself together. I inserted my key into the lock, and went in with a candle in my hand. I kicked open my half-open bedroom door, and gave a frightened look toward the fireplace; there was nothing there. A — h!

What a relief and what a delight! What a deliverance! I walked up and down briskly and boldly, but I was not altogether reassured, and kept turning round with a jump; the very shadows in the corners disquieted me.

I slept badly, and was constantly disturbed by imaginary noises, but I did not see *him;* no, that was all over.

Since that time I have been afraid of being alone at night. I feel that the specter is there, close to me, around me; but it has not appeared to me again.

And supposing it did, what would it matter, since I do not believe in it and know that it is nothing?

It still worries me, however, because I am constantly thinking of it: *his right arm hanging down and his head inclined to the left like a man who was asleep*—Enough of that, in Heaven's name! I don't want to think about it!

Why, however, am I so persistently possessed with this idea? His feet were close to the fire!

He haunts me; it is very stupid, but so it is. Who and what is HE? I know that he does not exist except in my cowardly imagination, in my fears, and in my agony! There—enough of that!

Yes, it is all very well for me to reason with myself, *to stiffen myself*, so to say; but I cannot remain at home, because I know he is there. I know I shall not see him again; he will not show himself again; that is all over. But he is there all the same in my thoughts. He remains invisible, but that does not prevent his being there. He is behind the doors, in the closed cupboards, in the wardrobe, under the bed, in every dark corner. If I open the door or the cupboard, if I take the candle to look under the bed and throw a light on to the dark places, he is there no longer, but I feel that he is behind me. I turn round, certain that I shall not see him, that I shall never see him again; but he is, none the less, behind me.

It is very stupid, it is dreadful; but what am I to do? I cannot help it.

But if there were two of us in the place, I feel certain that he would not be there any longer, for he is there just because I am alone, simply and solely because I am alone!

THE TAILOR'S DAUGHTER

THE steamboat "Kleber" had stopped, and I was admiring the beautiful bay of Bougie, that was opened out before us. The high hills were covered with forests, and in the distance the yellow sands formed a beach of powdered gold, while the sun shed its fiery rays on the white houses of the town.

The warm African breeze blew the odor of that great, mysterious continent, into which men of the Northern races but rarely penetrate, into my face. For three months I had been wandering on the borders of that great unknown world, on the outskirts of that strange world of the ostrich, the camel, the gazelle, the hippopotamus, the gorilla, the lion and the tiger, and the negro. I had seen the Arab galloping like the wind and passing like a floating standard, and I had slept under those brown tents, the moving habitation of the white birds of the desert, and felt, as it were, intoxicated with light with fancy, and with space.

But now, after this present and final excursion, I should have to return to France and to Paris, that city of useless chatter, of commonplace cares, and of continual hand-shaking, and should bid adieu to all that I had got to like so much, which was so new to me, which I had scarcely had time to see thoroughly, and which I so much regretted to leave.

A fleet of small boats surrounded the steamer, and, jumping into one rowed by a negro lad, I soon reached the quay near the old Saracen gate, whose gray ruins at the entrance of the Kabyle town looked like an old escutcheon of nobility. While I was standing by the side of my portmanteau, looking at the great steamer lying at anchor in the roads, and filled with admiration at that unique shore, and that semicircle of hills, bathed in blue light, more beautiful than those of Ajaccio, or of Porto, in Corsica, a heavy hand was laid on my shoulder. Turning round I saw a tall man with a long beard, dressed in white flannel, and wearing a straw hat, standing by my side and looking at me with his blue eyes.

"Are you not an old schoolfellow of mine?" he said.

"It is very possible. What is your name?"

"Trémoulin."

"By Jove! You were in the same class as I."

"Yes! Old fellow, I recognized you immediately."

He seemed so pleased, so happy at seeing me, that in an outburst of friendly selfishness, I shook both the hands of my former schoolfellow heartily, and felt very pleased at meeting him thus.

For four years, Trémoulin had been one of my best and most intimate school friends, one of those

whom we are too apt to forget as soon as we leave.
In those days, he had been a tall, thin fellow, whose
head seemed to be too heavy for his body; it was a
large, round head, and hung sometimes to the right
and sometimes to the left, on to his chest. Trémoulin
was very clever, however; he had a marvelous aptitude for learning, an instinctive intuition for all literary studies, and gained nearly all the prizes in our
class.

We were fully convinced at school that he would
turn out a celebrated man, a poet, no doubt, for he
wrote verses, and was full of ingeniously sentimental
ideas. His father, who kept a chemist's shop near
the Pantheon, was not supposed to be very well off,
and I had lost sight of him as soon as he had taken
his bachelor's degree. I naturally asked him what he
was doing there.

"I am a planter," he replied.

"Bah! You really plant?"

"And I have my harvest."

"What is it?"

"Grapes, from which I make wine."

"Is your wine-growing a success?"

"A great success."

"So much the better, old fellow."

"Were you going to the hotel?"

"Of course I was."

"Well, then, you must just come home with me,
instead."

"But!—"

"The matter is settled."

And he said to the young negro who was watching our movements: "Take that home, Al."

The lad put my portmanteau on his shoulder, and set off, raising the dust with his black feet, while Trémoulin took my arm and led me off. First of all, he asked about my journey and what impressions it had made on me, and seeing how enthusiastic I was about it, he seemed to like me better than ever. He lived in an old Moorish house, in an interior street, commanded by a terrace. It had a windowless court-yard and commanded the neighboring houses as well as the bay, and the forests, the hill, and the open sea. I could not help exclaiming:

"Ah! This is what I like; the whole of the East lays hold of me in this place. You are indeed lucky to be living here! What nights you must spend upon that terrace! Do you sleep there?"

"Yes, in the summer. We will go on to it this evening. Are you fond of fishing?"

"What kind of fishing?"

"Fishing by torchlight"

"Yes, I am particularly fond of it."

"Very well, then, we will go after dinner, and we will come back and drink sherbet on my roof."

After I had had a bath, he took me to see the charming Kabyle town, a veritable cascade of white houses toppling down to the sea, and then, when it was getting dusk, we went in, and after an excellent dinner went down to the quay. We saw nothing except the fires and the stars, those large, bright, scintillating African stars. A boat was waiting for us, and as soon as we had got in, a man whose face I could not distinguish began to row. My friend was getting ready the brazier which he would light later, and he said to me: "You know I have a

mania for using a fish-spear, and few can handle it
it better than l."

"Allow me to compliment you on your skill."
We had rowed round a kind of mole, and now were
in a small bay full of high rocks, whose shadows
looked like towers built in the water. I suddenly
perceived that the sea was phosphorescent, and as
the oars moved gently, they seemed to light up moving flames, that followed in our wake, and then died
out. I leaned over the side of the boat and watched
it as we glided over the glimmer in the darkness.

Where were we going to? I could not see my
neighbors; in fact, I could see nothing but the lumi-
nous ripple, and the sparks of water dropping from
the oars. It was hot, very hot, the darkness seemed
as hot as a furnace, and this mysterious motion with
these two men in that silent boat had a peculiar
effect upon me.

Suddenly the rower stopped. Where were we?
I heard a slight scratching noise close to me, and I
saw a hand, nothing but a hand applying a lighted
match to the iron grating which was fastened over
the bows of the boat and was heaped high with
wood, as if it had been a floating funeral pile. It was
soon blazing brightly, illuminating the boat and the
two men, an old, thin, pale, wrinkled sailor, with a
pocket handkerchief tied round his head instead of a
cap, and Trémoulin, whose fair beard glistened in the
light.

The other began to row again, while Trémoulin
kept throwing wood on to the brazier, which burned
red and brightly. I leaned over the side again, and
could see the bottom. A few feet below us there

was that strange country of the water, which vivifies plants and animals, just like the air of heaven does. Trémoulin, who was standing in the bows with his body bent forward and holding the sharp-pointed trident in his hand, was on the lookout with the ardent gaze of a beast of prey watching for its spoil. Suddenly, with a swift movement, he darted his forked weapon into the sea so vigorously that it secured a large fish swimming near the bottom. It was a conger eel, which managed to wriggle, half dead as it was, into a puddle of the brackish water.

Trémoulin again threw his spear, and when he pulled it up, I saw a great lump of red flesh which palpitated, moved, and rolled and unrolled long, strong, soft feelers round the handle of the trident. It was an octopus, and Trémoulin opened his knife, and with a swift movement plunged it between the eyes and killed it. And so our fishing continued, until the wood began to run short. When there was not enough left to keep up the fire, Trémoulin dipped the braziers into the sea, and we were again buried in darkness.

The old sailor began to row again, slowly and regularly, though I could not tell where the land or where the port was. By and by, however, I saw lights. We were nearing the harbor.

"Are you sleepy?" my friend said to me.

"Not the slightest."

"Then we will go and have a chat on the roof."

"I shall be delighted."

Just as we got on to the terrace, I saw the crescent moon rising behind the mountains, and around us the white houses, with their flat roofs, sloping down

toward the sea, while human forms were standing or lying on them, sleeping or dreaming under
the stars; whole families wrapped in long gowns, and
resting in the calm night, after the heat of the day.

It seemed to me as if the Eastern mind were
taking possession of me, the poetical and legendary
spirit of a people with simple and flowery thoughts.
My head was full of the Bible and of "The Arabian
Nights"; I could hear the prophets proclaiming miracles, and I could see princesses wearing silk robes
on the roofs of the palaces, while delicate perfumes,
whose smoke assumed the forms of genii, were burning on silver dishes. I said to Trémoulin:

"You are very fortunate in living here."

"I came here quite by accident," he replied.

"By accident?"

"Yes, accident and unhappiness brought me
here."

"You have been unhappy?"

"Very unhappy."

He was standing in front of me, wrapped in his
burnous, and his voice had such a painful ring in it,
that it almost made me shiver. After a moment's
silence, however, he continued:

"I will tell you what my troubles have been; perhaps it will do me good to speak about them."

"Let me hear them."

"Do you really wish it?"

"Yes."

"Very well, then. You remember what I was at
school; a sort of a poet, brought up in a chemist's
shop. I dreamed of writing books, and I tried it,
after taking my degree, but I did not succeed. I

published a volume of verse, and then a novel, and neither of them sold; then I wrote a play, which was never acted.

"Next, I lost my heart, but I will not give you an account of my passion. Next door to my father's shop, there was a tailor, who had a daughter with whom I fell in love. She was very clever, had obtained her certificates for higher education, and her mind was bright and active, quite in keeping indeed with her body. She might have been taken for fifteen, although she was two-and-twenty. She was very small, with delicate features, outlines and tints, just like some beautiful water-color. Her nose, her mouth, her blue eyes, her light hair, her smile, her waist, her hands, all looked as if they were fit for a stained window, and not for everyday life, but she was lively, supple, and incredibly active, and I was very much in love with her. I remember two or three walks in the Luxembourg Garden, near the Medicis fountain, which were certainly the happiest hours of my life. I dare say you have known that foolish condition of tender madness, which causes us to think of nothing but of acts of adoration! One really becomes possessed, haunted by a woman, and nothing exists for us when by her side.

"We soon became engaged, and I told her my projects for the future, which she did not approve. She did not believe that I was either a poet, a novelist, or a dramatic author, and thought a prosperous business could afford perfect happiness. So I gave up the idea of writing books, and resigned myself to selling them, and I bought a bookseller's business at Marseilles, the owner of which had just died.

"I had three very prosperous years. We had made our shop into a sort of literary drawing-room, where all the men of letters in the town used to come and talk. They came in, as if it had been a club, and exchanged ideas on books, on poets, and especially on politics. My wife, who took a very active part in the business, enjoyed quite a reputation in the town, but as for me, while they were all talking downstairs, I was working in my studio upstairs, which communicated with the shop by a winding staircase. I could hear their voices, their laughter, and their discussions, and sometimes I left off writing in order to listen. I remained in my own room to write a novel—which I never finished.

"The most regular frequenters of the shop were Monsieur Montina, a man of good private means, a tall, handsome man, such as one meets with in the south of France, with an olive skin and dark, expressive eyes; Monsieur Barbet, a magistrate; two merchants, who were partners, Messrs. Faucil and Labarrègue; and General the Marquis de la Flèche, the head of the Royalist party, the principal man in the whole district, an old fellow of sixty-six.

"My business prospered, and I was happy, very happy. One day, however, about three o'clock when I was out on business, as I was going through the Rue Saint Ferréol, I suddenly saw a woman come out of a house, whose figure and appearance were so much like my wife's, that I should have said to myself, 'There she is!' if I had not left her in the shop half an hour before, suffering from a headache. She was walking quickly on before me, without turning round, and, in spite of myself, I followed her, as I felt surprised and uneasy. I said to myself: 'It is she; no, it is quite impossible, as she has a sick headache. And then, what could she have to do in that house?' However, as I wished to have the matter cleared up, I made haste after her. I do not know whether she felt or guessed that I was behind her, or whether she recognized my step, but she turned round suddenly. It was she! When she saw me, she grew very red and stopped, and then, with a smile, she said: 'Oh! Here you are?' I felt choking.

"'Yes; so you have come out? And how is your headache?'

"'It is better, and I have been out on an errand.'

"'Where?'

"'To Lacaussade's, in the Rue Cassinelli to order some pencils.'

"She looked me full in the face. She was not flushed now, but rather pale, on the contrary. Her clear, limpid eyes—ah! those women's eyes!—appeared to be full of truth, but I felt vaguely and painfully, that they were full of lies. I was much more confused and embarrassed than she was herself, without venturing to suspect, but sure that she was lying, though I did not know why, and so I merely said:

"'You were quite right to go out, if you felt better.'

"'Oh! yes; my head is much better.'

"'Are you going home?'

"'Yes, of course I am.'

"I left her, and wandered about the streets by myself. What was going on? While I was talking to her, I had an intuitive feeling of her falseness, but now I could not believe that it was so, and when

I returned home to dinner, I was angry for having suspected her, even for a moment.

"Have you ever been jealous? It does not matter whether you have or not, but the first drop of jealousy had fallen into my heart, and that is always like a spark of fire. It did not accuse her of anything, and I did not think anything, I only knew that she had lied. You must remember that every night, after the customers and clerks had left, we were alone, and either strolled as far as the harbor, when it was fine, or remained talking in my office, if the weather was bad, and I used to open my heart to her without any reserve, because I loved her. She was part of my life, the greater part, and all my happiness, and in her small hands she held my trusting, faithful heart captive.

"During the first days, those days of doubt, and before my suspicions increased and assumed a precise shape, I felt depressed and chilly as if I were going to be seriously ill. I was continually cold, really cold, and could neither eat nor sleep. Why had she told me a lie? What was she doing in that house? I went there to try and find out something, but I could discover nothing. The man who rented the first floor, and who was an upholsterer, had told me all about his neighbors, but without helping me the least. A midwife had lived on the second floor, a dressmaker and a manicure and chiropodist on the third, and two coachmen and their families in the attics.

"Why had she told me a lie? It would have been so easy for her to have said that she had been to the dressmaker's or chiropodist's. Oh! how I longed to

question them, also! I did not say so, for fear that
she might guess my suspicions. One thing, however,
was certain: she had been into that house, and had
concealed the fact from me, so there was some mystery in it. But what? At one moment, I thought
there might be some laudable purpose in it, some
charitable deed which she wished to hide, some information which she wished to obtain, and I found
fault with myself for suspecting her. Have not all of
us the right to our little, innocent secrets, a kind of
second, interior life, for which one ought not to be
responsible to anybody? Can a man, because he has
taken a girl to be his companion through life, de-
mand that she shall neither think nor do anything
without telling him, either before or afterward? Does
the word marriage mean renouncing all liberty and
independence? Was is not quite possible that she
was going to the dressmaker's without telling me, or
that she was going to assist the family of one of the
coachmen? Or she might have thought that I might
criticise, if not blame, her visit to the house. She
knew me thoroughly, and my slightest peculiarities,
and perhaps she feared a discussion, even if she did
not think that I should find fault with her. She had
very pretty hands, and I ended by supposing that she
was having them secretly attended to by the manicure in the house which I suspected, and that she
did not tell me of it for fear that I should think her
extravagant. She was very methodical and economical,
and looked after all her household duties most carefully, and no doubt she thought that she should
lower herself in my eyes, were she to confess that
slight piece of feminine extravagance. Women have

very many subtleties and innate intricacies in their souls!

"But none of my own arguments reassured me. I was jealous, and I felt that my suspicion was affecting me terribly, that I was being devoured by it. I felt secret grief and anguish, and a thought which I still veiled. I did not dare to lift the veil, for beneath it I should find a terrible doubt. A lover? Had not she a lover? It was unlikely, impossible. A mere dream — and yet?

"I continually saw Montina's face before my eyes. I saw the tall, silly-looking, handsome man, with his bright hair, smiling into her face, and I said to myself: 'He is the one.' I concocted a story of their intrigues. They had talked a book over together, had discussed the love adventures it contained, had found something in it that resembled them, and they had turned that analogy into reality. And so I watched them, a prey to the most terrible sufferings that a man can endure. I bought shoes with india-rubber soles, so that I might be able to walk about the house without making any noise, and I spent half my time in going up and down my little spiral staircase, in the hope of surprising them, but I always found that the clerk was with them.

"I lived in a constant state of suffering. I could no longer work nor attend to my business. As soon as I went out, as soon as I had walked a hundred yards along the street, I said to myself: 'He is there!' and when I found he was not there, I went out again! But almost immediately, I went back again, thinking: 'He has come now!' and that went on every day.

"At night it was still worse, for I felt her by my side in bed asleep, or pretending to be asleep! Was she really sleeping? No, most likely not. Was that another lie?

"I remained motionless on my back, hot from the warmth of her body, panting and tormented. Oh! how intensely I longed to get up, to get a hammer and to split her head open, so as to be able to see inside it! I knew that I should have seen nothing except what is to be found in every head, and I should have discovered nothing, for that would have been impossible. And her eyes! When she looked at me, I felt furious with rage. I looked at her — she looked at me! Her eyes were transparent, candid — and false, false! Nobody could tell what she was thinking of, and I felt inclined to run pins into them and to destroy those mirrors of falseness.

"Ah! how well I could understand the Inquisition! I would have applied the torture, the boot — Speak! Confess! You will not? Then wait! And I would have seized her by the throat until I choked her. Or else I would have held her fingers into the fire. Oh! how I should have enjoyed doing it! Speak! Speak! You will not? I would have held them on the coals, and when the tips were burned, she would have confessed — certainly she would have confessed!"

Trémoulin was sitting up, shouting, with clenched fists. Around us, on the neighboring roofs, people awoke and sat up, as he was disturbing their sleep. As for me, I was moved and powerfully interested, and in the darkness I could see that little woman, that little, fair, lively, artful woman, as if I had known her personally. I saw her selling her books, talking with the men whom **her** childish ways attracted, and in her delicate, doll-like head, I could see little crafty ideas, silly ideas, the dreams which a milliner smelling of musk attaches to all heroes of romantic adventures. I suspected her just as he did, I hated and detested her, and would willingly have burned her fingers and made her confess.

Presently, he continued more calmly: "I do not know why I have told you all this, for I have never mentioned it to anyone, but then I have not seen anybody for two years! And it was seething in my heart like a fermenting wine. I have got rid of it, and so much the worse for you. Well, I had made a mistake, but it was worse than I thought, much worse. Just listen. I employed the means which a man always does under such circumstances, and pretended that I was going to be away from home for a day, and whenever I did this my wife went out to lunch. I need not tell you how I bribed a waiter in the restaurant to which they used to go, so that I might surprise them.

"He was to open the door of their private room for me. I arrived at the appointed time, with the fixed determination of killing them both. I could see the whole scene, just as if it had already occurred! I could see myself going in. A small table covered with glasses, bottles, and plates separated her from Montina. They would be so surprised when they saw me that they would not even attempt to move, and without a word, I should bring down the loaded stick which I had in my hand on the man's head. Killed by one blow, he would fall with his head on the table, and then, turning toward her, I should leave her a few moments to understand it all and to stretch out her arms toward me, mad with terror, before dying in her turn. Oh! I was ready, strong, determined, and pleased, madly pleased at the idea. The idea of the terrified look that she would throw at my raised stick, of her arms that she would stretch out to me, of her horrified cry, of her livid and convulsed looks, avenged me beforehand. I would not kill her at one blow. 'You will think me cruel, I daresay; but you do not know what a man suffers. To think that a woman, whether she be wife or mistress, whom one loves, gives herself to another, yields herself up to him as she does to you, and receives kisses from his lips, as she does from yours! It is a terrible, an atrocious thing to think of. When one feels that torture, one is ready for anything. I only wonder that more women are not murdered, for every man who has been deceived longs to commit murder, has dreamed of it in the solitude of his own room, or on a deserted road, and has been haunted by the one fixed idea of satisfied vengeance.

"I arrived at the restaurant, and asked whether they were there. The waiter whom I had bribed replied: 'Yes, Monsieur,' and taking me upstairs, he pointed to a door, and said: 'That is the room!' So I grasped my stick, as if my fingers had been made of iron, and went in. I had chosen a most appropriate moment, for they were kissing most lovingly, but it was not Montina, it was General de la Flèche, who was sixty-six years old. I had so fully made up my mind that I should find the other one there, I was motionless from astonishment.

"And then — and then I really do not quite know

what I thought, no, I really do not know. If I had found myself face to face with the other, I should have been convulsed with rage, but on seeing this old man, with fat stomach and pendulous cheeks, I was nearly choked with disgust. She, who did not look fifteen, small and slim as she was, had given herself to this fat man, who was nearly paralyzed, because he was a marquis and a general, the friend and representative of dethroned kings. No, I do not know what I felt, nor what I thought. I could not have lifted my hand against this old man; it would have been a disgrace to me, and I no longer felt inclined to kill my wife, but all women who could be guilty of such things! I was no longer jealous, but felt distracted, as if I had seen the horror of horrors!

"Let people say what they like of men, they are not so vile as that! If a man is known to have given himself up to an old woman in that fashion, people point their finger at him. The husband or lover of an old woman is more despised than a thief. We men are a decent lot, as a rule, but many women, especially in Paris, are absolutely bad. They will give themselves to all men, old or young, from the most contemptible and different motives, because it is their profession, their vocation, and their function. They are the eternal, unconscious, and serene prostitutes, who give up their bodies, because they are the merchandise of love, which they sell or give, to the old man who frequents the pavements with money in his pocket, or else for glory, to a lecherous old king, or to a celebrated and disgusting old man."

He vociferated like a prophet of old, in a furious voice, under the starry sky, and with the rage of a

man in despair he repeated all the glorified disgrace
of the mistresses of old kings, the respectable shame
of those virgins who marry old husbands, the toler-
ated disgrace of those young women, who accept old
kisses with a smile.

I could see them, as he evoked their memory,
since the beginning of the world, surging round us
in that Eastern night, girls, beautiful girls, with vile
souls, who, like the lower animals who know nothing of the age of the male, are docile to senile desires.
They rose up before one, the handmaids of the patri-
archs, who are mentioned in the Bible, Hagar, Ruth,
the daughters of Lot, Abigail, Abishag; the virgin of
Shunam, who reanimated David with her caresses
when he was dying, and the others, young, stout,
white, patricians or plebeians, irresponsible females
belonging to a master, and submissive slaves, whether
caught by the attraction of royalty or bought as
slaves!

"What did you do?" I asked.

"I went away," he replied simply. And we remained sitting side by side for a long time without
speaking, only dreaming!

I have retained an impression of that evening that
will never be dispelled. All that I saw, felt, and
heard, our fishing excursion, the octopus also, perhaps that harrowing story, amid those white figures
on the neighboring roofs, all seemed to concur in
producing a unique sensation. Certain meetings, certain inexplicable combinations of things, contain a
larger quantity of the secret quintessence of life than
that which is spread over the ordinary events of our
days, when nothing exceptional happens.

THE AVENGER

WHEN M. Antoine Leuillet married the Widow Mathilde Souris, he had been in love with her for nearly ten years.

M. Souris had been his friend, his old college chum. Leuillet was very fond of him, but found him rather a muff. He often used to say: "That poor Souris will never set the Seine on fire."

When Souris married Mlle. Mathilde Duval, Leuillet was surprised and somewhat vexed, for he had a slight weakness for her. She was the daughter of a neighbor of his, a retired haberdasher with a good deal of money. She was pretty, well-mannered, and intelligent. She accepted Souris on account of his money.

Then Leuillet cherished hopes of another sort. He began paying attentions to his friend's wife. He was a handsome man, not at all stupid, and also well off. He was confident that he would succeed; he failed. Then he fell really in love with her, and he was the

(117)

sort of lover who is rendered timid, prudent, and embarrassed by intimacy with the husband. Mme.
Souris fancied that he no longer meant anything serious by his attentions to her, and she became simply
his friend. This state of affairs lasted nine years.

Now, one morning, Leuillet received a startling
communication from the poor woman. Souris had
died suddenly of aneurism of the heart.

He got a terrible shock, for they were of the same
age; but, the very next moment, a sensation of profound joy, of infinite relief, of deliverance, penetrated
his body and soul. Mme. Souris was free.

He had the tact, however, to make such a display
of grief as the occasion required; he waited for the
proper time to elapse, and attended to all the conventional usages. At the end of fifteen months, he
married the widow.

His conduct was regarded as not only natural but
generous. He had acted like a good friend and an
honest man. In short, he was happy, quite happy.

They lived on terms of the closest confidence,
having from the first understood and appreciated each
other. One kept nothing secret from the other, and
they told each other their inmost thoughts. Leuillet
now loved his wife with a calm, trustful affection; he
loved her as a tender, devoted partner, who is an
equal and a confidant. But there still lingered in his
soul a singular and unaccountable grudge against the
deceased Souris, who had been the first to possess
this woman, who had had the flower of her youth
and of her soul, and who had even robbed her of her
poetic attributes. The memory of the dead husband
spoiled the happiness of the living husband; and this

posthumous jealousy now began to torment Leuillet's heart day and night.

The result was that he was incessantly talking about Souris, asking a thousand minute and intimate questions about him, and seeking for information as to all his habits and personal characteristics. And he pursued him with railleries even into the depths of the tomb, recalling with self-satisfaction his oddities, emphasizing his absurdities, and pointing out his defects.

Constantly he would call out to his wife from one end to the other of the house:

"Hallo, Mathilde!"

"Here I am, dear."

"Come and let us have a chat."

She always came over to him, smiling, well aware that Souris was to be the subject of the chat, and anxious to gratify her second husband's harmless fad.

"I say! do you remember how Souris wanted one day to prove to me that small men are always better loved than big men?"

And he launched out into reflections unfavorable to the defunct husband, who was small, and discreetly complimentary to himself, as he happened to be tall.

And Mme. Leuillet let him think that he was quite right; and she laughed very heartily, turned the first husband into ridicule in a playful fashion for the amusement of his successor, who always ended by remarking:

"Never mind! Souris was a muff!"

They were happy, quite happy. And Leuillet never ceased to testify his unabated attachment to his wife by all the usual manifestations.

Now, one night, when they happened to be both kept awake by a renewal of youthful ardor, Leuillet, who held his wife clasped tightly in his arms and had his lips glued to hers, said:

"Tell me this, darling."

"What?"

"Souris—'tisn't easy to put the question—was he very—very loving?"

She gave him a warm kiss, as she murmured:

"Not as much as you, my sweet."

His male vanity was flattered, and he went on:

"He must have been—rather a flat—eh?"

She did not answer. There was merely a sly little laugh on her face, which she pressed close to her husband's neck.

He persisted in his questions:

"Come now! Don't deny that he was a flat—well, I mean, rather an awkward sort of fellow?"

She nodded slightly.

"Well, yes, rather awkward."

He went on:

"I'm sure he used to weary you many a night—isn't that so?"

This time she had an access of frankness, and she replied:

"Oh! yes."

He embraced her once more when she made this acknowledgment, and murmured:

"What an ass he was! You were not happy with him?"

She answered:

"No. He was not always jolly."

Leuillet felt quite delighted, making a comparison

in his own mind between his wife's former situation and her present one.

He remained silent for some time; then, with a fresh outburst of curiosity, he said:

"Tell me this!"

"What?"

"Will you be quite candid — quite candid with me?"

"Certainly, dear."

"Well, look here! Were you never tempted to — to deceive this imbecile, Souris?"

Mme. Leuillet uttered a little "Oh!" in a shame-faced way, and again cuddled her face closer to her husband's chest. But he could see that she was laughing.

He persisted:

"Come now, confess it! He had a head just suited for a cuckold, this blockhead! It would be so funny! The good Souris! Oh! I say, darling, you might tell it to me — only to me!"

He emphasized the words "to me," feeling certain that if she wanted to show any taste when she deceived her husband, he, Leuillet, would have been the man; and he quivered with joy at the expectation of this avowal, sure that if she had not been the virtuous woman she was he could have won her then.

But she did not reply, laughing incessantly as if at the recollection of something infinitely comic.

Leuillet, in his turn, burst out laughing at the notion that he might have made a cuckold of Souris. What a good joke! What a capital lot of fun, to be sure!

He exclaimed in a voice broken by convulsions of laughter:

"Oh! poor Souris! poor Souris! Ah! yes, he had that sort of head — oh, certainly he had!"

And Mme. Leuillet now twisted herself under the sheets, laughing till the tears almost came into her eyes.

And Leuillet repeated: "Come, confess it! confess it! Be candid. You must know that it cannot be unpleasant to me to hear such a thing."

Then she stammered, still choking with laughter: "Yes, yes."

Her husband pressed her for an answer:

"Yes, what? Look here! tell me everything."

She was now laughing in a more subdued fashion, and, raising her mouth up to Leuillet's ear, which was held toward her in anticipation of some pleasant piece of confidence she whispered: "Yes — I did deceive him!"

He felt a cold shiver down his back, and utterly dumfounded, he gasped:

"You — you — did — really — deceive him?"

She was still under the impression that he thought the thing infinitely pleasant, and replied:

"Yes — really — really."

He was obliged to sit up in bed so great was the shock he received, holding his breath, just as overwhelmed as if he had just been told that he was a cuckold himself. At first he was unable to articulate properly; then after the lapse of a minute or so, he merely ejaculated:

"Ah!"

She, too, had stopped laughing now, realizing her mistake too late.

Leuillet, at length asked:

"And with whom?"

She kept silent, cudgeling her brain to find some excuse.

He repeated his question:

"With whom?"

At last, she said:

"With a young man."

He turned toward her abruptly, and in a dry tone, said:

"Well, I suppose it wasn't with some kitchen-slut. I ask you who was the young man—do you understand?"

She did not answer. He tore away the sheet which she had drawn over her head and pushed her into the middle of the bed, repeating:

"I want to know with what young man—do you understand?"

Then, she replied, having some difficulty in uttering the words:

"I only wanted to laugh." But he fairly shook with rage:

"What? How is that? You only wanted to laugh? So then you were making game of me? I'm not going to be satisfied with these evasions, let me tell you! I ask you what was the young man's name?"

She did not reply, but lay motionless on her back.

He caught hold of her arm and pressed it tightly:

"Do you hear me, I say? I want you to give me an answer when I speak to you."

Then she said, in nervous tones:

"I think you must be going mad! Let me alone!"

He trembled with fury, so exasperated that he scarcely knew what he was saying, and, shaking her with all his strength, he repeated:

"Do you hear me? do you hear me?"

She wrenched herself out of his grasp with a sudden movement and with the tips of her fingers slapped her husband on the nose. He entirely lost his temper, feeling that he had been struck, and angrily pounced down on her.

He now held her under him, boxing her ears in a most violent manner, and exclaiming:

"Take that — and that — and that — there you are, you trollop, you strumpet — you strumpet!"

Then when he was out of breath, exhausted from beating her, he got up and went over to the bureau to get himself a glass of sugared orange-water, almost ready to faint after his exertion.

And she lay huddled up in bed, crying and heaving great sobs, feeling that there was an end of her happiness, and that it was all her own fault.

Then in the midst of her tears, she faltered:

"Listen, Antoine, come here! I told you a lie — listen! I'll explain it to you."

And now, prepared to defend herself, armed with excuses and subterfuges, she slightly raised her head all disheveled under her crumpled nightcap.

And he turning toward her, drew close to her, ashamed at having whacked her, but feeling still in his heart's core as a husband an inexhaustible hatred against the woman who had deceived his predecessor, Souris.

THE CONSERVATORY

MONSIEUR and Mme. Lerebour were about the same age. But Monsieur looked younger, although he was the weaker of the two. They lived near Mantes in a pretty estate which they had bought after having made a fortune by selling printed cottons.

The house was surrounded by a beautiful garden containing a poultry yard, Chinese *kiosques*, and a little conservatory at the end of the avenue. M. Lerebour was short, round, and jovial, with the joviality of a shopkeeper of epicurean tastes. His wife, lean, self-willed, and always discontented, had not succeeded in overcoming her husband's good-humor. She dyed her hair, and sometimes read novels, which made dreams pass through her soul, although she affected to despise writings of this kind. People said she was a woman of strong passions without her having ever done anything to sustain that opinion. But her husband sometimes said: "My wife is a gay woman," with a certain knowing air which awakened suppositions.

For some years past, however, she had shown herself aggressive toward M. Lerebour, always irritated and hard, as if a secret and unavowable grief tormented her. A sort of misunderstanding was the result. They scarcely spoke to each other, and Madame, whose name was Palmyre, was incessantly heaping unkind compliments, wounding allusions, bitter words, without any apparent reason, on Monsieur, whose name was Gustave.

He bent his back, bored though gay, all the same, endowed with such a fund of contentment that he endured her domestic bickerings. He asked himself, nevertheless, what unknown cause could have thus embittered his spouse, for he had a strong feeling that her irritation had a hidden reason, but so difficult to penetrate that his efforts to do so were in vain.

He often said to her: "Look here, my dear, tell me what you have against me. I feel that you are concealing something."

She invariably replied: "But there is nothing the matter with me, absolutely nothing. Besides, if I had some cause for discontent, it would be for you to guess at it. I don't like men who understand nothing, who are so soft and incapable that one must come to their assistance to make them grasp the slightest thing."

He murmured dejectedly: "I see clearly that you don't want to say anything."

And he went away still striving to unravel the mystery.

The nights especially became very painful to him; for they always shared the same bed, as one does in good and simple households. It was not, therefore,

mere ordinary ill-temper that she displayed toward
him. She chose the moment when they were lying
side by side to load him with the liveliest raillery.
She reproached him principally with his corpulence:
"You take up all the room, you are becoming so
fat."

And she forced him to get up on the slightest
pretext, sending him downstairs to look for a newspaper she had forgotten, or a bottle of orange-water,
which he failed to find as she had herself hidden it
away. And she exclaimed in a furious and sarcastic
tone: "You might, however, know where to find it,
you big booby!" When he had been wandering
about the sleeping house for a whole hour, and returned to the room empty-handed, the only thanks
she gave him was to say: "Come, get back to bed,
it will make you thin to take a little walking; you
are becoming as flabby as a sponge."

She kept waking him every moment by declaring
that she was suffering from cramps in her stomach,
and insisting on his rubbing her with flannel soaked
in eau de Cologne. He would make efforts to cure
her, grieved at seeing her ill, and would propose to
go and rouse up Céleste, their maid. Then she would
get angry, crying: "You must be a fool. Well! it is
over; I am better now, so go back to bed, you big
lout."

To his question: "Are you quite sure you have
got better?" she would fling this harsh answer in his
face:

"Yes, hold your tongue! let me sleep! Don't
worry me any more about it! You are incapable of
doing anything, even of rubbing a woman."

He got into a state of deep dejection: "But, my darling—"

She became exasperated: "I want no 'buts.' Enough, isn't it? Give me some rest now." And she turned her face to the wall.

Now, one night, she shook him so abruptly that he started up in terror, and found himself in a sitting posture with a rapidity which was not habitual to him. He stammered:

"What? What's the matter?"

She caught him by the arm and pinched him till he cried out. Then she gave him a box on the ear: "I hear some noise in the house."

Accustomed to the frequent alarms of Mme. Lerebour, he did not disturb himself very much, and quietly asked:

"What sort of noise, my darling?"

She trembled, as if she were in a state of terror, and replied: "Noise—why, noise—the noise of footsteps. There is some one."

He remained incredulous: "Some one? You think so? But no; you must be mistaken. Besides, whom do you think it can be?"

She shuddered:

"Who? Who? Why, thieves, of course, you imbecile!"

He plunged softly under the sheets:

"Ah! no, my darling! There is nobody. I dare say you only dreamed it."

Then, she flung off the coverlet, and, jumping out of bed, in a rage: "Why, then, you are just as cowardly as you are incapable! In any case, I shall not let myself be massacred owing to your pusillanimity." And snatching up the tongs from the fire-place, she placed herself in a fighting attitude in front of the bolted door.

Moved by his wife's display of valor, perhaps ashamed, he rose up in his turn sulkily, and without taking off his nightcap he seized the shovel, and placed himself face to face with his better half.

They waited for twenty minutes in the deepest silence. No fresh noise disturbed the repose of the house. Then, Madame, becoming furious, got back into bed saying: "Nevertheless I'm sure there is some one."

In order to avoid anything like a quarrel, he did not make an allusion during the next day to this panic. But, next night, Mme. Lerebour woke up her husband with more violence still than the night before, and, panting, she stammered: "Gustave, Gustave, somebody has just opened the garden-gate!"

Astonished at this persistence, he fancied that his wife must have had an attack of somnambulism, and was about to make an effort to shake off this danger-ous state when he thought he heard, in fact, a slight sound under the walls of the house. He rose up, rushed to the window, and he saw—yes, he saw—a white figure quickly passing along one of the garden-walks.

He murmured, as if he were on the point of faint-ing: "There is some one." Then, he recovered his self-possession, felt more resolute, and suddenly carried away by the formidable anger of a proprietor whose territory has been encroached upon, he said: "Wait! wait, and you shall see!"

5 G. de M.—9

He rushed toward the writing-desk, opened it, took out the revolver, and dashed out into the stairs. His wife, filled with consternation, followed him, exclaiming: "Gustave, Gustave, don't abandon me, don't leave me alone! Gustave! Gustave!"

But he scarcely heard her; he had by this time laid his hand on the garden-gate.

Then she went back rapidly and barricaded herself in the conjugal chamber.

    *   *   *   *   *   *   *

She waited five minutes, ten minutes, a quarter of an hour. Wild terror took possession of her. Without doubt, they had killed him; they had seized, garroted, strangled him. She would have preferred to hear the report of the six barrels of the revolver, to know that he was fighting, that he was defending himself. But this great silence, this terrifying silence of the country overwhelmed her.

She rang for Céleste. Céleste did not come in answer to the bell. She rang again, on the point of swooning, of sinking into unconsciousness. The entire house remained without a sound. She pressed her burning forehead to the window, seeking to peer through the darkness without. She distinguished nothing but the blacker shadows of a row of trees beside the gray ruts on the roads.

It struck half past twelve. Her husband had been absent for forty-five minutes. She would never see him again. No! she would never see him again. And she fell on her knees sobbing.

Two light knocks at the door of the apartment made her spring up with a bound. M. Lerebour

called out to her: "Open, pray, Palmyre—'tis I."
She rushed forward, opened the door, and standing in
front of him, with her arms akimbo, and her eyes
full of tears, exclaimed: "Where have you been, you
dirty brute? Ah! you left me here by myself nearly
dead of fright. You care no more about me than if
I never existed."

He closed the bedroom door; then he laughed and
laughed like a madman, grinning from ear to ear,
with his hands on his sides, till the tears came into
his eyes.

Mme. Lerebour, stupefied, remained silent.

He stammered: "It was—it was—Céleste, who
had an appointment in the conservatory. If you knew
what—what I have seen—"

She had turned pale, choking with indignation.

"Eh? Do you tell me so? Céleste? In my
house? in—my—house—in my—my—in my conservatory. And you have not killed the man who
was her accomplice! You had a revolver and did not
kill him? In my house—in my house."

She sat down, not feeling able to do anything.

He danced a caper, snapped his fingers, smacked
his tongue, and, still laughing: "If you knew—if
you knew—" He suddenly gave her a kiss.

She tore herself away from him, and in a voice
broken with rage, she said: "I will not let this girl
remain one day longer in my house, do you hear?
Not one day—not one hour. When she returns to
the house, we will throw her out."

M. Lerebour had seized his wife by the waist, and
he planted rows of kisses on her neck, loud kisses,
as in bygone days. She became silent once more,

petrified with astonishment. But he, holding her clasped in his arms, drew her softly toward the bed.

*   *   *   *   *   *   *

Toward half past nine in the morning, Céleste, astonished at not having yet seen her master and mistress, who always rose early, came and knocked softly at their door.

They were in bed, and were gaily chatting side by side. She stood there astonished, and said: "Madame, it is the coffee."

Mme. Lerebour said in a very soft voice: "Bring it here to me, my girl. We are a little tired; we have slept very badly."

Scarcely had the servant-maid gone than M. Lerebour began to laugh again, tickling his wife under the chin, and repeating: "If you knew. Oh! if you knew."

But she caught his hands: "Look here! keep quiet, my darling, if you laugh like this you will make yourself ill."

And she kissed him softly on the eyes.

*   *   *   *   *   *   *

Mme. Lerebour has no more fits of sourness. Sometimes on bright nights the husband and wife come, with furtive steps, along by the clumps of trees and flower-beds as far as the little conservatory at the end of the garden. And they remain there planted side by side with their faces pressed against the glass as if they were looking at something strange and full of interest going on within.

They have increased Céleste's wages.

But M. Lerebour has got thin.

LETTER FOUND ON A CORPSE

You ask me, Madame, whether I am laughing at you? You cannot believe that a man has never been smitten with love. Well, no, I have never loved, never!

What is the cause of this? I really cannot tell. Never have I been under the influence of that sort of intoxication of the heart which we call love! Never have I lived in that dream, in that exaltation, in that state of madness into which the image of a woman casts us. I have never been pursued, haunted, roused to fever-heat, lifted up to Paradise by the thought of meeting, or by the possession of, a being who had suddenly become for me more desirable than any good fortune, more beautiful than any other creature, more important than the whole world! I have never wept, I have never suffered on account of any of you. I have not passed my nights thinking of one woman without closing my eyes. I have no experience of waking up with the thought and the mem-

(133)

ory of her shedding their illumination on me. I have never known the wild desperation of hope when she was about to come, or the divine sadness of regret when she parted with me, leaving behind her in the room a delicate odor of violet-powder.

I have never been in love.

I, too, have often asked myself why is this. And truly I can scarcely tell. Nevertheless, I have found some reasons for it; but they are of a metaphysical character, and perhaps you will not be able to appreciate them.

I suppose I sit too much in judgment on women to submit much to their fascination. I ask you to forgive me for this remark. I am going to explain what I mean. In every creature there is a moral being and a physical being. In order to love, it would be necessary for me to find a harmony between these two beings which I have never found. One has always too great a predominance over the other, sometimes the moral, sometimes the physical.

The intellect which we have a right to require in a woman, in order to love her, is not the same as virile intellect. It is more and it is less. A woman must have a mind open, delicate, sensitive, refined, impressionable. She has no need of either power or initiative in thought, but she must have kindness, elegance, tenderness, coquetry, and that faculty of assimilation which, in a little while, raises her to an equality with him who shares her life. Her greatest quality must be tact, that subtle sense which is to the mind what touch is to the body. It reveals to her a thousand little things, contours, angles, and forms in the intellectual life.

Very frequently pretty women have not intellect to correspond with their personal charms. Now the slightest lack of harmony strikes me and pains me at the first glance. In friendship, this is not of importance. Friendship is a compact in which one fairly divides defects and merits. We may judge of friends, whether man or woman, take into account the good they possess, neglect the evil that is in them, and appreciate their value exactly, while giving ourselves up to an intimate sympathy of a deep and fascinating character.

In order to love, one must be blind, surrender oneself absolutely, see nothing, reason from nothing, understand nothing. One must adore the weakness as well as the beauty of the beloved object, renounce all judgment, all reflection, all perspicacity.

I am incapable of such blindness, and rebel against a seductiveness not founded on reason. This is not all. I have such a high and subtle idea of harmony that nothing can ever realize my ideal. But you will call me a madman. Listen to me. A woman, in my opinion, may have an exquisite soul and a charming body without that body and that soul being in perfect accord with one another. I mean that persons who have noses made in a certain shape are not to be expected to think in a certain fashion. The fat have no right to make use of the same words and phrases as the thin. You, who have blue eyes, Madame, cannot look at life, and judge of things and events as if you had black eyes. The shades of your eyes should correspond, by a sort of fatality, with the shades of your thought. In perceiving these things I have the scent of a bloodhound. Laugh if you like, but it is so.

And yet I imagined that I was in love for an hour, for a day. I had foolishly yielded to the influence of surrounding circumstances. I allowed myself to be beguiled by the mirage of an aurora. Would you like to hear this short history?

*   *   *   *   *   *

I met, one evening, a pretty, enthusiastic woman who wanted, for the purpose of humoring a poetic fancy, to spend a night with me in a boat on a river. I would have preferred — but, no matter, I consented.

It was in the month of June. My fair companion chose a moonlight night in order to excite her imagination all the better.

We had dined at a riverside inn, and then we set out in the boat about ten o'clock. I thought it a rather foolish kind of adventure; but as my companion pleased me I did not bother myself too much about this. I sat down on the seat facing her, seized the oars, and off we started.

I could not deny that the scene was picturesque. We glided past a wooded isle full of nightingales, and the current carried us rapidly over the river covered with silvery ripples. The grasshoppers uttered their shrill, monotonous cry; the frogs croaked in the grass by the river's bank, and the lapping of the water as it flowed on made around us a kind of confused, almost imperceptible murmur, disquieting, which gave us a vague sensation of mysterious fear.

The sweet charm of warm nights and of streams glittering in the moonlight penetrated us. It seemed bliss to live and to float thus, to dream and to feel by one's side a young woman sympathetic and beautiful.

I was somewhat affected, somewhat agitated, some-what intoxicated by the pale brightness of the night and the consciousness of my proximity to a lovely woman.

"Come and sit beside me," she said.

I obeyed. She went on:

"Recite some verses for me."

This appeared to me rather too much. I declined; she persisted. She certainly wanted to have the ut-most pleasure, the whole orchestra of sentiment, from the moon to the rhymes of poets. In the end, I had to yield, and, as if in mockery, I recited for her a charming little poem by Louis Bouilhet, of which the following are a few strophes:

> "I hate the poet who with tearful eye
>   Murmurs some name while gazing tow'rds a star,
> Who sees no magic in the earth or sky,
>   Unless Lizette or Ninon be not far.
> The bard who in all Nature nothing sees
>   Divine, unless a petticoat he ties
> Amorously to the branches of the trees,
>   Or nightcap to the grass, is scarcely wise.
> He has not heard the eternal's thundertone,
>   The voice of Nature in her various moods,
> He cannot tread the dim ravines alone,
>   And of no woman dream 'mid whispering woods."

I expected some reproaches. Nothing of the sort. She murmured:

"How true it is!"

I remained stupefied. Had she understood?

Our boat was gradually drawing nearer to the bank, and got entangled under a willow which im-peded its progress. I drew my arm around my companion's waist, and very gently moved my lips toward her neck. But she repulsed me with an abrupt, angry movement:

"Have done, pray! You are rude!"

I tried to draw her toward me. She resisted, caught hold of the tree, and nearly upset us both into the water. I deemed it the prudent course to cease my importunities.

She said:

"I would rather have you capsized. I feel so happy. I want to dream—that is so nice." Then, in a slightly malicious tone, she added:

"Have you, then, already forgotten the verses you recited for me just now?"

She was right. I became silent.

She went on:

"Come! row!"

And I plied the oars once more. I began to find the night long and to see the absurdity of my conduct. My companion said to me:

"Will you make me a promise?"

"Yes. What is it?"

"To remain quiet, well-behaved, and discreet, if I permit you—"

"What? Say what you mean!"

"Here is what I mean! I want to lie down on my back in the bottom of the boat with you by my side. But I forbid you to touch me, to embrace me—in short to—to caress me."

I promised. She warned me:

"If you move, I'll capsize the boat."

And then we lay down side by side, our eyes turned toward the sky, while the boat glided slowly through

the water. We were rocked by the gentle movements of the shallop. The light sounds of the night
came to us more distinctly in the bottom of the boat,
sometimes causing us to start. And I felt springing
up within me a strange, poignant emotion, an infinite
tenderness, something like an irresistible impulse to
open my arms in order to embrace, to open my
heart in order to love, to give myself, to give my
thoughts, my body, my life, my entire being to some
one.

My companion murmured, like one in a dream:

"Where are we? Where are we going? It seems
to me that I am quitting the earth. How sweet it is!
Ah! if you loved me — a little!"

My heart began to throb. I had no answer to
give. It seemed to me that I loved her. I had no
longer any violent desire. I felt happy there by her
side, and that was enough for me.

And thus we remained for a long, long time without stirring. We caught each other's hands; some
delightful force rendered us motionless, an unknown
force stronger than ourselves, an alliance, chaste, intimate, absolute, of our persons lying there side by
side which belonged to without touching each other.
What was this? How do I know? Love, perhaps.

Little by little, the dawn appeared. It was three
o'clock in the morning. Slowly, a great brightness
spread over the sky. The boat knocked against
something. I rose up. We had come close to a
tiny islet.

But I remained ravished, in a state of ecstasy. In
front of us stretched the shining firmament, red, rosy,
violet, spotted with fiery clouds resembling golden

vapors. The river was glowing with purple, and three houses on one side of it seemed to be burning.

I bent toward my companion. I was going to say: "Oh! look!" But I held my tongue, quite dazed, and I could no longer see anything except her. She, too, was rosy, with the rosy flesh tints with which must have mingled a little the hue of the sky. Her tresses were rosy; her eyes were rosy; her teeth were rosy; her dress, her laces, her smile, all were rosy. And in truth I believed, so overpowering was the illusion, that the aurora was there before me.

She rose softly to her feet, holding out her lips to me; and I moved toward her, trembling, delirious, feeling indeed that I was going to kiss Heaven, to kiss happiness, to kiss a dream which had become a woman, to kiss an ideal which had descended into human flesh.

She said to me: "You have a caterpillar in your hair." And suddenly I felt myself becoming as sad as if I had lost all hope in life.

That is all, Madame. It is puerile, silly, stupid. But I am sure that since that day it would be impossible for me to love. And yet — who can tell?

[The young man upon whom this letter was found was yesterday taken out of the Seine between Bougival and Marly. An obliging bargeman, who had searched the pockets in order to ascertain the name of the deceased, brought this paper to the author.]

THE LITTLE CASK

JULES CHICOT, the innkeeper, who lived at Épreville, pulled up his tilbury in front of Mother Magloire's farmhouse. He was a tall man of about forty, fat and with a red face and was generally said to be a very knowing customer.

He hitched his horse up to the gatepost and went in. He owned some land adjoining that of the old woman. He had been coveting her plot for a long while, and had tried in vain to buy it a score of times, but she had always obstinately refused to part with it.

"I was born here, and here I mean to die," was all she said.

He found her peeling potatoes outside the farmhouse door. She was a woman of about seventy-two, very thin, shriveled and wrinkled, almost dried-up, in fact, and much bent, but as active and untiring as a girl. Chicot patted her on the back in a very friendly fashion, and then sat down by her on a stool.

"Well, Mother, you are always pretty well and hearty, I am glad to see."

"Nothing to complain of, considering, thank you. And how are you, Monsieur Chicot?"

"Oh! pretty well, thank you, except a few rheumatic pains occasionally; otherwise, I should have nothing to complain of."

"That's all the better!"

And she said no more, while Chicot watched her going on with her work. Her crooked, knotty fingers, hard as a lobster's claws, seized the tubers, which were lying in a pail, as if they had been a pair of pincers, and peeled them rapidly, cutting off long strips of skin with an old knife which she held in the other hand, throwing the potatoes into the water as they were done. Three daring fowls jumped one after the other into her lap, seized a bit of peel, and then ran away as fast as their legs would carry them with it in their beaks.

Chicot seemed embarrassed, anxious, with something on the tip of his tongue which he could not get out. At last he said hurriedly:

"I say, Mother Magloire—"

"Well, what is it?"

"You are quite sure that you do not want to sell your farm?"

"Certainly not; you may make up your mind to that. What I have said, I have said, so don't refer to it again."

"Very well; only I fancy I have thought of an arrangement that might suit us both very well."

"What is it?"

"Here you are: You shall sell it to me, and

keep it all the same. You don't understand? Very well, so just follow me in what I am going to say."

The old woman left off peeling her potatoes, and looked at the innkeeper attentively from under her bushy eyebrows, and he went on:

"Let me explain myself: Every month I will give you a hundred and fifty francs.* You understand me, I suppose? Every month I will come and bring you thirty crowns,† and it will not make the slightest difference in your life — not the very slightest. You will have your own home just as you have now, will not trouble yourself about me, and will owe me nothing; all you will have to do will be to take my money. Will that arrangement suit you?"

He looked at her good-humoredly, one might almost have said benevolently, and the old woman returned his looks distrustfully, as if she suspected a trap, and said:

"It seems all right, as far as I am concerned, but it will not give you the farm."

"Never mind about that," he said, "you will remain here as long as it pleases God Almighty to let you live; it will be your home. Only you will sign a deed before a lawyer making it over to me after your death. You have no children, only nephews and nieces for whom you don't care a straw. Will that suit you? You will keep everything during your life, and I will give you the thirty crowns a month. It is pure gain as far as you are concerned."

---

* As near as possible $30.
† The old name, still applied locally to a five-franc piece.

The old woman was surprised, rather uneasy, but, nevertheless, very much tempted to agree, and answered:

"I don't say that I will not agree to it, but I must think about it. Come back in a week and we will talk it over again, and I will then give you my definite answer."

And Chicot went off, as happy as a king who had conquered an empire.

Mother Magloire was thoughtful, and did not sleep at all that night; in fact, for four days she was in a fever of hesitation. She *smelled*, so to say, that there was something underneath the offer which was not to her advantage; but then the thought of thirty crowns a month, of all those coins chinking in her apron, falling to her, as it were, from the skies, without her doing anything for it, filled her with covetousness.

She went to the notary and told him about it. He advised her to accept Chicot's offer, but said she ought to ask for a monthly payment of fifty crowns instead of thirty, as her farm was worth sixty thousand francs* at the lowest calculation.

"If you live for fifteen years longer," he said, "even then he will only have paid forty-five thousand francs† for it."

The old woman trembled with joy at this prospect of getting fifty crowns a month; but she was still suspicious, fearing some trick, and she remained a long time with the lawyer asking questions without being able to make up her mind to go. At last she

---

* $12000.   † $9000.

gave him instructions to draw up the deed, and returned home with her head in a whirl, just as if she had drunk four jugs of new cider.

When Chicot came again to receive her answer she took a lot of persuading, and declared that she could not make up her mind to agree to his proposal, though she was all the time on tenter-hooks lest he should not consent to give the fifty crowns. At last, when he grew urgent, she told him what she expected for her farm.

He looked surprised and disappointed, and refused.

Then, in order to convince him, she began to talk about the probable duration of her life.

"I am certainly not likely to live for more than five or six years longer. I am nearly seventy-three, and far from strong, even considering my age. The other evening I thought I was going to die, and could hardly manage to crawl into bed."

But Chicot was not going to be taken in.

"Come, come, old lady, you are as strong as the church tower, and will live till you are a hundred at least; you will be sure to see me put underground first."

The whole day was spent in discussing the money, and as the old woman would not give way, the landlord consented to give the fifty crowns, and she insisted upon having ten crowns over and above to strike the bargain.

Three years passed by, and the old dame did not seem to have grown a day older. Chicot was in despair. It seemed to him as if he had been paying that annuity for fifty years, that he had been taken

5   G. de M.—10

in, outwitted, and ruined. From time to time he went to see his annuitant, just as one goes in July to see when the harvest is likely to begin. She always met him with a cunning look, and one would have felt inclined to think that she was congratulating herself on the trick she had played him. Seeing how well and hearty she seemed, he very soon got into his tilbury again, growling to himself:

"Will you never die, you old brute?"

He did not know what to do, and felt inclined to strangle her when he saw her. He hated her with a ferocious, cunning hatred, the hatred of a peasant who has been robbed, and began to cast about for means of getting rid of her.

One day he came to see her again, rubbing his hands like he did the first time when he proposed the bargain, and, after having chatted for a few minutes, he said:

"Why do you never come and have a bit of dinner at my place when you are in Épreville? The people are talking about it and saying that we are not on friendly terms, and that pains me. You know it will cost you nothing if you come, for I don't look at the price of a dinner. Come whenever you feel inclined; I shall be very glad to see you."

Old Mother Magloire did not need to be told twice, and the next day but one—she was going to the town in any case, it being market-day, in her gig, driven by her man—she, without any demur, put her trap up in Chicot's stable, and went in search of her promised dinner.

The publican was delighted, and treated her like a princess, giving her roast fowl, black pudding, leg of mutton, and bacon and cabbage. But she ate next to nothing. She had always been a small eater and had generally lived on a little soup and a crust of bread-and-butter.

Chicot was disappointed, and pressed her to eat more, but she refused. She would drink next to nothing either, and declined any coffee, so he asked her:

"But surely, you will take a little drop of brandy or liquor?"

"Well, as to that, I don't know that I will refuse." Whereupon he shouted out:

"Rosalie, bring the superfine brandy,—*the special*, —you know."

The servant appeared, carrying a long bottle ornamented with a paper vine-leaf, and he filled two liquor glasses.

"Just try that; you will find it first-rate."

The good woman drank it slowly in sips, so as to make the pleasure last all the longer, and when she had finished her glass, draining the last drops so as to make sure of all, she said:

"Yes, that is first-rate!"

Almost before she had said it, Chicot had poured her out another glassful. She wished to refuse, but it was too late, and she drank it very slowly, as she had done the first, and he asked her to have a third. She objected, but he persisted.

"It is as mild as milk, you know. I can drink ten or a dozen without any ill effect; it goes down like sugar, and leaves no headache behind; one would think that it evaporated on the tongue. It is the most wholesome thing you can drink."

She took it, for she really wished to have it, but she left half the glass.

Then Chicot, in an excess of generosity, said:

"Look here, as it is so much to your taste, I will give you a small keg of it, just to show that you and I are still excellent friends." Then she took her leave, feeling slightly overcome by the effects of what she had drunk.

The next day the innkeeper drove into her yard, and took a little iron-hooped keg out of his gig. He insisted on her tasting the contents, to make sure it was the same delicious article, and, when they had each of them drunk three more glasses, he said, as he was going away:

"Well, you know, when it is all gone, there is more left; don't be modest, for I shall not mind. The sooner it is finished the better pleased I shall be."

Four days later he came again. The old woman was outside her door cutting up the bread for her soup.

He went up to her, and put his face close to hers, so that he might smell her breath; and when he smelled the alcohol he felt pleased.

"I suppose you will give me a glass of *the special?*" he said. And they had three glasses each.

Soon, however, it began to be whispered abroad that Mother Magloire was in the habit of getting drunk all by herself. She was picked up in her kitchen, then in her yard, then in the roads in the neighborhood, and was often brought home like a log.

Chicot did not go near her any more, and, when people spoke to him about her, he used to say, putting on a distressed look:

"It is a great pity that she should have taken to drink at her age; but when people get old there is no remedy. It will be the death of her in the long run."

And it certainly was the death of her. She died the next winter. About Christmas time she fell down unconscious in the snow, and was found dead the next morning.

And when Chicot came in for the farm he said:

"It was very stupid of her; if she had not taken to drink she might very well have lived for ten years longer."

POOR ANDREW

THE lawyer's house looked on to the Square. Behind it, there was a nice, well-kept garden, with a back entrance into a narrow street which was almost always deserted, and from which it was separated by a wall.

At the bottom of that garden Maître* Moreau's wife had promised, for the first time, to meet Captain Sommerive, who had been making love to her for a long time.

Her husband had gone to Paris for a week, so she was quite free for the time being. The Captain had begged so hard, and had used such loving words; she was certain that he loved her so ardently, and she felt so isolated, so misunderstood, so neglected amid all the law business which seemed to be her husband's sole pleasure, that she had given away her heart without even asking herself whether he would give her anything else at some future time.

---

*Maître (Master) is the official title of French lawyers.

Then, after some months of Platonic love, of pressing of hands, of kisses rapidly stolen behind a door, the Captain had declared that he would ask permission to exchange, and leave the town immediately, if she would not grant him a meeting, a real meeting, during her husband's absence. So at length she yielded to his importunity.

Just then she was waiting, close against the wall, with a beating heart, trembling at the slightest sound, and when at length she heard somebody climbing up the wall, she very nearly ran away.

Suppose it were not he, but a thief? But no; some one called out softly, "Matilda!" and when she replied, "Etienne!" a man jumped on to the path with a crash.

It was he,—and what a kiss!

For a long time they remained in each other's arms, with united lips. But suddenly a fine rain began to fall, and the drops from the leaves fell on to her neck and made her start. Whereupon he said:

"Matilda, my adored one, my darling, my angel, let us go indoors. It is twelve o'clock, we can have nothing to fear; please let us go in."

"No, dearest; I am too frightened."

But he held her in his arms, and whispered in her ear:

"Your servants sleep on the third floor, looking on to the Square, and your room, on the first, looks on to the garden, so nobody can hear us. I love you so that I wish to love you entirely, from head to foot." And he embraced her vehemently.

She resisted still, frightened and even ashamed. But he put his arms round her, lifted her up, and carried her off through the rain, which was by this time descending in torrents.

The door was open; they groped their way up-stairs; and when they were in the room he bolted the door while she lit a candle.

Then she fell, half fainting, into a chair, while he kneeled down beside her.

At last, she said, panting:

"No! no! Etienne, please let me remain a virtuous woman; I should be too angry with you afterward; and after all, it is so horrid, so common. Cannot we love each other with a spiritual love only? Oh! Etienne!"

But he was inexorable, and then she tried to get up and escape from his attacks. In her fright she ran to the bed in order to hide herself behind the curtains; but it was a dangerous place of refuge, and he followed her. But in haste he took off his sword too quickly, and it fell on to the floor with a crash. And then a prolonged, shrill child's cry came from the next room, the door of which had remained open.

"You have awakened the child," she whispered, "and perhaps he will not go to sleep again."

He was only fifteen months old and slept in a room opening out of hers, so that she might be able to hear him.

The Captain exclaimed ardently:

"What does it matter, Matilda? How I love you; you must come to me, Matilda."

But she struggled and resisted in her fright.

"No! no! Just listen how he is crying; he will wake up the nurse, and what should we do if she were to come? We should be lost. Just listen to me, Etienne. When he screams at night his father always takes him into our bed, and he is quiet immediately; it is the only means of keeping him still. Do let me take him."

The child roared, uttering shrill screams, which pierced the thickest walls and could be heard by passers-by in the streets.

In his consternation the Captain got up, and Matilda jumped out and took the child into her bed, when he was quiet at once.

Etienne sat astride on a chair, and made a cigarette, and in about five minutes Andrew went to sleep again.

"I will take him back," his mother said; and she took him back very carefully to his bed.

When she returned, the Captain was waiting for her with open arms, and put his arms round her in a transport of love, while she, embracing him more closely, said, stammering:

"Oh! Etienne, my darling, if you only knew how I love you; how—"

Andrew began to cry again, and he, in a rage, exclaimed:

"Confound it all, won't the little brute be quiet?"

No, the little brute would not be quiet, but howled all the louder, on the contrary.

She thought she heard a noise downstairs; no doubt the nurse was coming, so she jumped up and took the child into bed, and he grew quiet directly.

Three times she put him back, and three times she had to fetch him again, and an hour before daybreak the Captain had to go, swearing like the proverbial trooper; and, to calm his impatience, Matilda promised to receive him again the next night. Of course, he came, more impatient and ardent than ever, excited by the delay.

He took care to put his sword carefully into a corner; he took off his boots like a thief, and spoke so low that Matilda could hardly hear him. At last, he was just going to be really happy when the floor, or some piece of furniture, or perhaps the bed itself, creaked; it sounded as if something had broken; and in a moment a cry, feeble at first, but which grew louder every moment, made itself heard. Andrew was awake again.

He yapped like a fox, and there was not the slightest doubt that if he went on like that the whole house would awake; so his mother, not knowing what to do, got up and brought him. The Captain was more furious than ever, but did not move, and very carefully he put out his hand, took a small piece of the child's skin between his two fingers, no matter where it was, the thighs or elsewhere, and pinched it. The little one struggled and screamed in a deafening manner, but his tormentor pinched everywhere, furiously and more vigorously. He took a morsel of flesh and twisted and turned it, and then let go in order to take hold of another piece, and then another and another.

The child screamed like a chicken having its throat cut, or a dog being mercilessly beaten. His mother caressed him, kissed him, and tried to stifle his cries by her tenderness; but Andrew grew purple, as if he were going into convulsions, and kicked and struggled with his little arms and legs in an alarming manner.

The Captain said, softly:

"Try and take him back to his cradle; perhaps he will be quiet."

And Matilda went into the other room with the child in her arms. As soon as he was out of his mother's bed he cried less loudly, and when he was in his own he was quiet, with the exception of a few broken sobs. The rest of the night was tranquil.

The next night the Captain came again. As he happened to speak rather loudly, Andrew awoke again and began to scream. His mother went and fetched him immediately, but the Captain pinched so hard and long that the child was nearly suffocated by its cries, its eyes turned in its head and it foamed at the mouth. As soon as it was back in its cradle it was quiet, and in four days Andrew did not cry any more to come into his mother's bed.

On Saturday evening the lawyer returned, and took his place again at the domestic hearth and in the conjugal chamber. As he was tired with his journey he went to bed early; but he had not long lain down when he said to his wife:

"Why, how is it that Andrew is not crying? Just go and fetch him, Matilda; I like to feel that he is between us."

She got up and brought the child, but as soon as he saw that he was in that bed, in which he had been so fond of sleeping a few days previous, he wriggled and screamed so violently in his fright that she had to take him back to his cradle.

M. Moreau could not get over his surprise. "What a very funny thing! What is the matter with him this evening? I suppose he is sleepy?"

"He has been like that all the time that you were away; I have never been able to have him in bed with me once."

In the morning the child woke up and began to laugh and play with his toys.

The lawyer, who was an affectionate man, got up, kissed his offspring, and took him into his arms to carry him to their bed. Andrew laughed, with that vacant laugh of little creatures whose ideas are still vague. He suddenly saw the bed and his mother in it, and his happy little face puckered up, till suddenly he began to scream furiously, and struggled as if he were going to be put to the torture.

In his astonishment his father said:

"There must be something the matter with the child," and mechanically he lifted up his little nightshirt.

He uttered a prolonged "O—o—h!" of astonishment. The child's calves, thighs, and buttocks were covered with blue spots as big as half-pennies.

"Just look, Matilda!" the father exclaimed; "this is horrible!" And the mother rushed forward in a fright. It was horrible; no doubt the beginning of some sort of leprosy, of one of those strange affections of the skin which doctors are often at a loss to account for. The parents looked at one another in consternation.

"We must send for the doctor," the father said.

But Matilda, pale as death, was looking at her child, who was spotted like a leopard. Then suddenly uttering a violent cry as if she had seen something that filled her with horror, she exclaimed:

"Oh! the wretch!"

In his astonishment M. Moreau asked: "What are you talking about? What wretch?"

She got red up to the roots of her hair, and stammered:

"Oh, nothing! but I think I can guess — it must be — we ought to send for the doctor. It must be that wretch of a nurse who has been pinching the poor child to make him keep quiet when he cries."

In his rage the lawyer sent for the nurse, and very nearly beat her. She denied it most impudently, but was instantly dismissed, and the Municipality having been informed of her conduct, she will find it a hard matter to get another situation.

A FISHING EXCURSION

PARIS was blockaded, desolate, famished. The sparrows were few, and anything that was to be had was good to eat.

On a bright morning in January, Mr. Morissot, a watchmaker by trade, but idler through circumstances, was walking along the boulevard, sad, hungry, with his hands in the pockets of his uniform trousers, when he came face to face with a brother-in-arms whom he recognized as an old-time friend.

Before the war, Morissot could be seen at daybreak every Sunday, trudging along with a cane in one hand and a tin box on his back. He would take the train to Colombes and walk from there to the Isle of Marante where he would fish until dark.

It was there he had met Mr. Sauvage who kept a little notion store in the Rue Notre Dame de Lorette, a jovial fellow and passionately fond of fishing like himself. A warm friendship had sprung up between these two and they would fish side by side all day, very often without saying a word. Some days, when everything looked fresh and new and the beautiful spring sun gladdened every heart, Mr. Morissot would exclaim:

"How delightful!" and Mr. Sauvage would answer:

"There is nothing to equal it."

Then again on a fall evening, when the glorious setting sun, spreading its golden mantle on the already tinted leaves, would throw strange shadows around the two friends, Sauvage would say:

"What a grand picture!"

"It beats the boulevard!" would answer Morissot. But they understood each other quite as well without speaking.

The two friends had greeted each other warmly and had resumed their walk side by side, both thinking deeply of the past and present events. They entered a *café*, and when a glass of absinthe had been placed before each Sauvage sighed:

"What terrible events, my friend!"

"And what weather!" said Morissot sadly; "this is the first nice day we have had this year. Do you remember our fishing excursions?"

"Do I! Alas! when shall we go again!"

After a second absinthe they emerged from the *café*, feeling rather dizzy—that light-headed effect which alcohol has on an empty stomach. The balmy air had made Sauvage exuberant and he exclaimed:

"Suppose we go!"

"Where?"

"Fishing."

"Fishing! Where?"

"To our old spot, to Colombes. The French soldiers are stationed near there and I know Colonel Dumoulin will give us a pass."

"It's a go; I am with you."

An hour after, having supplied themselves with their fishing tackle, they arrived at the colonel's villa. He had smiled at their request and had given them a pass in due form.

At about eleven o'clock they reached the advance-guard, and after presenting their pass, walked through Colombes and found themselves very near their destination. Argenteuil, across the way, and the great plains toward Nanterre were all deserted. Solitary the hills of Orgemont and Sannois rose clearly above the plains; a splendid point of observation.

"See," said Sauvage pointing to the hills, "the Prussians are there."

Prussians! They had never seen one, but they knew that they were all around Paris, invisible and powerful; plundering, devastating, and slaughtering. To their superstitious terror they added a deep hatred for this unknown and victorious people.

"What if we should meet some?" said Morissot.

"We would ask them to join us," said Sauvage in true Parisian style.

Still they hesitated to advance. The silence frightened them. Finally Sauvage picked up courage.

"Come, let us go on cautiously."

They proceeded slowly, hiding behind bushes, looking anxiously on every side, listening to every sound. A bare strip of land had to be crossed before reaching the river. They started to run. At last, they reached the bank and sank into the bushes; breathless, but relieved.

Morissot thought he heard some one walking. He listened attentively, but no, he heard no sound. They were indeed alone! The little island shielded them from view. The house where the restaurant used to be seemed deserted; feeling reassured, they settled themselves for a good day's sport.

Sauvage caught the first fish, Morissot the second; and every minute they would bring one out which they would place in a net at their feet. It was indeed miraculous! They felt that supreme joy which one feels after having been deprived for months of a pleasant pastime. They had forgotten everything; even the war!

Suddenly, they heard a rumbling sound and the earth shook beneath them. It was the cannon on Mont Valérien. Morissot looked up and saw a trail of smoke, which was instantly followed by another explosion. Then they followed in quick succession.

"They are at it again," said Sauvage shrugging his shoulders. Morissot, who was naturally peaceful, felt a sudden, uncontrollable anger.

"Stupid fools! What pleasure can they find in killing each other!"

"They are worse than brutes!"

"It will always be thus as long as we have governments."

"Well, such is life!"

"You mean death!" said Morissot laughing.

They continued to discuss the different political problems, while the cannon on Mont Valérien sent death and desolation among the French.

5 G. de M.—11

Suddenly they started. They had heard a step be-hind them. They turned and beheld four big men in dark uniforms, with guns pointed right at them. Their fishing-lines dropped out of their hands and floated away with the current.

In a few minutes, the Prussian soldiers had bound them, cast them into a boat, and rowed across the river to the island which our friends had thought de-serted. They soon found out their mistake when they reached the house, behind which stood a score or more of soldiers. A big burly officer, seated astride a chair, smoking an immense pipe, addressed them in excellent French:

" Well, gentlemen, have you made a good haul?"

Just then, a soldier deposited at his feet the net full of fish which he had taken good care to take along with him. The officer smiled and said:

"I see you have done pretty well; but let us change the subject. You are evidently sent to spy upon me. You pretended to fish so as to put me off the scent, but I am not so simple. I have caught you and shall have you shot. I am sorry, but war is war. As you passed the advance-guard you certainly must have the password; give it to me, and I will set you free."

The two friends stood side by side, pale and slightly trembling, but they answered nothing.

"No one will ever know. You will go back home quietly and the secret will disappear with you. If you refuse, it is instant death! Choose!"

They remained motionless; silent. The Prussian officer calmly pointed to the river.

"In five minutes you will be at the bottom of this

AFTER THE ORIGINAL DRAWING BY L. VALLET.

———

" Farewell, Sauvage ! "
" Farewell, Morissot ! "

river! Surely, you have a family, friends waiting for
you?"

Still they kept silent. The cannon rumbled incessantly. The officer gave orders in his own tongue,
then moved his chair away from the prisoners.
A squad of men advanced within twenty feet of them,
ready for command.

"I give you one minute; not a second more!"

Suddenly approaching the two Frenchmen, he took
Morissot aside and whispered:

"Quick; the password. Your friend will not
know; he will think I have changed my mind."
Morissot said nothing.

Then taking Sauvage aside he asked him the same
thing, but he also was silent. The officer gave further
orders and the men leveled their guns. At that
moment, Morissot's eyes rested on the net full of fish
lying in the grass a few feet away. The sight made
him feel faint and, though he struggled against it, his
eyes filled with tears. Then turning to his friend:

"Farewell! Mr. Sauvage!"

"Farewell! Mr. Morissot."

They stood for a minute, hand in hand, trembling
with emotion which they were unable to control.

"Fire!" commanded the officer.

The squad of men fired as one. Sauvage fell
straight on his face. Morissot, who was taller,
swayed, pivoted, and fell across his friend's body, his
face to the sky; while blood flowed freely from the
wound in his breast. The officer gave further orders
and his men disappeared. They came back presently
with ropes and stones, which they tied to the feet
of the two friends, and four of them carried them to

the edge of the river. They swung them and threw
them in as far as they could. The bodies weighted
by stones sank immediately. A splash, a few ripples
and the water resumed its usual calmness. The only
thing to be seen was a little blood floating on the
surface. The officer calmly retraced his steps toward
the house muttering:

"The fish will get even now."

He perceived the net full of fish, picked it up,
smiled, and called:

"Wilhelm!"

A soldier in a white apron approached. The officer handed him the fish saying:

"Fry these little things while they are still alive;
They will make a delicious meal."

And having resumed his position on the chair, he
puffed away at his pipe."

A WARNING NOTE

I HAVE received the following letter. Thinking that it may be profitable to many readers, I make it my business to communicate it to them:

"PARIS, November 15, 1886.

"MONSIEUR: You often treat, either in the shape of short stories or chronicles, of subjects which have relation to what I may describe as 'current morals.' I am going to submit to you some reflections which, it seems to me, ought to furnish you with the materials for one of your tales.

"I am not married; I am a bachelor, and, as it seems to me, a rather simple man. But I fancy that many men, the greater part of men, are simple in the way that I am. As I am always, or nearly always, a plain dealer, I am not always able to see through the natural cunning of my neighbors, and I go straight ahead, with my eyes open, without sufficiently looking out for what is behind things — behind people's external behavior.

"We are nearly all accustomed, as a rule, to take appearances for realities, and to look on people as what they pretend to be. Very few possess that scent which enables certain men to divine the real and hidden nature of others. From this peculiar and conventional method of regarding life comes the fact that we pass, like moles, through the midst of events; and that we never believe in what is, but in what seems to be, that we declare a thing to be improbable as soon as we are shown the fact behind the veil, and that everything which displeases our idealistic morality is classed by us as an exception, without taking into account that these exceptions all brought together constitute nearly the total number of cases. It further results that credulous and good people like me are deceived by everybody, especially by women, who have a talent in this direction.

"I have started far afield in order to come to the particular fact which interests me. I have a mistress, a married woman. Like many others, I imagined (do you understand?) that I had chanced on an exception, on an unhappy little woman who was deceiving her husband for the first time. I had paid attentions to her, or rather I had looked on myself as having paid attention to her for a long time, as having overcome her virtue by dint of kindness and love, and as having triumphed by the sheer force of perseverance. In fact, I had made use of a thousand precautions, a thousand devices, and a thousand subtle dallyings in order to succeed.

"Now here is what happened last week: Her husband being absent for some days, she suggested that we should both dine together, and that I should attend on myself so as to avoid the presence of a manservant. She had a fixed idea which had haunted her for the last four or five months: She wanted to get tipsy, but to get tipsy altogether without being afraid of consequences, without having to go back home, speak to her chambermaid, and walk before witnesses. She had often obtained what she called 'a gay agitation' without going farther, and she had found it delightful. So she had promised herself that she would get tipsy once, only once, but thoroughly so. At her own house she pretended that she was going to spend twenty-four hours with some friends near Paris, and she reached my abode just about dinner-hour.

"A woman naturally ought not to get fuddled except when she has had too much champagne. If she drinks a big glass of it fasting, and before the oysters arrive, she begins to ramble in her talk.

"We had a cold dinner prepared on a table behind me. It was enough for me to stretch out my arm to take the dishes or the plates, and I attended on myself as best I could while I listened to her chattering.

"She kept swallowing glass after glass, haunted by her fixed idea. She began by making me the recipient of meaningless and interminable confidences with regard to her sensations as a young girl. She went on and on, her eyes wandering and brilliant, her tongue untied, and her light ideas rolling themselves out endlessly like the blue telegraph-paper which is moved on without stopping by the bobbin and keeps extending in response to the click of the electric apparatus which covers it with words.

"From time to time she asked me:

" 'Am I tipsy?'

" 'No, not yet.'

"And she went on drinking.

"She was so in a little while—not so tipsy as to lose her senses, but tipsy enough to tell the truth, as it seemed to me.

"To her confidences as to her emotions while a young girl succeeded more intimate confidences as to her relations with her husband. She made them to me without restraint, till she wearied me with them, under this pretext, which she repeated a hundred times: 'I can surely tell everything to you. To whom could I tell everything if it were not to you?' So I was made acquainted with all the habits, all the defects, all the fads and the most secret fancies of her husband.

"And by way of claiming my approval she asked: 'Isn't he a fool? Do you think he has taken a feather out of me, eh? So, the first time I saw you, I said to myself: "Let me see! I like him, and I'll take him for my lover." It was then you began flirting with me.'

"I must have presented an odd face to her eyes at that moment, for she could see it, tipsy though she was; and with great outbursts of laughter, she exclaimed: 'Ah! you big simpleton, you did go about it cautiously; but, when men pay attentions to us, you dear blockhead, you see we like it, and then they must make quick work of it, and not keep us waiting. A man must be a ninny not to understand, by a mere glance at us, that we mean "Yes." Ah! I believe I was waiting for you, you stupid! I did

not know what to do in order to make you see that
I was in a hurry. Oh! yes — flowers — verses — compliments — more verses — and nothing else at all! I
was very near letting you go, my fine fellow, you
were so long in making up your mind. And only to
think that half the men in the world are like you,
while the other half — ha! ha! ha!'

"This laugh of hers sent a cold shiver down my
back. I stammered: 'The other half — what about
the other half?'

"She still went on drinking, her eyes steeped in
the fumes of sparkling wine, her mind impelled by
that imperious necessity for telling the truth which
sometimes takes possession of drunkards.

"She replied: 'Ah! the other half makes quick
work of it — too quick; but, all the same, they are
right. There are days when we don't hit it off with
them; but there are days too, when it all goes right,
in spite of everything. My dear, if you only knew
how funny it is — the way the two kinds of men act!
You see, the timid ones, such as you — you never
could imagine what sort the others are and what
they do — immediately — as soon as they find themselves alone with us. They are regular dare-devils!
They get many a slap in the face from us — no doubt
of that — but what does that matter? They know
we're the sort that kiss and don't tell! They know
us well — they do!'

"I stared at her with the eyes of an Inquisitor,
and with a mad desire to make her speak, to learn
everything from her. How often had I put this question to myself: 'How do the other men behave
toward the women who belong to us?' I was fully

conscious of the fact that from the way I saw two men talking to the same woman publicly in a drawing-room, these two men, if they found themselves, one after the other, all alone with her, would conduct themselves quite differently, although they were both equally well acquainted with her. We can guess at the first glance of the eye that certain beings, naturally endowed with the power of seduction, more lively, more daring than we are, reach, after an hour's chat with a woman who pleases them, a degree of intimacy to which we would not attain in a year. Well, do these men, these seducers, these bold adventurers, take, when the occasion presents itself to them, liberties with their hands and lips which to us, the timid ones, would appear odious outrages, but which women perhaps look on merely as pardonable effrontery or as indecent homage to their irresistible grace?

"So I asked her: 'There are women, though, who think these men very improper?'

"She threw herself back on her chair in order to laugh more at her ease, but with a nerveless, unhealthy laugh, one of those laughs which end in hysteria. Then, a little more calmly, she replied: 'Ha! ha! my dear, improper—that is to say, that they dare everything—at once—all—you understand—and many other things, too.'

"I felt myself horrified as if she had just revealed to me a monstrous thing.

"'And you permit this, you women?'

"'No, we don't permit it; we slap them in the face—but, for all that, they amuse us! And then with them one is always afraid—one is never easy.

You must keep watching them the whole time — it is like fighting a duel. You have to keep staring into their eyes to see what they are thinking of or what they intend. They are blackguards, if you like, but they love us better than you do!'

"A singular and unexpected sensation stole over me. Although a bachelor, and determined to remain a bachelor, I suddenly felt in my breast the spirit of a husband in the face of this impudent confidence. I felt myself the friend, the ally, the brother of all these confiding men who are, if not robbed, at least defrauded by all the rufflers of women's waists.

"It is this strange emotion, Monsieur, that I am obeying at this moment, in writing to you, in begging of you to address a warning note to the great army of easy-going husbands.

"However, I had still some lingering doubts. This woman was drunk and must be lying.

"I went on to inquire: 'How is it that you never relate these adventures to anyone, you women?'

"She gazed at me with profound pity, and with such an air of sincerity that, for the moment, I thought she had been sobered by astonishment.

"'We? My dear fellow, you are very foolish. Why do we never talk to you about these things? Ha! ha! ha! Does your valet tell you about his tips, his odd sous? Well, this is our little tip. The husband ought not to complain when we don't go farther. But how dull you are! To talk of these things would be to give the alarm to all ninnies! Ah! how dull you are! And then what harm does it do as long as we don't yield?'

"I felt myself in a state of great confusion as I put the question to her:

"'So then you have often been embraced by men?'

"She answered, with an air of sovereign contempt for the man who could have any doubt on the subject:

"'Faith! Why, every woman has been often embraced. Try it on with any of them, no matter whom, in order to see for yourself, you great goose! Look here! embrace Mme. de X——! She is quite young, and quite virtuous. Embrace, my friend — embrace — and touch — you shall see — ha! ha! ha!'

"All of a sudden, she flung her glass straight at the chandelier. The champagne fell down in a shower, extinguished three wax-candles, stained the hangings, and deluged the table, while the broken glass was scattered about the dining-room. Then, she made an effort to seize the bottle to do the same with it, but I prevented her. After that, she burst out crying in a very loud tone — the hysteria had come on, as I had anticipated.

* * * * * * *

"Some days later, I had almost forgotten this avowal of a tipsy woman when I chanced to find myself at an evening party with this Mme. de X——, whom my mistress had advised me to embrace. As I lived in the same direction as she did, I offered to drive her to her own door, for she was alone this evening. She accepted my offer.

"As soon as we were in the carriage, I said to myself: 'Come! I must try it on!' But I had not the courage. I did not know how to make a start, how to begin the attack.

"Then, suddenly, the desperate courage of cowards came to my aid. I said to her: 'How pretty you were, this evening.'

"She replied with a laugh: 'So then, this evening was an exception, since you only remarked it for the first time?'

"I did not know what rejoinder to make. Certainly my gallantry was not making progress. After a little reflection, however, I managed to say:

"'No, but I never dared to tell it to you.'

"She was astonished:

"'Why?'

"'Because it is—it is a little difficult.'

"'Difficult to tell a woman that she's pretty? Why, where did you come from? You should always tell us so, even when you only half think it, because it always gives us pleasure to hear.'

"I felt myself suddenly animated by a fantastic audacity, and, catching her round the waist, I raised my lips toward her mouth.

"Nevertheless I seemed to be rather nervous about it, and not to appear so terrible to her. I must also have arranged and executed my movement very badly, for she managed to turn her head aside so as to avoid contact with my face, saying:

"'Oh, no—this is rather too much—too much. You are too quick! Take care of my hair. You cannot embrace a woman who has her hair dressed like mine!'

"I resumed my former position in the carriage, disconcerted, unnerved by this repulse. But the carriage drew up before her gate; and she, as she stepped out of it, held out her hand to me, saying, in her most gracious tones:

"'Thanks, dear Monsieur, for having seen me home—and don't forget my advice!'

"I saw her three days later. She had forgotten everything.

"And I, Monsieur, I am incessantly thinking on the other sort of men—the sort of men to whom a lady's hair is no obstacle, and who know how to seize every opportunity."

AFTER

"MY DARLINGS," said the Comtesse, "you must go to bed."

The three children, two girls and a boy, rose up to kiss their grandmother.

Then they said "Good night" to M. le Curé, who had dined at the château, as he did every Thursday.

The Abbé Mauduit sat two of the young ones on his knees, passing his long arms clad in black behind the children's necks; and, drawing their heads toward him with a paternal movement, he kissed each of them on the forehead with a long, tender kiss.

Then, he again set them down on the floor, and the little beings went off, the boy in front, and the girls behind.

"You are fond of children, M. le Curé," said the Comtesse.

"Very fond, Madame."

The old woman raised her bright eyes toward the priest.

"And—has your solitude never weighed too heavily on you?"

"Yes, sometimes."

He became silent, hesitated, and then added: "But I was never made for ordinary life."

"What do you know about it?"

"Oh! I know very well. I was made to be a priest; I followed my own path."

The Comtesse kept staring at him:

"Look here, M. le Curé, tell me this—tell me how it was you resolved to renounce forever what makes us love life—the rest of us—all that consoles and sustains us? What is it that drove you, impelled you, to separate yourself from the great natural path of marriage and the family. You are neither an enthusiast nor a fanatic, neither a gloomy person nor a sad person. Was it some strange occurrence, some sorrow, that led you to take lifelong vows?"

The Abbé Mauduit rose up and drew near to the fire, stretching out to the flames the big shoes that country priests generally wear. He seemed still hesitating as to what reply he should make.

He was a tall old man with white hair, and for the last twenty years had been the pastor of the parish of Sainte-Antoine-du-Rocher. The peasants said of him, "There's a good man for you!" And indeed he was a good man, benevolent, friendly to all, gentle, and, to crown all, generous. Like Saint Martin, he had cut his cloak in two. He freely laughed, and wept too, for very little, just like a woman,—a thing that prejudiced him more or less in the hard minds of the country people.

The old Comtesse de Saville, living in retirement in her château of Rocher, in order to bring up her grandchildren, after the successive deaths of her son and her daughter-in-law, was very much attached to the curé, and used to say of him: "He has a kind heart!"

The abbé came every Thursday to spend the evening at the château, and they were close friends, with the open and honest friendship of old people.

She persisted:

"Look here M. le Curé! 'tis your turn now to make a confession!"

He repeated: "I was not made for a life like everybody else. I saw it myself, fortunately, in time, and have had many proofs since that I made no mistake on that point.

"My parents, who were mercers in Verdiers, and rather rich, had much ambition on my account. They sent me to a boarding-school while I was very young. You cannot conceive what a boy may suffer at college, by the mere fact of separation, of isolation. This monotonous life without affection is good for some and detestable for others. Young people often have hearts more sensitive than one supposes, and by shutting them up thus too soon, far from those they love, we may develop to an excessive extent a sensibility which is of an overstrung kind, and which becomes sickly and dangerous.

"I scarcely ever played; I never had companions; I passed my hours in looking back to my home with regret; I spent the whole night weeping in my bed. I sought to bring up before my mind recollections of my own home, trifling recollections of little things, little events. I thought incessantly of all I had left behind there. I became almost imperceptibly an over-sensitive youth, to whom the slightest annoyances were dreadful griefs.

"Together with this, I remained taciturn, self-absorbed, without expansion, without confidants. This work of mental exaltation was brought about obscurely but surely. The nerves of children are quickly excited; one ought to realize the fact that they live in a state of deep quiescence up to the time of almost complete development. But does anyone reflect that, for certain students, an unjust imposition can be as great a pang as the death of a friend afterward? Does anyone realize the fact that certain young souls have, with very little cause, terrible emotions, and are in a very short time diseased and incurable souls?

"This was my case. This faculty of regret developed itself in me in such a fashion that my existence became a martyrdom.

"I did not speak about it; I said nothing about it; but gradually I acquired a sensibility, or rather a sensitivity, so lively that my soul resembled a living wound. Everything that touched it produced in it twitchings of pain, frightful vibrations, and veritable ravages. Happy are the men whom nature has buttressed with indifference and cased in stoicism.

"I reached my sixteenth year. An excessive timidity had come to me from this aptitude to suffer on account of everything. Feeling myself unprotected against all the attacks of chance or fate, I feared every contact, every approach, every event. I lived on the watch as if under the constant threat of an unknown and always expected misfortune. I was afraid either to speak or to act publicly. I had, indeed, the sensation that life is a battle, a dreadful conflict in which one receives terrible blows, grievous, mortal wounds. In place of cherishing, like all men, the hope of good-

fortune on the morrow, I only kept a confused fear
of it, and I felt in my own mind a desire to conceal
myself—to avoid that combat in which I should be
vanquished and slain.

"As soon as my studies were finished, they gave
me six months' time to choose a career. Suddenly a very simple event made me see clearly
into myself, showed me the diseased condition of
my mind, made me understand the danger, and caused
me to make up my mind to fly from it.

"Verdiers is a little town surrounded with plains
and woods. In the central street stands my parents'
house. I now passed my days far from this dwelling
which I had so much regretted, so much desired.
Dreams were awakened in me, and I walked all alone
in the fields in order to let them escape and fly away.
My father and my mother, quite occupied with business, and anxious about my future, talked to me only
about their profits or about my possible plans. They
were fond of me in the way that hard-headed, practical people are; they had more reason than heart in
their affection for me. I lived imprisoned in my
thoughts, and trembling with eternal uneasiness.

"Now, one evening, after a long walk, as I was
making my way home with quick strides so as not to
be late, I met a dog trotting toward me. He was a
species of red spaniel, very lean, with long curly ears.

"When he was ten paces away from me, he
stopped. I did the same. Then he began wagging
his tail, and came over to me with short steps and
nervous movements of his whole body, going down
on his paws as if appealing to me, and softly shaking his head. He then made a show of crawling

with an air so humble, so sad, so suppliant, that I
felt the tears coming into my eyes. I came near
him; he ran away; then he came back again; and I
bent down, trying to coax him to approach me with
soft words. At last, he was within reach and I
gently caressed him with the most careful hands.

"He grew bold, rose up bit by bit, laid his paws
on my shoulders, and began to lick my face. He
followed me into the house.

"This was really the first being I had passionately
loved, because he returned my affection. My attachment to this animal was certainly exaggerated and
ridiculous. It seemed to me in a confused sort of
way that we were two brothers, lost on this earth,
and therefore isolated and without defense, one as
well as the other. He never again quitted my side.
He slept at the foot of my bed, ate at the table in
spite of the objections of my parents, and followed
me in my solitary walks.

"I often stopped at the side of a ditch, and I sat
down in the grass. Sam would lie on my knees,
and lift up my hand with the end of his nose so that
I might caress him.

"One day toward the end of June, as we were
on the road from Saint-Pierre-de-Chavrol, I saw the
diligence from Pavereau coming along. Its four horses
were going at a gallop. It had a yellow box-seat, and
imperial crowned with black leather. The coachman
cracked his whip; a cloud of dust rose up under the
wheels of the heavy vehicle, then floated behind, just
as a cloud would do.

"And, all of a sudden, as the vehicle came close to
me. Sam, perhaps frightened by the noise and wishing

to join me, jumped in front of it. A horse's foot
knocked him down. I saw him rolling over, turning
round, falling back again on all fours, and then the
entire coach gave two big jolts and behind it I saw
something quivering in the dust on the road. He
was nearly cut in two; all his intestines were hanging
through his stomach, which had been ripped open,
and spurts of blood fell to the ground. He tried to
get up, to walk, but he could only move his two front
paws, and scratch the ground with them, as if to
make a hole. The two others were already dead.
And he howled dreadfully, mad with pain.

"He died in a few minutes. I cannot describe
how much I felt and suffered. I was confined to my
own room for a month.

"Now, one night, my father, enraged at seeing
me in such a state for so little, exclaimed:

"'How then will it be when you have real griefs,
if you lose your wife or children?'

"And I began to see clearly into myself. I understood why all the small miseries of each day assumed
in my eyes the importance of a catastrophe; I saw
that I was organized in such a way that I suffered
dreadfully from everything, that every painful impression was multiplied by my diseased sensibility, and
an atrocious fear of life took possession of me. I was
without passions, without ambitions; I resolved to
sacrifice possible joys in order to avoid sure sorrows.
Existence is short, but I made up my mind to spend
it in the service of others, in relieving their troubles
and enjoying their happiness. By having no direct
experience of either one or the other, I would only
be conscious of passionless emotions.

"And if you only knew how, in spite of this, misery tortures me, ravages me. But what would be for me an intolerable affliction has become commiseration, pity.

"The sorrows which I have every day to concern myself about I could not endure if they fell on my own heart. I could not have seen one of my children die without dying myself. And I have, in spite of everything, preserved such a deep and penetrating fear of circumstances that the sight of the postman entering my house makes a shiver pass every day through my veins, and yet I have nothing to be afraid of now."

The Abbé Mauduit ceased speaking. He stared into the fire in the huge grate, as if he saw there mysterious things, all the unknown portion of existence which he would have been able to live if he had been more fearless in the face of suffering.

He added, then, in a subdued tone:

"I was right. I was not made for this world."

The Comtesse said nothing at first; but at length, after a long silence, she remarked:

"For my part, if I had not my grandchildren, I believe I would not have the courage to live."

And the Curé rose up without saying another word.

As the servants were asleep in the kitchen, she conducted him herself to the door which looked out on the garden, and she saw his tall shadow, revealed by the reflection of the lamp, disappearing through the gloom of night.

Then she came back, sat down before the fire, and pondered over many things on which we never think when we are young.

THE SPASM

THE hotel-guests slowly entered the dining-room, and sat down in their places. The waiters began to attend on them in a leisurely fashion so as to enable those who were late to arrive, and to avoid bringing back the dishes. The old bathers, the *habitués*, those whose season was advancing, gazed with interest toward the door, whenever it opened, with a desire to see new faces appearing.

This is the principal distraction of health-resorts. People look forward to the dinner hour in order to inspect each day's new arrivals, to find out who they are, what they do, and what they think. A vague longing springs up in the mind, a longing for agreeable meetings, for pleasant acquaintances, perhaps for love-adventures. In this life of elbowings, strangers, as well as those with whom we have come into daily contact, assume an extreme importance. Curiosity is aroused, sympathy is ready to exhibit itself, and sociability is the order of the day.

We cherish antipathies for a week and friendships for a month; we see other people with different eyes, when we view them through the medium of the acquaintanceship that is brought about at health-resorts. We discover in men suddenly, after an hour's chat in the evening after dinner, or under the trees in the park where the generous spring bubbles up, a high intelligence and astonishing merits, and, a month afterward, we have completely forgotten these new friends, so fascinating when we first met them.

There also are formed lasting and serious ties more quickly than anywhere else. People see each other every day; they become acquainted very quickly; and with the affection thus originated is mingled something of the sweetness and self-abandonment of long-standing intimacies. We cherish in after years the dear and tender memories of those first hours of friendship, the memory of those first conversations through which we have been able to unveil a soul, of those first glances which interrogate and respond to the questions and secret thoughts which the mouth has not as yet uttered, the memory of that first cordial confidence, the memory of that delightful sensation of opening our hearts to those who are willing to open theirs to us.

And the melancholy of health-resorts, the monotony of days that are alike, help from hour to hour in this rapid development of affection.

* * * * * * *

Well, this evening, as on every other evening, we awaited the appearance of strange faces.

Only two appeared, but they were very remarkable looking, a man and a woman — father and daughter.

They immediately produced the same effect on my mind as some of Edgar Poe's characters; and yet there was about them a charm, the charm associated with misfortune. I looked upon them as the victims of fatality. The man was very tall and thin, rather stooping, with hair perfectly white, too white for his comparatively youthful physiognomy; and there was in his bearing and in his person that austerity peculiar to Protestants. The daughter, who was probably twenty-four or twenty-five, was small in stature, and was also very thin, very pale, and had the air of one worn out with utter lassitude. We meet people like this from time to time, people who seem too weak for the tasks and the needs of daily life, too weak to move about, to walk, to do all that we do every day. This young girl was very pretty, with the diaphanous beauty of a phantom; and she ate with extreme slowness, as if she were almost incapable of moving her arms. It must have been she assuredly who had come to take the waters.

They found themselves facing me at the opposite side of the table; and I at once noticed that the father had a very singular nervous spasm. Every time he wanted to reach an object, his hand made a hook-like movement, a sort of irregular zigzag, before it succeeded in touching what it was in search of; and, after a little while, this action was so wearisome to me that I turned aside my head in order not to see it. I noticed, too, that the young girl, during meals, wore a glove on her left hand.

After dinner, I went for a stroll in the park of the thermal establishment. This led toward the little Auvergnese station of Châtel Guyon, hidden in a gorge at the foot of the high mountain, of that mountain from which flow so many boiling springs, rising from the deep bed of extinct volcanoes. Over there, above us, the domes, which had once been craters, raised their mutilated heads on the summit of the long chain. For Châtel Guyon is situated at the spot where the region of domes begins. Beyond it stretches out the region of peaks, and, further on again, the region of precipices.

The Puy de Dôme is the highest of the domes, the Peak of Sancy is the loftiest of the peaks, and Cantal is the most precipitous of these mountain heights.

This evening, it was very warm. I walked up and down a shady path, on the side of the mountain overlooking the park, listening to the opening strains of the Casino band. I saw the father and the daughter advancing slowly in my direction. I saluted them, as we are accustomed to salute our hotel-companions at health-resorts; and the man, coming to a sudden halt, said to me:

"Could you not, Monsieur, point out to us a short walk, nice and easy, if that is possible, and excuse my intrusion on you?"

I offered to show them the way toward the valley through which the little river flowed, a deep valley forming a gorge between two tall, craggy, wooded slopes. They gladly accepted my offer, and we talked naturally about the virtues of the waters.

"Oh!" he said, "my daughter has a strange malady, the seat of which is unknown. She suffers from incomprehensible nervous disorders. At one time, the doctors think she has an attack of heart disease, at another time, they imagine it is some affection of the liver, and at another time they declare it to be a disease of the spine. To-day, her condition is attributed to the stomach, which is the great caldron and regulator of the body, the Protean source of diseases with a thousand forms and a thousand susceptibilities to attack. This is why we have come here. For my part, I am rather inclined to think it is the nerves. In any case it is very sad."

Immediately the remembrance of the violent spasmodic movement of his hand came back to my mind, and I asked him:

"But is this not the result of heredity? Are not your own nerves somewhat affected?"

He replied calmly:

"Mine? Oh! no — my nerves have always been very steady."

Then suddenly, after a pause, he went on:

"Ah! You were alluding to the spasm in my hand every time I want to reach for anything? This arises from a terrible experience which I had. Just imagine! this daughter of mine was actually buried alive!"

I could only give utterance to the word "Ah!" so great were my astonishment and emotion.

* * * * * * *

He continued:

"Here is the story. It is simple. Juliette had been subject for some time to serious attacks of the heart. We believed that she had disease of that organ and we were prepared for the worst.

"One day, she was carried into the house cold, lifeless, dead. She had fallen down unconscious in the garden. The doctor certified that life was extinct. I watched by her side for a day and two nights. I laid her with my own hands in the coffin, which I accompanied to the cemetery where she was deposited in the family vault. It is situated in the very heart of Lorraine.

"I wished to have her interred with her jewels, bracelets, necklaces, rings, all presents which she had got from me, and with her first ball-dress on.

"You may easily imagine the state of mind in which I was when I returned home. She was the only companion I had, for my wife has been dead for many years. I found my way to my own apartment in a half-distracted condition, utterly exhausted, and I sank into my easy-chair, without the capacity to think or the strength to move. I was nothing better now than a suffering, vibrating machine, a human being who had, as it were, been flayed alive; my soul was like a living wound.

"My old valet, Prosper, who had assisted me in placing Juliette in her coffin, and preparing her for her last sleep, entered the room noiselessly, and asked:

"'Does Monsieur want anything?'

"I merely shook my head, by way of answering 'No.'

"He urged: 'Monsieur is wrong. He will bring some illness on himself. Would Monsieur like me to put him to bed?'

"I answered: 'No! let me alone!' And he left the room.

"I know not how many hours slipped away. Oh! what a night, what a night! It was cold. My fire had died out in the huge grate; and the wind, the winter wind, an icy wind, a hurricane accompanied by frost and snow, kept blowing against the window with a sinister and regular noise.

"How many hours slipped away? There I was without sleeping, powerless, crushed, my eyes wide open, my legs stretched out, my body limp, inanimate, and my mind torpid with despair. Suddenly, the great bell of the entrance gate, the bell of the vestibule, rang out.

"I got such a shock that my chair cracked under me. The solemn ponderous sound vibrated through the empty château as if through a vault. I turned round to see what the hour was by my clock. It was just two in the morning. Who could be coming at such an hour?

"And abruptly the bell again rang twice. The servants, without doubt, were afraid to get up. I took a wax-candle and descended the stairs. I was on the point of asking: 'Who is there?'

"Then, I felt ashamed of my weakness, and I slowly opened the huge door. My heart was throbbing wildly; I was frightened; I hurriedly drew back the door, and in the darkness, I distinguished a white figure standing erect, something that resembled an apparition.

"I recoiled, petrified with horror, faltering:

"'Who—who—who are you?'

"A voice replied:

"'It is I, father.'

"It was my daughter. I really thought I must be mad, and I retreated backward before this advancing specter. I kept moving away, making a sign with my hand, as if to drive the phantom away, that gesture which you have noticed,—that gesture of which since then I have never got rid.

"The apparition spoke again:

"'Do not be afraid, papa; I was not dead. Somebody tried to steal my rings, and cut one of my fingers, the blood began to flow, and this reanimated me.'

"And, in fact, I could see that her hand was covered with blood.

"I fell on my knees, choking with sobs and with a rattling in my throat.

"Then, when I had somewhat collected my thoughts, though I was still so much dismayed that I scarcely realized the gruesome good-fortune that had fallen to my lot, I made her go up to my room, and sit down in my easy-chair; then I rang excitedly for Prosper to get him to light up the fire again and to get her some wine and summon the rest of the servants to her assistance.

"The man entered, stared at my daughter, opened his mouth with a gasp of alarm and stupefaction, and then fell back, insensible.

"It was he who had opened the vault, and who had mutilated and then abandoned my daughter, for he could not efface the traces of the theft. He had not even taken the trouble to put back the coffin into its place, feeling sure, besides, that he would not be suspected by me, as I completely trusted him.

"You see, Monsieur, that we are very unhappy people."

*   *   *   *   *   *   *

He stopped.

The night had fallen, casting its shadows over the desolate, mournful vale, and a sort of mysterious fear possessed me at finding myself by the side of those strange beings, of this young girl who had come back from the tomb and this father with his uncanny spasm.

I found it impossible to make any comment on this dreadful story. I only murmured:

"What a horrible thing!"

Then, after a minute's silence, I added:

"Suppose we go back, I think it is getting cold."

And we made our way back to the hotel.

A MEETING

I T was all an accident, a pure accident. Tired of standing, Baron d'Etraille went — as all the Princess's rooms were open on that particular evening — into an empty bedroom, which appeared almost dark after coming out of the brilliantly-lighted drawing-rooms.

He looked round for a chair in which to have a doze, as he was sure his wife would not go away before daylight. As soon as he got inside the door he saw the big bed with its azure-and-gold hangings, in the middle of the great room, looking like a catafalque in which love was buried, for the Princess was no longer young. Behind it, a large bright spot looked like a lake seen at a distance from a window It was a big looking-glass, which, discreetly covered with dark drapery very rarely let down, seemed to look at the bed, which was its accomplice. One might almost fancy that it felt regrets, and that one was going to see in it

(192)

charming shapes of nude women and the gentle movement of arms about to embrace them.

The Baron stood still for a moment, smiling and rather moved, on the threshold of this chamber dedicated to love. But suddenly something appeared in the looking-glass, as if the phantoms which he had evoked had come up before him. A man and a woman who had been sitting on a low couch hidden in the shade had risen, and the polished surface, reflecting their figures, showed that they were kissing each other before separating.

The Baron recognized his wife and the Marquis de Cervigné. He turned and went away like a man fully master of himself, and waited till it was day before taking away the Baroness. But he had no longer any thoughts of sleeping.

As soon as they were alone, he said:

"Madame, I saw you just now in the Princess de Raynes's room. I need say no more, for I am not fond either of reproaches, acts of violence, or of ridicule. As I wish to avoid all such things, we shall separate without any scandal. Our lawyers will settle your position according to my orders. You will be free to live as you please when you are no longer under my roof; but, as you will continue to bear my name, I must warn you that should any scandal arise, I shall show myself inflexible."

She tried to speak, but he stopped her, bowed, and left the room.

He was more astonished and sad than unhappy. He had loved her dearly during the first period of their married life; but his ardor had cooled, and now he often had a caprice, either in a theater or in soci-

5 G. de M.—13

ety, though he always preserved a certain liking for the Baroness.

She was very young, hardly four-and-twenty, small, slight,—too slight,—and very fair. She was a true Parisian doll: clever, spoiled, elegant, coquettish, witty, with more charm than real beauty. He used to say familiarly to his brother, when speaking of her:

"My wife is charming, attractive, but—there is nothing to lay hold of. She is like a glass of champagne that is all froth—when you have got to the wine it is very good, but there is too little of it, unfortunately."

He walked up and down the room in great agitation, thinking of a thousand things. At one moment he felt in a great rage, and felt inclined to give the Marquis a good thrashing, to horsewhip him publicly, in the club. But he thought that would not do, it would not be the thing; *he* would be laughed at, and not the other, and he felt that his anger proceeded more from wounded vanity than from a broken heart. So he went to bed, but could not get to sleep.

A few days afterward it was known in Paris that the Baron and Baroness d'Etraille had agreed to an amicable separation on account of incompatibility of temper. Nobody suspected anything, nobody laughed, and nobody was astonished.

The Baron, however, to avoid meeting her, traveled for a year; then he spent the summer at the seaside, and the autumn in shooting, returning to Paris for the winter. He did not meet his wife once.

He did not even know what people said about her. At any rate, she took care to save appearances, and that was all he asked for.

He got dreadfully bored, traveled again, restored his old castle of Villebosc — which took him two years; then for over a year he received relays of friends there, till at last, tired of all these common-place, so-called pleasures, he returned to his mansion in the Rue de Lills, just six years after their sepa-ration.

He was then forty-five, with a good crop of gray hair, rather stout, and with that melancholy look of people who have been handsome, sought after, much liked, and are deteriorating daily.

A month after his return to Paris he took cold on coming out of his club, and had a bad cough, so his medical man ordered him to Nice for the rest of the winter.

He started by the express on Monday evening. He was late, got to the station only a very short time before the departure of the train, and had barely time to get into a carriage, with only one other oc-cupant, who was sitting in a corner so wrapped in furs and cloaks that he could not even make out whether it were a man or a woman, as nothing of the figure could be seen. When he perceived that he could not find out, he put on his traveling-cap, rolled himself up in his rugs, and stretched himself out comfortably to sleep.

He did not wake up till the day was breaking, and looked immediately at his fellow-traveler. He had not stirred all night, and seemed still to be sound asleep.

M. d'Etraille made use of the opportunity to brush his hair and his beard, and to try and freshen him-self up a little generally, for a night's traveling changes one's looks very much when one has attained a certain age.

A great poet has said:

"When we are young, our mornings are triumphant!"

Then we wake up with a cool skin, a bright eye, and glossy hair. When one grows older one wakes up in a very different state. Dull eyes, red, swollen cheeks, dry lips, the hair and beard all disarranged, impart an old, fatigued, worn-out look to the face.

The Baron opened his traveling dressing-case, made himself as tidy as he could, and then waited.

The engine whistled and the train stopped, and his neighbor moved. No doubt he was awake. They started off again, and then an oblique ray of the sun shone into the carriage just on to the sleeper, who moved again, shook himself, and then calmly showed his face.

It was a young, fair, pretty, stout woman, and the Baron looked at her in amazement. He did not know what to believe. He could really have sworn that it was his wife—but wonderfully changed for the better: stouter—why, she had grown as stout as he was —only it suited her much better than it did him.

She looked at him quietly, did not seem to recognize him, and then slowly laid aside her wraps. She had that calm assurance of a woman who is sure of herself, the insolent audacity of a first awaking, knowing and feeling that she was in her full beauty and freshness.

The Baron really lost his head. Was it his wife, or somebody else who was as like her as any sister could be? As he had not seen her for six years he might be mistaken.

She yawned, and he knew her by the gesture. She turned and looked at him again, calmly, indifferently, as if she scarcely saw him, and then looked out at the country again.

He was upset and dreadfully perplexed, and waited, looking at her sideways, steadfastly.

Yes; it was certainly his wife. How could he possibly have doubted? There could certainly not be two noses like that, and a thousand recollections flashed through him, slight details of her body, a beauty-spot on one of her limbs and another on her back. How often he had kissed them! He felt the old feeling of the intoxication of love stealing over him, and he called to mind the sweet odor of her skin, her smile when she put her arms on to his shoulders, the soft intonations of her voice, all her graceful, coaxing ways.

But how she had changed and improved! It was she and yet not she. He thought her riper, more developed, more of a woman, more seductive, more desirable, adorably desirable.

And this strange, unknown woman, whom he had accidentally met in a railway-carriage belonged to him; he had only to say to her:

"I insist upon it."

He had formerly slept in her arms, existed only in her love, and now he had found her again certainly, but so changed that he scarcely knew her. It was another, and yet she at the same time. It was another who had been born, formed, and grown since he had left her. It was she, indeed; she whom he had possessed but who was now altered, with a more assured smile and greater self-possession. There were two women in one, mingling a great deal of what was new and unknown with many sweet recollections of the past. There was something singular, disturbing, exciting about it—a kind of mystery of love in which there floated a delicious confusion. It was his wife in a new body and in new flesh which his lips had never pressed.

And he remembered that in six or seven years everything changes in us, only outlines can be recognized, and sometimes even they disappear.

The blood, the hair, the skin, all change, and are reconstituted, and when people have not seen each other for a long time they find, when they meet, another totally different being, although it be the same and bear the same name.

And the heart also can change. Ideas may be modified and renewed, so that in forty years of life we may, by gradual and constant transformations, become four or five totally new and different beings.

He dwelt on this thought till it troubled him; it had first taken possession of him when he surprised her in the Princess's room. He was not the least angry; it was not the same woman that he was looking at—that thin, excitable little doll of those days.

What was he to do? How should he address her? and what could he say to her? Had she recognized him?

The train stopped again. He got up, bowed, and said: "Bertha, do you want anything I can bring you?"

She looked at him from head to foot, and answered, without showing the slightest surprise or confusion or anger, but with the most perfect indifference:

"I do not want anything—thank you."

He got out and walked up and down the platform a little in order to think, and, as it were, to recover his senses after a fall. What should he do now? If he got into another carriage it would look as if he were running away. Should he be polite or importunate? That would look as if he were asking for forgiveness. Should he speak as if he were her master? He would look like a fool, and besides, he really had no right to do so.

He got in again and took his place.

During his absence she had hastily arranged her dress and hair, and was now lying stretched out on the seat, radiant, but without showing any emotion.

He turned to her, and said: "My dear Bertha, since this singular chance has brought us together after a separation of six years—a quite friendly separation—are we to continue to look upon each other as irreconcilable enemies? We are shut up together, *tête-à-tête*, which is so much the better or so much the worse. I am not going to get into another carriage, so don't you think it is preferable to talk as friends till the end of our journey?"

She answered quite calmly again:

"Just as you please."

Then he suddenly stopped, really not knowing what to say; but as he had plenty of assurance, he sat down on the middle seat, and said:

"Well, I see I must pay my court to you; so much the better. It is, however, really a pleasure,

for you are charming. You cannot imagine how you
have improved in the last six years. I do not know
any woman who could give me that delightful sensation which I experienced just now when you emerged
from your wraps. I could really have thought such a
change impossible."

Without moving her head or looking at him, she
said: "I cannot say the same with regard to you;
you have certainly deteriorated a great deal."

He got red and confused, and then, with a smile
of resignation, he said:

"You are rather hard."

"Why?" was her reply. "I am only stating
facts. I don't suppose you intend to offer me your
love? It must, therefore, be a matter of perfect indifference to you what I think about you. But I
see it is a painful subject, so let us talk of something else. What have you been doing since I last
saw you?"

He felt rather out of countenance, and stammered:

"I? I have traveled, shot, and grown old, as you
see. And you?"

She said, quite calmly: "I have taken care of appearances, as you ordered me."

He was very nearly saying something brutal, but
he checked himself, and kissed his wife's hand:

"And I thank you," he said.

She was surprised. He was indeed strong and
always master of himself.

He went on: "As you have acceded to my first
request, shall we now talk without any bitterness?"

She made a little movement of surprise.

"Bitterness! I don't feel any; you are a complete stranger to me; I am only trying to keep up a difficult conversation."

He was still looking at her, carried away in spite of her harshness, and he felt seized with a brutal desire, the desire of the master.

Perceiving that she had hurt his feelings, she said:

"How old are you now? I thought you were younger than you look."

He grew rather pale:

"I am forty-five"; and then he added: "I forgot to ask after Princess de Raynes. Are you still intimate with her?"

She looked at him as if she hated him:

"Yes, certainly I am. She is very well, thank you."

They remained sitting side by side, agitated and irritated. Suddenly he said:

"My dear Bertha, I have changed my mind. You are my wife, and I expect you to come with me to-day. You have, I think, improved both morally and physically, and I am going to take you back again. I am your husband and it is my right to do so."

She was stupefied, and looked at him, trying to divine his thoughts; but his face was resolute and impenetrable.

"I am very sorry," she said, "but I have made other engagements."

"So much the worse for you," was his reply. "The law gives me the power, and I mean to use it."

They were getting to Marseilles, and the train whistled and slackened speed. The Baroness got

up, carefully rolled up her wraps, and then turning to
her husband, she said:

"My dear Raymond, do not make a bad use of
the *tête-à-tête* which I had carefully prepared. I
wished to take precautions, according to your advice,
so that I might have nothing to fear from you or
from other people, whatever might happen. You
are going to Nice, are you not?"

"I shall go wherever you go."

"Not at all; just listen to me, and I am sure that
you will leave me in peace. In a few moments,
when we get to the station, you will see the Princess de Raynes and Countess Hermit waiting for me
with their husbands. I wished them to see us, and
to know that we had spent the night together in the
railway-carriage. Don't be alarmed; they will tell it
everywhere as a most surprising fact.

"I told you just now that I had most carefully
followed your advice and saved appearances. Anything else does not matter, does it? Well, in order
to do so, I wished to be seen with you. You told
me carefully to avoid any scandal, and I am avoiding
it, for, I am afraid—I am afraid—"

She waited till the train had quite stopped, and as
her friends ran up to open the carriage door, she
said:

"I am afraid that I am *enceinte.*"

The Princess stretched out her arms to embrace
her, and the Baroness said, pointing to the Baron,
who was dumb with astonishment, and trying to get
at the truth:

"You do not recognize Raymond? He has certainly changed a good deal, and he agreed to come

with me so that I might not travel alone. We take little trips like this occasionally, like good friends who cannot live together. We are going to separate here; he has had enough of me already."

She put out her hand, which he took mechanically, and then she jumped out on to the platform among her friends, who were waiting for her.

The Baron hastily shut the carriage door, for he was too much disturbed to say a word or come to any determination. He heard his wife's voice, and their merry laughter as they went away.

He never saw her again, nor did he ever discover whether she had told him a lie or was speaking the truth.

A NEW YEAR'S GIFT

JACQUES DE RANDAL, having dined at home alone, told his valet he might go, and then sat down at a table to write his letters.

He finished out every year by writing and dreaming, making for himself a sort of review of things that had happened since last New Year's Day, things that were now all over and dead; and, in proportion as the faces of his friends rose up before his eyes, he wrote them a few lines, a cordial "Good morning" on the first of January.

So he sat down, opened a drawer, took out of it a woman's photograph, gazed at it a few moments, and kissed it. Then, having laid it beside a sheet of note-paper, he began:

"MY DEAR IRÈNE: You must have by this time the little souvenir which I sent you. I have shut myself up this evening in order to tell you—"

The pen here ceased to move. Jacques rose up and began walking up and down the room.

(204)

For the last six months he had a mistress, not a mistress like the others, a woman with whom one engages in a passing intrigue, of the theatrical world or the *demi-monde*, but a woman whom he loved and won. He was no longer a young man, although still comparatively young, and he looked on life seriously in a positive and practical spirit.

Accordingly, he drew up the balance-sheet of his passion, as he drew up every year the balance-sheet of friendships that were ended or freshly contracted, of circumstances and persons that had entered into his life. His first ardor of love having grown calmer, he asked himself, with the precision of a merchant making a calculation, what was the state of his heart with regard to her, and he tried to form an idea of what it would be in the future. He found there a great and deep affection, made up of tenderness, gratitude, and the thousand subtleties which give birth to long and powerful attachments.

A ring of the bell made him start. He hesitated. Should he open? But he deemed it was his duty to open, on this New Year's night, to the Unknown who knocks while passing, no matter whom it may be.

So he took a wax-candle, passed through the ante-chamber, removed the bolts, turned the key, drew the door back, and saw his mistress standing pale as a corpse, leaning against the wall.

He stammered: "What is the matter with you?"
She replied: "Are you alone?"
"Yes."
"Without servants?"
"Yes."

"You are not going out?"

"No."

She entered with the air of a woman who knew the house. As soon as she was in the drawing-room, she sank into the sofa, and, covering her face with her hands, began to weep dreadfully.

He kneeled down at her feet, seized hold of her hands to remove them from her eyes, so that he might look at them, and exclaimed:

"Irène, Irène, what is the matter with you? I implore of you to tell me what is the matter with you?"

Then, in the midst of her sobs she murmured: "I can no longer live like this."

He did not understand.

"Like this? What do you mean?"

"Yes. I can no longer live like this. I have endured so much. He struck me this afternoon."

"Who—your husband?"

"Yes—my husband."

"Ha!"

He was astonished, having never suspected that her husband could be brutal. He was a man of the world, of the better class, a clubman, a lover of horses, a theater-goer, and an expert swordsman; he was known, talked about, appreciated everywhere, having very courteous manners, but a very mediocre intellect, an absence of education and of the real culture needed in order to think like all well-bred people, and finally a respect for all conventional prejudices.

He appeared to devote himself to his wife, as a man ought to do in the case of wealthy and well-bred people. He displayed enough of anxiety about her wishes, her health, her dresses, and, beyond that, left her perfectly free.

Randal, having become Irène's friend, had a right to the affectionate hand-clasp which every husband endowed with good manners owes to his wife's intimate acquaintances. Then, when Jacques, after having been for some time the friend, became the lover, his relations with the husband were more cordial.

Jacques had never dreamed that there were storms in this household, and he was scared at this unexpected revelation.

He asked:

"How did it happen? Tell me."

Thereupon she related a long history, the entire history of her life, since the day of her marriage — the first discussion arising out of a mere nothing, then accentuating itself in the estrangement which grows up each day between two opposite types of character.

Then came quarrels, a complete separation, not apparent, but real; next, her husband showed himself aggressive, suspicious, violent. Now, he was jealous, jealous of Jacques, and this day even, after a scene, he had struck her.

She added with decision: "I will not go back to him. Do with me what you like."

Jacques sat down opposite to her, their knees touching each other. He caught hold of her hands:

"My dear love, you are going to commit a gross, an irreparable folly. If you want to quit your husband, put wrongs on one side, so that your situation as a woman of the world may be saved."

She asked, as she cast at him a restless glance:

"Then, what do you advise me?"

"To go back home, and to put up with your life there till the day when you can obtain either a separation or a divorce, with the honors of war."

"Is not this thing which you advise me to do a little cowardly?"

"No; it is wise and reasonable. You have a high position, a reputation to safeguard, friends to preserve, and relations to deal with. You must not lose all these through a mere caprice."

She rose up, and said with violence:

"Well, no! I cannot have any more of it! It is at an end! it is at an end!"

Then, placing her two hands on her lover's shoulders and looking at him straight in the face, she asked:

"Do you love me?"

"Yes."

"Really and truly?"

"Yes."

"Then keep me!"

He exclaimed:

"Keep you? In my own house? Here? Why, you are mad. It would mean losing you forever; losing you beyond hope of recall! You are mad!"

She replied, slowly and seriously, like a woman who feels the weight of her words:

"Listen, Jacques. He has forbidden me to see you again, and I will not play this comedy of coming secretly to your house. You must either lose me or take me."

"My dear Irène, in that case, obtain your divorce, and I will marry you."

"Yes, you will marry me in—two years at the soonest. Yours is a patient love."

"Look here! Reflect! If you remain here, he'll come to-morrow to take you away, seeing that he is your husband, seeing that he has right and law on his side."

"I did not ask you to keep me in your own house, Jacques, but to take me anywhere you like. I thought you loved me enough to do that. I have made a mistake. Good-bye!"

She turned round, and went toward the door so quickly that he was only able to catch hold of her when she was outside the room.

"Listen, Irène."

She struggled, and did not want to listen to him any longer, her eyes full of tears, and with these words only on her lips:

"Let me alone! let me alone! let me alone!"

He made her sit down by force, and falling once more on his knees at her feet, he now brought forward a number of arguments and counsels to make her understand the folly and terrible risk of her project. He omitted nothing which he deemed it necessary to say to convince her, finding in his very affection for her strong motives of persuasion.

As she remained silent and cold, he begged of her, implored of her to listen to him, to trust him, to follow his advice.

When he had finished speaking, she only replied:

"Are you disposed to let me go away now? Take away your hands, so that I may rise up."

"Look here, Irène."

"Will you let go?"

5   G. de M.—14

"Irène—is your resolution irrevocable?"

"Do let me go."

"Tell me only whether this resolution, this foolish resolution of yours, which you will bitterly regret, is irrevocable?"

"Yes: let me go!"

"Then stay. You know well that you are at home here. We shall go away to-morrow morning."

She rose up, in spite of him, and said in a hard tone:

"No. It is too late. I do not want sacrifice; I want devotion."

"Stay! I have done what I ought to do; I have said what I ought to say. I have no further responsibility on your behalf. My conscience is at peace. Tell me what you want me to do, and I will obey."

She resumed her seat, looked at him for a long time, and then asked, in a very calm voice:

"Explain, then."

"How is that? What do you wish me to explain?"

"Everything—everything that you have thought about before coming to this resolution. Then I will see what I ought to do."

"But I have thought about nothing at all. I ought to warn you that you are going to accomplish an act of folly. You persist; then I ask to share in this act of folly, and I even insist on it."

"It is not natural to change one's opinion so quickly."

"Listen, my dear love. It is not a question here of sacrifice or devotion. On the day when I realized that I loved you, I said this to myself, which every lover ought to say to himself in the same case: 'The man who loves a woman, who makes an effort to win her, who gets her and who takes her, contracts so far as he is himself and so far as she is concerned, a sacred engagement.' It is, mark you, a question of dealing with a woman like you, and not with a woman of an impulsive and yielding disposition.

"Marriage, which has a great social value, a great legal value, possesses in my eyes only a very slight moral value, taking into account the conditions under which it generally takes place.

"Therefore, when a woman, united by this lawful bond, but having no attachment to a husband whom she cannot love, a woman whose heart is free, meets a man for whom she cares, and gives herself to him, when a man who has no other tie takes a woman in this way, I say that they pledge themselves toward each other by this mutual and free agreement much more than by the 'Yes' uttered in the presence of the Mayor.

"I say that, if they are both honorable persons, their union must be more intimate, more real, more healthy than if all the sacraments had consecrated it.

"This woman risks everything. And it is exactly because she knows it, because she gives everything, her heart, her body, her soul, her honor, her life, because she has foreseen all miseries, all dangers, all catastrophes, because she dares to do a bold act, an intrepid act, because she is prepared, determined to brave everything — her husband who might kill her, and society which may cast her out. This is why she is heroic in her conjugal infidelity; this is why her lover in taking her must also have foreseen every-

thing, and preferred her to everything, whatever
might happen. I have nothing more to say. I spoke
in the beginning like a man of sense whose duty it
was to warn you; and now there is left in me only
one man—the man who loves you. Say, then, what
I am to do!"

Radiant, she closed his mouth with her lips, and
said to him in a low tone:

"It is not true, darling! There is nothing the
matter! My husband does not suspect anything. But
I wanted to see, I wanted to know, what you would
do. I wished for a New Year's gift—the gift of
your heart—another gift besides the necklace you
have just sent me. You have given it to me. Thanks!
thanks! God be thanked for the happiness you have
given me!"

MY UNCLE SOSTHENES

My uncle Sosthenes was a Free-thinker, like many others are, from pure stupidity; people are very often religious in the same way. The mere sight of a priest threw him into a violent rage; he would shake his fist and grimace at him, and touch a piece of iron when the priest's back was turned, forgetting that the latter action showed a belief after all, the belief in the evil eye.

Now when beliefs are unreasonable one should have all or none at all. I myself am a Freethinker; I revolt at all the dogmas which have invented the fear of death, but I feel no anger toward places of worship, be they Catholic Apostolic, Roman, Protestant, Greek, Russian, Buddhist, Jewish, or Mohammedan. I have a peculiar manner of looking at them and explaining them. A place of worship represents the homage paid by man to "The Unknown." The more extended our thoughts and our views become, the more The Unknown diminishes, and the more places of worship will decay. I, however, in the place of church furniture, in the place of pulpits, reading desks, altars, and so on, would fit them up with telescopes, microscopes, and electrical machines; that is all.

My uncle and I differed on nearly every point. He was a patriot, while I was not — for after all patriotism is a kind of religion; it is the egg from which wars are hatched.

My uncle was a Freemason, and I used to declare that they are stupider than old women devotees. That is my opinion, and I maintain it; if we must have any religion at all the old one is good enough for me.

What is their object? Mutual help to be obtained by tickling the palms of each other's hands. I see no harm in it, for they put into practice the Christian precept: "Do unto others as ye would they should do unto you." The only difference consists in the tickling, but it does not seem worth while to make such a fuss about lending a poor devil half-a-crown.

To all my arguments my uncle's reply used to be: "We are raising up a religion against a religion; Freethought will kill clericalism. Freemasonry is the headquarters of those who are demolishing all deities."

"Very well, my dear uncle," I would reply (in my heart I felt inclined to say, "You old idiot!"); "it is just that which I am blaming you for. Instead of destroying, you are organizing competition; it is only a case of lowering the prices. And then, if you only admitted Freethinkers among you I could understand it, but you admit anybody. You have a number of Catholics among you, even the leaders of the

party. Pius IX. is said to have been one of you before he became Pope. If you call a society with
such an organization a bulwark against clericalism, I
think it is an extremely weak one."

"My dear boy," my uncle would reply, with a
wink, "our most formidable actions are political;
slowly and surely we are everywhere undermining
the monarchical spirit."

Then I broke out: "Yes, you are very clever! If
you tell me that Freemasonry is an election-machine,
I will grant it you. I will never deny that it is used
as a machine to control candidates of all shades; if
you say that it is only used to hoodwink people, to
drill them to go to the voting-urn as soldiers are
sent under fire, I agree with you; if you declare that
it is indispensable to all political ambitions because
it changes all its members into electoral agents, I
should say to you, 'That is as clear as the sun.'
But when you tell me that it serves to undermine the
monarchical spirit, I can only laugh in your face.

"Just consider that vast and democratic associa-
tion which had Prince Napoleon for its Grand Master
under the Empire; which has the Crown Prince for its
Grand Master in Germany, the Czar's brother in Russia,
and to which the Prince of Wales and King Hum-
bert and nearly all the royalists of the globe belong."

"You are quite right," my uncle said; "but all
these persons are serving our projects without guessing it."

I felt inclined to tell him he was talking a pack of
nonsense.

It was, however, indeed a sight to see my uncle
when he had a Freemason to dinner.

On meeting they shook hands in a manner that was irresistibly funny; one could see that they were going through a series of secret mysterious pressures. When I wished to put my uncle in a rage, I had only to tell him that dogs also have a manner which savors very much of Freemasonry, when they greet one another on meeting.

Then my uncle would take his friend into a corner to tell him something important, and at dinner they had a peculiar way of looking at each other, and of drinking to each other, in a manner as if to say: "We know all about it, don't we?"

And to think that there are millions on the face of the globe who are amused at such monkey tricks! I would sooner be a Jesuit.

Now in our town there really was an old Jesuit who was my uncle's detestation. Every time he met him, or if he only saw him at a distance, he used to say: "Go on, you toad!" And then, taking my arm, he would whisper to me:

"Look here, that fellow will play me a trick some day or other, I feel sure of it."

My uncle spoke quite truly, and this was how it happened, through my fault also.

It was close on Holy Week, and my uncle made up his mind to give a dinner on Good Friday, a real dinner with his favorite chitterlings and black puddings. I resisted as much as I could, and said:

"I shall eat meat on that day, but at home, quite by myself. Your *manifestation,* as you call it, is an idiotic idea. Why should you manifest? What does it matter to you if people do not eat any meat?"

But my uncle would not be persuaded. He asked three of his friends to dine with him at one of the best restaurants in the town, and as he was going to pay the bill, I had certainly, after all, no scruples about *manifesting*.

At four o'clock we took a conspicuous place in the most frequented restaurant in the town, and my uncle ordered dinner in a loud voice, for six o'clock.

We sat down punctually, and at ten o'clock we had not finished. Five of us had drunk eighteen bottles of fine still wines, and four of champagne. Then my uncle proposed what he was in the habit of calling: "The archbishop's feat." Each man put six small glasses in front of him, each of them filled with a different liqueur, and then they had all to be emptied at one gulp, one after another, while one of the waiters counted twenty. It was very stupid, but my uncle thought it was very suitable to the occasion.

At eleven o'clock he was dead drunk. So we had to take him home in a cab and put him to bed, and one could easily foresee that his anti-clerical demonstration would end in a terrible fit of indigestion.

As I was going back to my lodgings, being rather drunk myself, with a cheerful Machiavelian drunkenness which quite satisfied all my instincts of scepticism, an idea struck me.

I arranged my necktie, put on a look of great distress, and went and rang loudly at the old Jesuit's door. As he was deaf he made me wait a longish while, but at length he appeared at his window in a cotton nightcap and asked what I wanted.

I shouted out at the top of my voice:

"Make haste, reverend Sir, and open the door; a poor, despairing, sick man is in need of your spiritual ministrations."

The good, kind man put on his trousers as quickly as he could and came down without his cassock. I told him in a breathless voice that my uncle, the Free-thinker, had been taken suddenly ill. Fearing it was going to be something serious he had been seized with a sudden fear of death, and wished to see a priest and talk to him; to have his advice and com-fort, to make up with the Church, and to confess, so as to be able to cross the dreaded threshold at peace with himself; and I added in a mocking tone:

"At any rate, he wishes it, and if it does him no good it can do him no harm."

The old Jesuit, who was startled, delighted, and almost trembling, said to me:

"Wait a moment, my son, I will come with you."

But I replied: "Pardon me, reverend Father, if I do not go with you; but my convictions will not al-low me to do so. I even refused to come and fetch you, so I beg you not to say that you have seen me, but to declare that you had a presentiment—a sort of revelation of his illness."

The priest consented, and went off quickly, knocked at my uncle's door, was soon let in, and I saw the black cassock disappear within that strong-hold of Freethought.

I hid under a neighboring gateway to wait for events. Had he been well, my uncle would have half murdered the Jesuit, but I knew that he would

scarcely be able to move an arm, and I asked myself, gleefully, what sort of a scene would take place
between these antagonists — what explanation would
be given, and what would be the issue of this situation, which my uncle's indignation would render
more tragic still?

I laughed till I had to hold my sides, and said to
myself, half aloud: "Oh! what a joke, what a joke!"

Meanwhile it was getting very cold. I noticed
that the Jesuit stayed a long time, and thought:
"They are having an explanation, I suppose."

One, two, three hours passed, and still the reverend Father did not come out. What had happened?
Had my uncle died in a fit when he saw him, or
had he killed the cassocked gentleman? Perhaps they
had mutually devoured each other? This last suppo-
sition appeared very unlikely, for I fancied that my
uncle was quite incapable of swallowing a grain more
nourishment at that moment.

At last the day broke. I was very uneasy, and,
not venturing to go into the house myself, I went
to one of my friends who lived opposite. I roused
him, explained matters to him, much to his amusement and astonishment, and took possession of his
window.

At nine o'clock he relieved me and I got a little
sleep. At two o'clock I, in my turn, replaced him.
We were utterly astonished.

At six o'clock the Jesuit left, with a very happy
and satisfied look on his face, and we saw him go
away with a quiet step.

Then, timid and ashamed, I went and knocked at
my uncle's door. When the servant opened it I did

not dare to ask her any questions, but went upstairs without saying a word.

My uncle was lying pale, exhausted, with weary, sorrowful eyes and heavy arms, on his bed. A little religious picture was fastened to one of the bed-curtains with a pin.

"Why, uncle," I said, "you in bed still? Are you not well?"

He replied in a feeble voice:

"Oh! my dear boy, I have been very ill; nearly dead."

"How was that, uncle?"

"I don't know; it was most surprising. But what is stranger still is, that the Jesuit priest who has just left—you know, that excellent man whom I have made such fun of—had a divine revelation of my state, and came to see me."

I was seized with an almost uncontrollable desire to laugh, and with difficulty said: "Oh, really!"

"Yes, he came. He heard a Voice telling him to get up and come to me, because I was going to die. It was a revelation."

I pretended to sneeze, so as not to burst out laughing; I felt inclined to roll on the ground with amusement.

In about a minute I managed to say, indignantly: "And you received him, uncle, you? You, a Free-thinker, a Freemason? You did not have him thrown out-of-doors?"

He seemed confused, and stammered:

"Listen a moment, it is so astonishing—so aston-ishing and providential! He also spoke to me about my father; it seems he knew him formerly."

"Your father, uncle? But that is no reason for receiving a Jesuit."

"I know that, but I was very ill, and he looked after me most devotedly all night long. He was perfect; no doubt he saved my life; those men are all more or less doctors."

"Oh! he looked after you all night? But you said just now that he had only been gone a very short time."

"That is quite true; I kept him to breakfast after all his kindness. He had it at a table by my bedside while I drank a cup of tea."

"And he ate meat?"

My uncle looked vexed, as if I had said something very much out of place, and then added:

"Don't joke, Gaston; such things are out of place at times. He has shown me more devotion than many a relation would have done and I expect to have his convictions respected."

This rather upset me, but I answered, nevertheless: "Very well, uncle; and what did you do after breakfast?"

"We played a game of bézique, and then he repeated his breviary while I read a little book which he happened to have in his pocket, and which was not by any means badly written."

"A religious book, uncle?"

"Yes, and no, or rather—no. It is the history of their missions in Central Africa, and is rather a book of travels and adventures. What these men have done is very grand."

I began to feel that matters were going badly, so I got up. "Well, good-bye, uncle," I said, "I see you are going to leave Freemasonry for religion; you are a renegade."

He was still rather confused, and stammered:

"Well, but religion is a sort of Freemasonry."

"When is your Jesuit coming back?" I asked.

"I don't—I don't know exactly; to-morrow, perhaps; but it is not certain."

I went out, altogether overwhelmed.

My joke turned out very badly for me! My uncle became radically converted, and if that had been all I should not have cared so much. Clerical or Freemason, to me it is all the same; six of one and half-a-dozen of the other; but the worst of it is that he has just made his will—yes, made his will—and has disinherited me in favor of that rascally Jesuit!

ALL OVER

THE Comte de Lormerin had just finished dressing himself. He cast a parting glance at the large glass, which occupied an entire panel of his dressing-room, and smiled.

He was really a fine-looking man still, though he was quite gray. Tall, slight, elegant, with no projecting paunch, with a scanty mustache of doubtful shade on his thin face· which seemed fair rather than white, he had presence, that "chic," in short, that indescribable something which establishes between two men more difference than millions of dollars.

He murmured: "Lormerin is still alive!"

And he made his way into the drawing-room, where his correspondence awaited him.

On his table, where everything had its place, the work-table of the gentleman who never works, there were a dozen letters lying beside three newspapers of different opinions. With a single touch of the finger he exposed to view all these letters, like a gambler giving the choice of a card; and he scanned the handwriting — a thing he did each morning before tearing open the envelopes.

It was for him a moment of delightful expectancy, of inquiry, and vague anxiety. What did these sealed mysterious papers bring him? What did they contain of pleasure, of happiness, or of grief? He surveyed them with a rapid sweep of the eye, recognizing in each case the hand that wrote them, selecting them, making two or three lots, according to what he expected from them. Here, friends; there, persons to whom he was indifferent; further on, strangers. The last kind always gave him a little uneasiness. What did they want from him? What hand had traced those curious characters full of thoughts, promises, or threats?

This day, one letter in particular caught his eye. It was simple nevertheless, without seeming to reveal anything; but he regarded it with disquietude, with a sort of internal shiver.

He thought: "From whom can it be? I certainly know this writing, and yet I can't identify it."

He raised it to a level with his face, holding it delicately between two fingers, striving to read through the envelope without making up his mind to open it.

Then he smelled it, and snatched up from the table a little magnifying glass which he used in studying all the niceties of handwriting. He suddenly felt unnerved. "Whom is it from? This hand is familiar to me, very familiar. I must have often read its prosings, yes, very often. But this must have been a long, long time ago. Who the deuce can it be from? Pooh! 'tis only from somebody asking for money."

And he tore open the letter. Then he read:

"MY DEAR FRIEND: You have, without doubt, forgotten me, for it is now twenty-five years since we saw each other. I was young; I am old. When I bade you farewell, I quitted Paris in order to follow into the provinces my husband, my old husband, whom you used to call 'my hospital.' Do you remember him? He died five years ago; and now I am returning to Paris to get my daughter married, for I have a daughter, a beautiful girl of eighteen, whom you have never seen. I informed you about her entrance into the world, but you certainly did not pay much attention to so trifling an event.

"You, you are always the handsome Lormerin; so I have been told. Well, if you still recollect little Lise, whom you used to call 'Lison,' come and dine this evening with her, with the elderly Baronne de Vance, your ever faithful friend, who, with some emotion, stretches out to you, without complaining at her lot, a devoted hand, which you must clasp but no longer kiss, my poor 'Jaquelet.'

"LISE DE VANCE."

Lormerin's heart began to throb. He remained sunk in his armchair, with the letter on his knees, staring straight before him, overcome by poignant feelings that made the tears mount up to his eyes!

If he had ever loved a woman in his life, it was this one, little Lise, Lise de Vance, whom he called "Cinder-Flower" on account of the strange color of her hair, and the pale gray of her eyes. Oh! what a fine, pretty, charming creature she was, this frail Baronne, the wife of that old, gouty, pimply Baron, who had abruptly carried her off to the provinces, shut her up, kept her apart through jealousy, through jealousy of the handsome Lormerin.

Yes, he had loved her, and he believed that he, too, had been truly loved. She gave him the name

5 G. de M.—15

cf Jaquelet, and used to pronounce the word in an exquisite fashion.

A thousand memories that had been effaced came back to him, far off and sweet and melancholy now. One evening, she called on him on her way home from a ball, and they went out for a stroll in the Bois de Boulogne, she in evening dress, he in his dressing-jacket. It was springtime; the weather was beautiful. The odor of her bodice embalmed the warm air,—the odor of her bodice, and also a little, the odor of her skin. What a divine night! When they reached the lake, as the moon's rays fell across the branches into the water, she began to weep. A little surprised, he asked her why.

She replied:

"I don't know. 'Tis the moon and the water that have affected me. Every time I see poetic things they seize hold of my heart and I have to cry."

He smiled, moved himself, considering her feminine emotion charming—the emotion of a poor little woman whom every sensation overwhelms. And he embraced her passionately, stammering:

"My little Lise, you are exquisite."

What a charming love affair, short-lived and dainty it had been, and all over too so quickly, cut short in the midst of its ardor by this old brute of a Baron, who had carried off his wife, and never shown her afterward to anyone!

Lormerin had forgotten, in good sooth, at the end of two or three months. One woman drives out the other so quickly in Paris, when one is a bachelor! No matter! he had kept a little chapel for her in his heart, for he had loved her alone! He assured himself now that this was so.

He rose up, and said aloud: "Certainly, I will go and dine with her this evening!"

And instinctively he turned round toward the glass in order to inspect himself from head to foot. He reflected: "She must have grown old unpleasantly, more than I have!" And he felt gratified at the thought of showing himself to her still handsome, still fresh, of astonishing her, perhaps of filling her with emotion, and making her regret those bygone days so far, far distant!

He turned his attention to the other letters. They were not of importance.

The whole day, he kept thinking of this phantom. What was she like now? How funny it was to meet in this way after twenty-five years! Would he alone recognize her?

He made his toilette with feminine coquetry, put on a white waistcoat, which suited him better, with the coat, sent for the hairdresser to give him a finishing touch with the curling-iron, for he had preserved his hair, and started very early in order to show his eagerness to see her.

The first thing he saw on entering a pretty drawing-room, freshly furnished, was his own portrait, an old, faded photograph, dating from the days of his good-fortune, hanging on the wall in an antique silk frame.

He sat down, and waited. A door opened behind him. He rose up abruptly, and, turning round, beheld an old woman with white hair who extended both hands toward him.

He seized them, kissed them one after the other with long, long kisses, then, lifting up his head, he gazed at the woman he had loved.

Yes, it was an old lady, an old lady whom he did not recognize, and who, while she smiled, seemed ready to weep.

He could not abstain from murmuring:

"It is you, Lise?"

She replied:

"Yes, it is I; it is I, indeed. You would not have known me, isn't that so? I have had so much sorrow—so much sorrow. Sorrow has consumed my life. Look at me now—or rather don't look at me! But how handsome you have kept—and young! If I had by chance met you in the street, I would have cried, 'Jaquelet!' Now sit down and let us, first of all, have a chat. And then I'll show you my daughter, my grown-up daughter. You'll see how she resembles me—or rather how I resembled her—no, it is not quite that: she is just like the 'me' of former days—you shall see! But I wanted to be alone with you first. I feared that there would be some emotion on my side, at the first moment. Now it is all over—it is past. Pray be seated, my friend."

He sat down beside her, holding her hand; but he did not know what to say; he did not know this woman—it seemed to him that he had never seen her before. What had he come to do in this house? Of what could he speak? Of the long ago? What was there in common between him and her? He could no longer recall anything to mind in the presonce of this grandmotherly face. He could no longer recall to mind all the nice, tender things so sweet, so bitter, that had assailed his heart, some time since, when he thought of the other, of little Lise, of the dainty Cinder-Flower. What then had become of her, the former one, the one he had loved — that woman of far-off dreams, the blonde with gray eyes, the young one who used to call him Jaquelet so prettily?

They remained side by side, motionless, both constrained, troubled, profoundly ill at ease.

As they only talked in commonplace phrases, broken and slow, she rose up and pressed the button of the bell.

"I am going to call Renée," she said.

There was a tap at the door, then the rustle of a dress; next, a young voice exclaimed:

"Here I am, mamma!"

Lormerin remained scared, as if at the sight of an apparition.

He stammered:

"Good day, Mademoiselle."

Then, turning toward the mother:

"Oh! it is you!"

In fact, it was she, she whom he had known in bygone days, the Lise who had vanished and came back! In her he found the woman he had won twenty-five years before. This one was even younger still, fresher, more childlike.

He felt a wild desire to open his arms, to clasp her to his heart again, murmuring in her ear:

"Good day, Lison!"

A man-servant announced: "Dinner is ready, Madame." And they proceeded toward the dining-room.

What passed at this dinner? What did they say to him, and what could he say in reply? He found himself plunged in one of those strange dreams which border on insanity. He gazed at the two women with a fixed idea in his mind, a morbid, self-contra-dictory idea: "Which is the real one?"

The mother smiled, repeating over and over again: "Do you remember?" And it was in the bright eye of the young girl that he found again his memories of the past. Twenty times, he opened his mouth to say to her: "Do you remember, Lison?—" forgetting this white-haired lady who was regarding him with looks of tenderness.

And yet there were moments when he no longer felt sure, when he lost his head. He could see that the woman of to-day was not exactly the woman of long ago. The other one, the former one, had in her voice, in her glance, in her entire being something which he did not find again in the mother. And he made efforts to recall his ladylove, to seize again what had escaped from her, what this resusci-tated one did not possess.

The Baronne said:

"You have lost your old sprightliness, my poor friend."

He murmured: "There are many other things that I have lost!"

But in his heart, touched with emotion, he felt his old love springing to life once more like an awakened wild beast ready to bite him.

The young girl went on chattering, and every now and then some familiar phrase of her mother which she had borrowed, a certain style of speaking and thinking, that resemblance of mind and manner which people acquire by living together, shook Lormerin from head to foot. All these things penetrated him, making the reopened wound of his passion bleed anew.

He got away early, and took a turn along the boulevard. But the image of this young girl pursued him, haunted him, quickened his heart, inflamed his blood. Instead of two women, he now saw only one, a young one, the one of former days returned, and he loved her as he had loved her prototype in bygone years. He loved her with greater ardor, after an interval of twenty-five years.

He went home to reflect on this strange and terrible thing, and to think on what he should do.

But as he was passing, with a wax-candle in his hand before the glass, the large glass in which he had contemplated himself and admired himself before he started, he saw reflected there an elderly, gray-haired man; and suddenly he recollected what he had been in olden days, in the days of little Lise. He saw himself charming and handsome, as he had been when he was loved! Then, drawing the light nearer, he looked at himself more closely, as one inspects a strange thing with a magnifying glass, tracing the wrinkles, discovering those frightful ravages which he had not perceived till now.

And he sat down, crushed at the sight of himself, at the sight of his lamentable image, murmuring:

"All over, Lormerin!"

MY LANDLADY

"A T THAT time," said George Kervelen, "I was living in furnished lodgings in the Rue des Saints-Pères. "When my father had made up his mind that I should go to Paris to continue my law studies, there had been a long discussion about settling everything. My allowance had been fixed at first at two thousand five hundred francs,* but my poor mother was so anxious, that she said to my father that if I spent my money badly I might not take enough to eat, and then my health would suffer, and so it was settled that a comfortable boarding-house should be found for me, and that the amount should be paid to the proprietor himself, or herself, every month.

"Some of our neighbors told us of a certain Mme. Kergaran, a native of Brittany, who took in boarders, and so my father arranged matters by letter with this respectable person, at whose house I and my luggage arrived one evening.

---

* $500 a year.

"Mme. Kergaran was a woman of about forty. She was very stout, had a voice like a drill-sergeant, and decided everything in a very abrupt manner. Her house was narrow, with only one window opening on to the street on each story, which rather gave it the appearance of a ladder of windows, or better, perhaps, of a slice of a house sandwiched in between two others.

"The landlady lived on the first floor with her servant, the kitchen and dining-room were on the second, and four boarders from Brittany lived on the third and fourth, and I had two rooms on the fifth.

"A little dark corkscrew staircase led up to these attics. All day long Mme. Kergaran was up and down these stairs like a captain on board ship. Ten times a day she would go into each room, noisily superintending everything, seeing that the beds were properly made, the clothes well brushed, that the attendance was all that it should be; in a word, she looked after her boarders like a mother, and better than a mother.

"I soon made the acquaintance of my four fellow-countrymen. Two were medical and two were law students, but all impartially endured the landlady's despotic yoke. They were as frightened of her as a boy robbing an orchard is of a rural policeman.

"I, however, immediately felt that I wished to be independent; it is my nature to rebel. I declared at once that I meant to come in at whatever time I liked, for Mme. Kergaran had fixed twelve o'clock at night as the limit. On hearing this she looked at me for a few moments, and then said:

"'It is quite impossible; I cannot have Annette called up at any hour of the night. You can have nothing to do out-of-doors at such a time.'

"I replied firmly that, according to the law, she was obliged to open the door for me at any time.

"'If you refuse,' I said, 'I shall get a policeman to witness the fact, and go and get a bed at some hotel, at your expense, in which I shall be fully justified. You will, therefore, be obliged either to open the door for me or to get rid of me. Do which you please.'

"I laughed in her face as I told her my conditions. She could not speak for a moment for surprise, then she tried to negotiate, but I was firm, and she was obliged to yield. It was agreed that I should have a latchkey, on my solemn undertaking that no one else should know it.

"My energy made such a wholesome impression on her that from that time she treated me with marked favor; she was most attentive, and even showed me a sort of rough tenderness which was not at all unpleasing. Sometimes when I was in a jovial mood I would kiss her by surprise, if only for the sake of getting the box on the ears which she gave me immediately afterward. When I managed to duck my head quickly enough, her hand would pass over me as swiftly as a ball, and I would run away laughing, while she would call after me:

"'Oh! you wretch, I will pay you out for that.'

"However, we soon became real friends.

"It was not long before I made the acquaintance of a girl who was employed in a shop, and whom I constantly met. You know what such sort of love affairs are in Paris. One fine day, going to a lecture, you meet a girl going to work arm-in-arm with a friend. You look at her and feel that pleasant little shock which the eyes of some women give you. The next day at the same time, going through the same street, you meet her again, and the next, and the succeeding days. At last you speak, and the love affair follows its course just like an illness.

"Well, by the end of three weeks I was on that footing with Emma which precedes intimacy. The fall would indeed have taken place much sooner had I known where to bring it about. The girl lived at home, and utterly refused to go to a hotel. I did not know how to manage, but at last I made the desperate resolve to take her to my room some night at about eleven o'clock, under the pretense of giving her a cup of tea. Mme. Kergaran always went to bed at ten, so that we could get in by means of my latchkey without exciting any attention, and go down again in an hour or two in the same way.

"After a good deal of entreaty on my part, Emma accepted my invitation.

"I did not spend a very pleasant day, for I was by no means easy in my mind. I was afraid of complications, of a catastrophe, of some scandal. At night I went into a *café,* and drank two cups of coffee and three or four glasses of cognac, to give me courage, and when I heard the clock strike half past ten, I went slowly to the place of meeting, where she was already waiting for me. She took my arm in a coaxing manner, and we set off slowly toward my lodgings. The nearer we got to the door the more nervous I got, and I thought to myself: 'If only Mme. Kergaran is in bed already.'

"I said to Emma two or three times:

"'Above all things, don't make any noise on the stairs,' to which she replied, laughing:

"'Are you afraid of being heard?'

"'No,' I said, 'but I am afraid of waking the man who sleeps in the room next to me, who is not at all well.'

"When I got near the house I felt as frightened as a man does who is going to the dentist's. All the windows were dark, so no doubt everybody was asleep, and I breathed again. I opened the door as carefully as a thief, let my fair companion in, shut it behind me, and went upstairs on tiptoe, holding my breath, and striking wax-matches lest the girl should make a false step.

"As we passed the landlady's door I felt my heart beating very quickly. But we reached the second floor, then the third, and at last the fifth, and got into my room. Victory!

"However, I only dared to speak in a whisper, and took off my boots so as not to make any noise. The tea, which I made over a spirit-lamp, was soon drunk, and then I became pressing, till little by little, as if in play, I, one by one, took off my companion's garments. She yielded while resisting, blushing, confused.

"She had absolutely nothing on except a short white petticoat when my door suddenly opened, and Mme. Kergaran appeared with a candle in her hand, in exactly the same costume as Emma.

"I jumped away from her and remained standing up, looking at the two women, who were looking at each other. What was going to happen?

"My landlady said, in a lofty tone of voice which I had never heard from her before:

"'Monsieur Kervelen, I will not have prostitutes in my house.'

"'But, Madame Kergaran,' I stammered, 'the young lady is a friend of mine. She just came in to have a cup of tea.'

"'People don't take tea in their chemises. You will please make this person go directly.'

"Emma, in a natural state of consternation, began to cry, and hid her face in her petticoat, and I lost my head, not knowing what to do or say. My landlady added, with irresistible authority:

"'Help her to dress, and take her out at once.'

"It was certainly the only thing I could do, so I picked up her dress from the floor, put it over her head, and began to fasten it as best I could. She helped me, crying all the time, hurrying and making all sorts of mistakes and unable to find either button-holes or laces, while Mme. Kergaran stood by motionless, with the candle in her hand, looking at us with the severity of a judge.

"As soon as Emma was dressed, without even stopping to button her boots, she rushed past the landlady and ran downstairs. I followed her in my slippers and half undressed, and kept repeating: 'Mademoiselle! Mademoiselle!'

"I felt that I ought to say something to her, but I could not find anything. I overtook her just by the street-door, and tried to take her into my arms, but she pushed me violently away, saying in a low, nervous voice:

"'Leave me alone, leave me alone!' and so ran out into the street, closing the door behind her.

"When I went upstairs again I found that Mme. Kergaran was waiting on the first landing. I went up slowly, expecting, and ready for, anything.

"Her door was open, and she called me in, saying in a severe voice:

"'I want to speak to you, M. Kervelen.'

"I went in, with my head bent. She put her candle on the mantlepiece, and then, folding her arms over her expansive bosom, which a fine white dressing-jacket hardly covered, she said:

"'So, Monsieur Kervelen, you think my house is a house of ill-fame?'

"I was not at all proud. I murmured:

"'Oh dear, no! But, Mme. Kergaran, you must not be angry; you know what young men are.'

"'I know,' was her answer, 'that I will not have such creatures here, so you will understand that. I expect to have my house respected, and I will not have it lose its reputation, you understand me? I know—'

"She went on thus for at least twenty minutes, overwhelming me with the good name of her house, with reasons for her indignation, and loading me with severe reproofs. I went to bed crestfallen, and resolved never again to try such an experiment, so long, at least, as I continued to be a lodger of Mme. Kergaran."

THE HORRIBLE

THE shadows of a balmy night were slowly falling. The women remained in the drawing-room of the villa. The men, seated or astride on garden-chairs, were smoking in front of the door, forming a circle round a table laden with cups and wineglasses.

Their cigars shone like eyes in the darkness which, minute by minute, was growing thicker. They had been talking about a frightful accident which had occurred the night before—two men and three women drowned before the eyes of the guests in the river opposite.

General de G—— remarked:

"Yes, these things are affecting, but they are not horrible.

"The horrible, that well-known word, means much more than the terrible. A frightful accident like this moves, upsets, scares; it does not horrify. In order that we should experience horror, something more is needed than the mere excitation of the soul, something more than the spectacle of the dreadful death; there must be a shuddering sense of mystery or a sensation of abnormal terror beyond the limits of nature. A man who dies, even in the most dramatic conditions, does not excite horror; a field of battle is not horrible; blood is not horrible; the vilest crimes are rarely horrible.

"Now, here are two personal examples, which have shown me what is the meaning of horror:

"It was during the war of 1870. We were retreating toward Pont-Audemer, after having passed through Rouen. The army, consisting of about twenty thousand men, twenty thousand men in disorder, disbanded, demoralized, exhausted, was going to reform at Havre.

"The earth was covered with snow. The night was falling. They had not eaten anything since the day before, and were flying rapidly, the Prussians not far off. The Norman country, livid, dotted with the shadows of the trees surrounding the farms, stretched away under a heavy and sinister black sky.

"Nothing else could be heard in the wan twilight save the confused sound, soft and undefined, of a marching throng, an endless tramping, mingled with the vague clink of canteens or sabers. The men, bent, round-shouldered, dirty, in many cases even in rags, dragged themselves along, hurrying through the snow, with a long broken-backed stride.

"The skin of their hands stuck to the steel of their muskets' butt-ends, for it was freezing dreadfully that night. I frequently saw a little soldier take off his shoes in order to walk barefooted, so much did his footgear bruise him; and with every step he left a track of blood. Then, after some time, he sat down in a field for a few minutes' rest, and never got up again. Every man who sat down died.

"Should we have left behind us those poor exhausted soldiers, who fondly counted on being able to start afresh as soon as they had somewhat refreshed their stiffened legs? Now, scarcely had they ceased to move, and to make their almost frozen blood circulate in their veins, than an unconquerable torpor congealed them, nailed them to the ground, closed their eyes, and in one second the overworked human mechanism collapsed. They gradually sank down, their heads falling toward their knees — without, however, quite tumbling over, for their loins and their limbs lost the capacity for moving, and became as hard as wood, impossible to bend or straighten.

"The rest of us, more robust, kept still straggling on, chilled to the marrow of our bones, advancing by dint of forced movement through the night, through that snow, through that cold and deadly country, crushed by pain, by defeat, by despair, above all overcome by the abominable sensation of abandonment, of death, of nothingness.

"I saw two gendarmes holding by the arm a curious-looking little man, old, beardless, of truly surprising aspect.

"They were looking out for an officer, believing that they had caught a spy. The word 'Spy' at once spread through the midst of the stragglers, and they gathered in a group round the prisoner. A voice exclaimed: 'He must be shot!' And all these soldiers who were falling from utter prostration, only holding themselves on their feet by leaning on their guns, felt of a sudden that thrill of furious and bestial anger which urges on a mob to massacre.

"I wanted to speak! I was at that time in command of a battalion; but they no longer recognized the authority of their commanding officers; they would have shot me.

"One of the gendarmes said: 'He has been following us for the last three days. He has been asking information from everyone about the artillery.'

"I took it on myself to question this person:

"'What are you doing? What do you want? Why are you accompanying the army?'

"He stammered out some words in some unintelligible dialect. He was, indeed, a strange being, with narrow shoulders, a sly look, and such an agitated air in my presence that I had no longer any real doubt that he was a spy. He seemed very aged and feeble. He kept staring at me from under his eyes with a humble, stupid, and crafty air.

"The men all round us exclaimed:

"'To the wall! to the wall!'

"I said to the gendarmes:

"'Do you answer for the prisoner?'

"I had not ceased speaking when a terrible push threw me on my back, and in a second I saw the man seized by the furious soldiers, thrown down, struck, dragged along the side of the road, and flung against a tree. He fell in the snow, nearly dead already.

"And immediately they shot him. The soldiers fired at him, reloaded their guns, fired again with the desperate energy of brutes. They fought with each other to have a shot at him, filed off in front of the corpse, and kept firing at him, just as people at a funeral keep sprinkling holy water in front of a coffin.

"But suddenly a cry arose of 'The Prussians! the Prussians!' and all along the horizon I heard the great noise of this panic-stricken army in full flight.

"The panic, generated by these shots fired at this vagabond, had filled his very executioners with terror; and, without realizing that they were themselves the originators of the scare, they rushed away and disappeared in the darkness.

"I remained alone in front of the corpse with the two gendarmes whom duty had compelled to stay with me.

"They lifted up this riddled piece of flesh, bruised and bleeding.

"'He must be examined,' said I to them.

"And I handed them a box of vestas which I had in my pocket. One of the soldiers had another box. I was standing between the two.

"The gendarme, who was feeling the body, called out:

"'Clothed in a blue blouse, trousers, and a pair of shoes.'

"The first match went out; we lighted a second. The man went on, as he turned out the pockets:

"'A horn knife, check handkerchief, a snuffbox, a bit of packthread, a piece of bread.'

"The second match went out; we lighted a third. The gendarme, after having handled the corpse for a long time, said:

"'That is all.'

"I said:

"'Strip him. We shall perhaps find something near the skin.'

"And, in order that the two soldiers might help each other in this task, I stood between them to give them light. I saw them, by the rapid and speedily extinguished flash of the match, take off the garments one by one, and expose to view that bleeding bundle of flesh still warm, though lifeless.

"And suddenly one of them exclaimed:

"'Good God, Colonel, it is a woman!'

"I cannot describe to you the strange and poignant sensation of pain that moved my heart. I could not believe it, and I kneeled down in the snow before this shapeless pulp of flesh to see for myself: it was a woman.

"The two gendarmes, speechless and stunned, waited for me to give my opinion on the matter. But I did not know what to think, what theory to adopt.

"Then the brigadier slowly drawled out:

"'Perhaps she came to look for a son of hers in the artillery, whom she had not heard from.'

"And the other chimed in:

"'Perhaps indeed that is so.'

"And I, who had seen some terrible things in my time, began to weep. I felt, in the presence of this corpse, in that icy cold night, the midst of that gloomy plain, at the sight of this mystery, at the sight of this murdered stranger, the meaning of that word 'horror.'

"Now, I had the same sensation last year while interrogating one of the survivors of the Flatters Mission, an Algerian sharpshooter.

"You probably know some of the details of this atrocious drama. It is possible, however, that you are unacquainted with all.

"The Colonel traveled through the desert into the Soudan, and passed through the immense territory of the Touaregs, who are, in that great ocean of sand which stretches from the Atlantic to Egypt and from the Soudan to Algeria, a sort of pirates resembling those who ravaged the seas in former days.

"The guides who accompanied the column belonged to the tribe of Chambaa, of Ouargla.

"One day, they pitched their camp in the middle of the desert, and the Arabs declared that, as the spring was a little farther away, they would go with all their camels to look for water.

"Only one man warned the Colonel that he had been betrayed. Flatters did not believe this, and accompanied the convoy with the engineers, the doctors, and nearly all his officers.

"They were massacred round the spring and all the camels captured.

"The Captain of the Arab Intelligence Department at Ouargla, who had remained in the camp, took command of the survivors, spahis and sharpshooters, and commenced the retreat, leaving behind the baggage and the provisions for want of camels to carry them.

"Then they started on their journey through this solitude without shade and without limit, under a devouring sun, which parched them from morning till night.

"One tribe came to tender its submission and brought dates as a tribute. They were poisoned.

Nearly all the French died, and among them, the last officer.

"There now only remained a few spahis, with their quartermaster, Pobéguin, and some native sharp-shooters of the Chambaa tribe. They had still two camels left. These disappeared one night along with two Arabs.

"Then the survivors feared that they would have to eat each other up. As soon as they discovered the flight of the two men with the two beasts, those who remained separated, and proceeded to march, one by one, through the soft sand, under the glare of a scorching sun, at a distance of more than a gunshot from each other.

"So they went on all day, and, when they reached a spring, each of them came up to drink at it in turn as soon as each solitary marcher had moved forward the number of yards arranged upon. And thus they continued marching the whole day, rais-ing, everywhere they passed in that level burned-up expanse, those little columns of dust which, at a dis-tance, indicate those who are trudging through the desert.

"But, one morning, one of the travelers made a sudden turn, and drew nearer to his neighbor. And they all stopped to look.

"The man toward whom the famished soldier drew near did not fly, but lay flat on the ground, and took aim at the one who was coming on. When he believed he was within gunshot, he fired. The other was not hit, and continued to advance, and cocking his gun in turn, killed his comrade.

"Then from the entire horizon, the others rushed

to seek their share. And he who had killed the fallen man, cutting the corpse into pieces, distributed it.

"Then they once more placed themselves at fixed distances, these irreconcilable allies, preparing for the next murder which would bring them together.

"For two days they lived on this human flesh, which they divided among each other. Then, the famine came back, and he who had killed the first man began killing afresh. And again, like a butcher, he cut up the corpse and offered it to his comrades, keeping only his own portion of it. This retreat of cannibals continued. The last Frenchman, Pobéguin, was massacred at the side of a well the very night before the supplies arrived.

"Do you understand now what I mean by the 'horrible?'"

This was the story told us a few nights ago by General de G——.

THE FIRST SNOWFALL

THE long promenade of La Croisette runs in a curve up to the edge of the blue water. Over there, at the right, the Esterel advances far into the sea. It obstructs the view, shutting in the horizon with the pretty southern aspect of its peaked, numerous, and fantastic summits.

At the left, the isles of Sainte-Marguerite and Saint-Honorat, lying in the water, present long aisles of fir-trees.

And all along the great gulf, all along the tall mountains that encircle Cannes, the white villa residences seem to be sleeping in the sunlight. You can see them from a distance, the bright houses, scattered from the top to the bottom of the mountains, dotting the dark greenery with specks of snow.

Those near the water open their gates on the vast promenade which is lashed by the quiet waves. The air is soft and balmy. It is one of those days when in this southern climate the chill of winter is not felt, Above the walls of the gardens may be seen orange-trees and citron-trees full of golden fruit. Ladies advance with slow steps over the sand of the avenue, followed by children rolling hoops or chatting with gentlemen.

      *   *   *   *   *   *   *

A young lady had just passed out through the door of her coquettish little house facing La Croisette. She stops for a moment to gaze at the promenaders, smiles, and, with the gait of one utterly enfeebled, makes her way toward an empty bench right in front of the sea. Fatigued after having gone twenty paces, she sits down out of breath. Her pale face seems that of a dead woman. She coughs, and raises to her lips her transparent fingers as if to stop those shakings that exhaust her.

She gazes at the sky full of sunshine and at the swallows, at the zigzag summits of the Esterel over there, and at the sea, quite close to her, so blue, so calm, so beautiful.

She smiles still, and murmurs:

"Oh! how happy I am!"

She knows, however, that she is going to die, that she will never see the springtime, that in a year, along the same promenade, these same people who pass before her now will come again to breathe the warm air of this charming spot, with their children a little bigger, with their hearts all filled with hopes, with tenderness, with happiness, while at the bottom of an oak coffin the poor flesh which is left to her still to-day will have fallen into a condition of rottenness, leaving only her bones lying in the silk robe which she has selected for a winding-sheet.

She will be no more. Everything in life will go

on as before for others. For her life will be over—over forever. She will be no more. She smiles, and inhales as well as she can, with her diseased lungs, the perfumed air of the gardens.

And she sinks into a reverie.

*   *   *   *   *   *   *

She recalls the past. She had been married, four years ago, to a Norman gentleman. He was a strong young man, bearded, healthy looking, with wide shoulders, narrow mind, and joyous disposition.

They had been united through worldly motives which she did not quite understand. She would willingly have said "Yes." She did say "Yes," with a movement of the head in order not to thwart her father and mother. She was a Parisian, gay and full of the joy of living.

Her husband brought her home to his Norman château. It was a huge stone building surrounded by tall trees of great age. A high clump of fir-trees shut out the view in front. On the right an opening in the trees presented a view of the plain which stretched out, quite flat, up to the distant farmsteads. A cross-road passed before the boundary-line leading to the highroad three kilometers away.

Oh! she could remember everything—her arrival, her first day in her new abode, and her isolated fate afterward.

When she stepped out of the carriage, she glanced at the old building and laughingly exclaimed:

"It does not look gay!"

Her husband began to laugh in his turn and replied:

"Pooh! we get used to it! You'll see. I never feel bored in it, for my part."

That day they passed their time in embracing each other, and she did not find it too long. This lasted for the best part of three months. The days passed one after the other in insignificant yet absorbing occupations. She learned the value and the importance of the little things of life. She knew that people can interest themselves in the price of eggs which cost a few centimes more or less according to the seasons.

It was summer. She went to the fields to see the harvest cut. The gaiety of the sunshine kept up the gaiety of her heart.

The autumn came. Her husband went hunting. He started in the morning with his two dogs, Medor and Mirza. Then she remained alone, without grieving herself, moreover, at Henry's absence. She was, however, very fond of him, but he was not missed by her. When he returned home, her affection was specially absorbed by the dogs. She took care of them every evening with a mother's affection, caressed them incessantly, gave them a thousand charming little names which she had no idea of applying to her husband.

He invariably told her all about his hunting. He pointed out the places where he found partridges, expressed his astonishment at not having caught any hares in Joseph Ledentu's clover, or else appeared indignant at the conduct of M. Lechapelier, of Havre, who always followed the border of his estates to shoot game that had been started by him, Henry de Parville.

She replied: "Yes, indeed; it is not right," thinking of something else all the while.

The winter came, the Norman winter, cold and rainy. The endless rain-storms came down on the slates of the great many-angled roof, rising like a blade toward the sky. The road seemed like streams of mud, the country a plain of mud, and no noise could be heard save that of water falling; no movement could be seen save the whirling flight of crows rolling themselves out like a cloud, alighting on a field, and then hurrying away again.

About four o'clock, the army of dark, flying creatures came and perched in the tall beeches at the left of the château, emitting deafening cries. During nearly an hour, they fluttered from tree-top to tree-top, seemed to be fighting, croaked, and made the gray branches move with their black wings. She gazed at them, each evening, with a pressure of the heart, so deeply was she penetrated by the lugubrious melancholy of the night falling on the desolate grounds.

Then she rang for the lamp, and she drew near the fire. She burned heaps of wood without succeeding in warming the spacious apartments invaded by the humidity. She felt cold every day, everywhere, in the drawing-room, at meals in her own apartment. It seemed to her she was cold even in the marrow of her bones. He only came in to dinner, he was always hunting, or else occupied with sowing seed, tilling the soil, and all the work of the country.

He used to come back jolly and covered with mud, rubbing his hands while he exclaimed:

"What wretched weather!" Or else: "It is a good thing to have a fire." Or sometimes: "Well, how are you to-day? Do you feel in good spirits?"

He was happy, in good health, without desires, thinking of nothing else save this simple, sound, and quiet life.

About December, when the snow had come, she suffered so much from the icy-cold air of the château which seemed to have acquired a chill with the centuries it had passed through, as human beings do with years, that she asked her husband one evening:

"Look here, Henry! You ought to have a hot-air plant put into the house; it would dry the walls. I assure you I cannot warm myself from morning till night."

At first he was stunned at this extravagant idea of introducing a hot-air plant into his manor-house. It would have seemed more natural to him to have his dogs fed out of his silver plate. Then, he gave a tremendous laugh which made his chest heave, while he exclaimed:

"A hot-air plant here! A hot-air plant here! Ha! ha! ha! what a good joke!"

She persisted:

"I assure you, dear, I feel frozen; you don't feel it because you are always moving about; but, all the same, I feel frozen."

He replied, still laughing:

"Pooh! you will get used to it, and besides it is excellent for the health. You will only be all the better for it. We are not Parisians, damn it! to live in hot-houses. And besides the spring is quite near."

* * * * * * *

About the beginning of January, a great misfortune befell her. Her father and her mother died of a carriage-accident. She came to Paris for the funeral. And her mind was entirely plunged in grief on account of it for about six months.

The softness of fine days at length awakened her, and she lived a sad, drifting life of languor until autumn.

When the cold weather came back, she was brought face to face, for the first time, with the gloomy future. What was she to do? Nothing. What was going to happen to her henceforth? Nothing. What expectation, what hope, could revive her heart? None. A doctor who was consulted declared that she would never have children.

Sharper, more penetrating still than the year before, the cold made her suffer continually.

She stretched out her shivering hands to the big flames. The glaring fire burned her face; but icy puffs seemed to slip down her back and to penetrate between the flesh and her underclothing. And she shook from head to foot. Innumerable currents of air appeared to have taken up their abode in the apartment, living, crafty currents of air, as cruel as enemies. She encountered them every moment; they were incessantly buffeting her, sometimes on the face, sometimes on the hands, sometimes on the neck, with their treacherous, frozen breath.

Once more she spoke of a hot-air plant; but her husband heard her request as if she were asking for the moon. The introduction of such an apparatus at Parville appeared to him as impossible as the discovery of the Philosopher's Stone.

Having been at Rouen on business one day he brought back to his wife a dainty foot-warmer made of copper, which he laughingly called a "portable hot-water heater"; and he considered that this would prevent her henceforth from ever being cold.

Toward the end of December she understood that she could not live thus always, and she said timidly one evening at dinner:

"Listen, dear! Are we not going to spend a week or two in Paris before spring?"

He was stupefied:

"In Paris? In Paris? But what are we to do there? No, by Jove! We are better off here. What odd ideas come into your head sometimes."

She faltered:

"It might distract us a little."

He did not understand:

"What is it you want to distract you? Theaters, evening parties, dinners in town? You know, however, well that in coming here you ought not to expect any distractions of that kind!"

She saw a reproach in these words and in the tone in which they were uttered. She relapsed into silence. She was timid and gentle, without resisting power and without strength of will.

In January, the cold weather returned with violence. Then the snow covered the earth.

One evening, as she watched the great whirling cloud of crows winding round the trees, she began to weep, in spite of herself.

Her husband came in. He asked, in great surprise:

"What is the matter with you?"

He was happy, quite happy, never having dreamed of another life or other pleasures. He had been born and had grown up in this melancholy district. He felt well in his own house, at his ease in body and mind.

He did not realize that we may desire events, have a thirst for changing pleasures; he did not understand that it does not seem natural to certain beings to remain in the same places during the four seasons; he seemed not to know that spring, summer, autumn, and winter, have, for multitudes of persons, new pleasures in new countries.

She could not say anything in reply, and she quickly dried her eyes. At last she murmured, in a distracted sort of way:

"I am—I—I am a little sad—I am a little bored."

But she was seized with terror for having even said so much, and she added very quickly:

"And besides—I am—I am a little cold."

At this statement he got angry:

"Ah! yes, still your idea of the hot-air plant. But look here, deuce take it! you have only had one cold since you came here."

* * * * * * *

The night came. She went up to her room, for she had insisted on having a separate apartment. She went to bed. Even in the bed, she felt cold. She thought: "Is it to be like this always, always till death?"

And she thought of her husband. How could he have said this:

"You have only had one cold since you came here?"

Then she must get ill; she must cough in order that he might understand what she suffered!

And she was filled with indignation, the angry indignation of a weak, a timid being.

She must cough. Then, without doubt, he would take pity on her. Well, she would cough; he would hear her coughing; the doctor should be called in; he would see that her husband would see.

She got up with her legs and her feet naked, and a childish idea made her smile:

"I want a hot-air plant, and I must have it. I shall cough so much that he'll have to put one into the house."

And she sat down almost naked in a chair. She waited an hour, two hours. She shivered, but she did not catch cold. Then she resolved to make use of a bold expedient.

She noiselessly left her room, descended the stairs, and opened the garden-gate.

The earth, covered with snow, seemed dead. She abruptly thrust forward her naked foot, and plunged it into the light and icy froth. A sensation of cold, painful as a wound, mounted up to her heart. However, she stretched out the other leg and began to descend the steps slowly.

Then she advanced through the grass, saying to herself:

"I'll go as far as the fir-trees."

She walked with quick steps, out of breath, choking every time she drove her foot through the snow.

She touched the first fir-tree with her hand, as if to convince herself that she carried out her plan to the end; then she went back into the house. She believed two or three times that she was going to fall, so torpid and weak did she feel. Before going

5   G. de M.—17

in, meanwhile, she sat in that icy snow, and she even gathered some in order to rub to her breast.

Then she went in, and got into bed. It seemed to her, at the end of an hour, that she had a swarm of ants in her throat, and that other ants were running all over her limbs. She slept, however.

Next day, she was coughing, and she could not get up.

She got inflammation of the lungs. She became delirious, and in her delirium she asked for a hot-air plant. The doctor insisted on having one put in. Henry yielded, but with an irritated repugnance.

    *   *   *   *   *   *

She could not be cured. The lungs, severely attacked, made those who attended on her uneasy about her life.

"If she remains here, she will not last as long as the next cold weather," said the doctor.

She was sent to the south. She came to Cannes, recognized the sun, loved the sea, and breathed the air of orange-blossoms. Then in the spring, she returned north. But she lived with the fear of being cured, with the fear of the long winters of Normandy; and as soon as she was better, she opened her window by night while thinking of the sweet banks of the Mediterranean. And now she was going to die. She knew it and yet she was contented.

She unfolds a newspaper which she had not already opened, and reads this heading:

"THE FIRST SNOW IN PARIS."

After this, she shivers and yet smiles. She looks across at the Esterel which is turning rose-colored

under the setting sun. She looks at the vast blue
sky, so blue, so very blue, and the vast blue sea, so
very blue also, and rises up and returns to the house,
with slow steps, only stopping to cough, for she had
remained out too long; and she has caught cold, a
slight cold.

She finds a letter from her husband. She opens it
still smiling, and she reads:

"MY DEAR LOVE: I hope you are going on well, and that you
do not regret too much our beautiful district. We have had for some
days past a good frost which announces snow. For my part, I adore
this weather, and you understand that I am keeping that cursed hot-
air plant of yours going.—"

She ceases reading, quite happy at the thought
that she has had her hot-air plant. Her right hand,
which holds the letter, falls down slowly over her
knees, while she raises her left hand to her mouth,
as if to calm the obstinate cough which is tearing
her chest.

BOITELLE

Père Boitelle (Antoine) had the reputation through the whole country of a specialist in dirty jobs. Every time a pit, a dunghill, or a cesspool required to be cleared away, or a dirt-hole to be cleansed out, he was the person employed to do it.

He would come there with his nightman's tools and his wooden shoes covered with dirt, and would set to work, whining incessantly about the nature of his occupation. When people asked him why he did this loathsome work, he would reply resignedly:

"Faith, 'tis for my children whom I must support. This brings in more than anything else."

He had, indeed, fourteen children. If anyone asked him what had become of them, he would say with an air of indifference:

"There are only eight of them left in the house. One is out at service, and five are married."

When the questioner wanted to know whether they were well married, he replied vivaciously:

"I did not cross them. I crossed them in nothing. They married just as they pleased. We shouldn't
go against people's likings — it turns out badly. I am
a night-cartman because my parents went against my
likings. But for that I would have become a workman like the others."

Here is the way his parents had thwarted him in
his likings:

He was at that time a soldier stationed at Havre,
not more stupid than another, or sharper either, a
rather simple fellow, in truth. During his hours of
freedom his greatest pleasure was to walk along the
quay, where the bird-dealers congregate. Sometimes
alone, sometimes with a soldier from his own part of
the country, he would slowly saunter along by cages
where parrots with green backs and yellow heads
from the banks of the Amazon, parrots with gray
backs and red heads from Senegal, enormous macaws,
which looked like birds brought up in conservatories,
with their flower-like feathers, plumes, and tufts, par-
oquets of every shape, painted with minute care by
that excellent miniaturist, God Almighty, with the
little young birds, hopping about, yellow, blue, and
variegated, mingling their cries with the noise of the
quay, added to the din caused by the unloading of
the vessels, as well as by passengers and vehicles —
a violent clamor, loud, shrill, and deafening, as if
from some distant, monstrous forest.

Boitelle would stop, with strained eyes, wide-open
mouth, laughing and enraptured, showing his teeth to
the captive cockatoos, who kept nodding their white
or yellow topknots toward the glaring red of his
breeches and the copper buckle of his belt. When

he found a bird that could talk, he put questions to it, and if it happened at the time to be disposed to reply and to hold a conversation with him, he would remain there till nightfall filled with gaiety and contentment. He also found heaps of fun in looking at the monkeys, and could conceive no greater luxury for a rich man than to possess these animals, just like cats and dogs. This taste for the exotic he had in his blood, as people have a taste for the chase, or for medicine, or for the priesthood. He could not refrain, every time the gates of the barracks opened, from going back to the quay, as if drawn toward it by an irresistible longing.

Now, on one occasion, having stopped almost in ecstasy before an enormous ararauna, which was swelling out its plumes, bending forward, and bridling up again, as if making the court-courtesies of parrot-land, he saw the door of a little tavern adjoining the bird-dealer's shop opening, and his attention was attracted by a young negress, with a silk kerchief tied round her head, sweeping into the street the rubbish and the sand of the establishment.

Boitelle's attention was soon divided between the bird and the woman, and he really could not tell which of these two beings he contemplated with the greater astonishment and delight.

The negress, having got rid of the sweepings of the tavern, raised her eyes, and, in her turn, was dazzled by the soldier's uniform. There she stood facing him with her broom in her hands as if she were presenting arms for him, while the ararauna continued making courtesies. Now at the end of a few seconds the soldier began to get embarrassed by this attention, and he walked away gingerly so as not to present the appearance of beating a retreat.

But he came back. Almost every day he passed in front of the Colonial tavern, and often he could distinguish through the windowpanes the figure of the little black-skinned maid filling out "bocks" or glasses of brandy for the sailors of the port. Frequently, too, she would come out to the door on seeing him. Soon, without even having exchanged a word, they smiled at one another like old acquaintances; and Boitelle felt his heart moved when he saw suddenly glittering between the dark lips of the girl her shining row of white teeth. At length, he ventured one day to enter, and was quite surprised to find that she could speak French like everyone else. The bottle of lemonade, of which she was good enough to accept a glassful, remained in the soldier's recollection memorably delicious; and it became habitual with him to come and absorb in this little tavern on the quay all the agreeable drinks which he could afford.

For him it was a treat, a happiness, on which his thoughts were constantly dwelling, to watch the black hand of the little maid pouring out something into his glass while her teeth, brighter than her eyes, showed themselves as she laughed. When they had kept company in this way for two months, they became fast friends, and Boitelle, after his first astonishment at discovering that this negress was in principle as good as the best girls in the country, that she exhibited a regard for economy, industry, religion, and good conduct, loved her more on that account, and became so much smitten with her that he wanted to marry her.

He told her about his intentions, which made her dance with joy. Besides, she had a little money, left her by a female oyster dealer, who had picked her up when she had been left on the quay at Havre by an American captain. This captain had found her, when she was only about six years old, lying on bales of cotton in the hold of his ship, some hours after his departure from New York. On his arrival in Havre, he there abandoned to the care of this compassionate oyster-dealer the little black creature, who had been hidden on board his vessel, he could not tell how or why.

The oyster-woman having died, the young negress became a servant at the Colonial tavern.

Antoine Boitelle added: "This will be all right if my parents don't go against it. I will never go against them, you understand — never! I'm going to say a word or two to them the first time I go back to the country."

On the following week, in fact, having obtained twenty-four hours' leave, he went to see his family, who cultivated a little farm at Tourteville near Yvetot.

He waited till the meal was finished, the hour when the coffee baptized with brandy makes people more open-hearted, before informing his parents that he had found a girl answering so well to his likings in every way that there could not exist any other in all the world so perfectly suited to him.

The old people, at this observation, immediately assumed a circumspect air, and wanted explanations.

At first he concealed nothing from them except the color of her skin.

She was a servant, without much means, but strong, thrifty, clean, well-conducted, and sensible. All these things were better than money would be in the hands of a bad housewife. Moreover, she had a few sous, left her by a woman who had reared her,— a good number of sous, almost a little dowry,— fifteen hundred francs in the savings' bank. The old people, overcome by his talk, and relying, too, on their own judgment, were gradually giving way, when he came to the delicate point. Laughing in rather a constrained fashion, he said:

"There's only one thing you may not like. She is not white."

They did not understand, and he had to explain at some length and very cautiously, to avoid shocking them, that she belonged to the dusky race of which they had only seen samples among figures exhibited at Epinal. Then, they became restless, perplexed, alarmed, as if he had proposed a union with the Devil.

The mother said: "Black? How much of her is black? Is it the whole of her?"

He replied: "Certainly. Everywhere, just as you are white everywhere."

The father interposed: "Black? Is it as black as the pot?"

The son answered: "Perhaps a little less than that. She is black, but not disgustingly black. The curé's cassock is black; but it is not uglier than a surplice, which is white."

The father said: "Are there more black people besides her in her country?"

And the son, with an air of conviction, exclaimed: "Certainly!"

But the old man shook his head: "This must be disagreeable!"

Said the son: "It isn't more disagreeable than anything else, seeing that you get used to it in no time."

The mother asked: "It doesn't soil linen more than other skins, this black skin?"

"Not more than your own, as it is her proper color."

Then, after many other questions, it was agreed that the parents should see this girl before coming to any decision and that the young fellow, whose period of service was coming to an end in the course of a month, should bring her to the house in order that they might examine her, and decide by talking the matter over whether or not she was too dark to enter the Boitelle family.

Antoine accordingly announced that on Sunday, the twenty-second of May, the day of his discharge, he would start for Tourteville with his sweetheart.

She had put on, for this journey to the house of her lover's parents, her most beautiful and most gaudy clothes, in which yellow, red, and blue were the prevailing colors, so that she had the appearance of one adorned for a national *fête*.

At the terminus, as they were leaving Havre, people stared at her very much, and Boitelle was proud of giving his arm to a person who commanded so much attention. Then, in the third-class carriage, in which she took a seat by his side, she excited so much astonishment among the peasants that the peo-

ple in the adjoining compartments got up on their
benches to get a look at her over the wooden partition which divided the different portions of the carriage from one another. A child, at sight of her,
began to cry with terror, another concealed his face
in his mother's apron. Everything went off well,
however, up to their arrival at their destination. But,
when the train slackened its rate of motion as they
drew near Yvetot, Antoine felt ill at ease, as he
would have done at an inspection when he did not
know his drill-practice. Then, as he put his head
out through the carriage door, he recognized, some
distance away, his father, who was holding the bridle of the horse yoked to a carriage, and his mother
who had made her way to the railed portion of the
platform where a number of spectators had gathered.

He stepped out first, gave his hand to his sweetheart, and holding himself erect, as if he were escort-
ing a general, he advanced toward his family.

The mother, on seeing this black lady, in variegated costume in her son's company, remained so
stupefied that she could not open her mouth; and the
father found it hard to hold the horse, which the engine or the negress caused to rear for some time
without stopping. But Antoine, suddenly seized with
the unmingled joy of seeing once more the old people, rushed forward with open arms, embraced his
mother, embraced his father, in spite of the nag's
fright, and then turning toward his companion, at
whom the passengers on the platform stopped to
stare with amazement, he proceeded to explain:

"Here she is! I told you that, at first sight, she

seems odd; but as soon as you know her, in very truth, there's not a better sort in the whole world. Say good morrow to her without making any bother about it."

Thereupon, Mère Boitelle, herself nearly frightened out of her wits, made a sort of courtesy, while the father took off his cap, murmuring: "I wish you good luck!"

Then, without further delay, they climbed up on the car, the two women at the lower end on seats, which made them jump up and down as the vehicle went jolting along the road, and the two men outside on the front seat.

Nobody spoke. Antoine, ill at ease, whistled a barrack-room air; his father lashed the nag; and his mother, from where she sat in the corner, kept casting sly glances at the negress, whose forehead and cheek-bones shone in the sunlight like well-blacked shoes.

Wishing to break the ice, Antoine turned round.

"Well," said he, "we don't seem inclined to talk."

"We must get time," replied the old woman.

He went on:

"Come! tell us the little story about that hen of yours that laid eight eggs."

It was a funny anecdote of long standing in the family. But, as his mother still remained silent, paralyzed by emotion, he started the talking himself and narrated, with much laughter on his own part, this memorable adventure. The father, who knew it by heart, brightened up at the opening words of the narrative; his wife soon followed his example; and the

negress herself, when he had reached the drollest part
of it, suddenly gave vent to a laugh so noisy, rolling,
and torrentlike that the horse, becoming excited,
broke into a gallop for a little while.

This served as the introduction to their acquaintanceship. The company at length began to chat.

On reaching the house they all alighted, and he
conducted his sweetheart to a room so that she
might take off her dress, to avoid staining it while
preparing a good dish intended to win the old people's affections by appealing to their stomachs. Then
he drew his parents aside near the door, and with
beating heart, asked:

"Well, what do you say now?"

The father said nothing. The mother, less timid,
exclaimed:

"She is too black. No, indeed, this is too much
for me. It turns my blood."

"That may be, but it is only for the moment."

They then made their way into the interior of the
house where the good woman was somewhat affected
at the spectacle of the negress engaged in cooking.
She at once proceeded to assist her, with petticoats
tucked up, active in spite of her age.

The meal was an excellent one — very long, very
enjoyable. When they had afterward taken a turn together, Antoine said to his father:

"Well, dad, what do you say to this?"

The peasant took care never to compromise himself.

"I have no opinion about it. Ask your mother."

So Antoine went back to his mother, and, leading
her to the end of the room, said:

"Well, mother, what do you think of her?"

"My poor lad, she is really too black. If she were only a little less black, I would not go against you, but this is too much. One would think it was Satan!"

He did not press her, knowing how obstinate the old woman had always been, but he felt a tempest of disappointment sweeping over his heart. He was turning over in his mind what he ought to do, what plan he could devise, surprised, moreover, that she had not conquered them already as she had captivated himself. And they all four set out with slow steps through the cornfields, having again relapsed into silence. Whenever they passed a fence, they saw a countryman sitting on the stile and a group of brats climbing up to stare at them. People rushed out into the road to see the "black" whom young Boitelle had brought home with him. At a distance they noticed people scampering across the fields as they do when the drum beats to draw public attention to some living phenomenon. Père and Mère Boitelle, scared by this curiosity, which was exhibited everywhere through the country at their approach, quickened their pace, walking side by side, leaving far behind their son, whom his dark companion asked what his parents thought of her.

He hesitatingly replied that they had not yet made up their minds.

But on the village-green, people rushed out of all the houses in a flutter of excitement; and, at the sight of the gathering rabble, old Boitelle took to his heels, and regained his abode, while Antoine, swelling with rage, his sweetheart on his arm, advanced majestically under the battery of staring eyes, opened wide in amazement.

He understood that it was at an end, that there was no hope for him, that he could not marry his negress. She also understood it; and as they drew near the farmhouse they both began to weep. As soon as they had got back to the house, she once more took off her dress to aid the mother in her household duties, and followed her everywhere, to the dairy, to the stable, to the henhouse, taking on herself the hardest part of the work, repeating always, "Let me do it, Madame Boitelle," so that, when night came on, the old woman, touched but inexorable, said to her son: "She is a good girl, all the same. 'Tis a pity she is so black; but indeed she is too much so. I couldn't get used to it. She must go back again. She is too black!"

And young Boitelle said to his sweetheart:

"She will not consent. She thinks you are too black. You must go back again. I will go with you to the train. No matter—don't fret. I am going to talk to them after you have started."

He then conducted her to the railway-station, still cheering her up with hope, and, when he had kissed her, he put her into the train, which he watched as it passed out of sight, his eyes swollen with tears. In vain did he appeal to the old people. They would not give their consent.

And when he had told this story, which was known all over the country, Antoine Boitelle would always add:

"From that time forward I have had no heart for anything—for anything at all. No trade suited me any longer, and so I became what I am—a night-cartman."

People would say to him: "Yet you got married."

"Yes, and I can't say that my wife didn't please me, seeing that I've got fourteen children; but she is not the other one, oh! no—certainly not! The other one, mark you, my negress, she had only to give me one glance and I felt as if I were in Heaven!"

THE ACCURSED BREAD

DADDY TAILLE had three daughters: Anna, the eldest, who was scarcely ever mentioned in the family; Rose, the second girl, who was eighteen; and Clara, the youngest, who was a girl of fifteen.

Old Taille was a widower, and a foreman in M. Lebrument's button-manufactory. He was a very upright man, very well thought of, abstemious; in fact a sort of model workman. He lived at Havre, in the Rue d'Angoulême.

When Anna ran away the old man flew into a fearful rage. He threatened to kill the seducer, who was head clerk in a large draper's establishment in that town. Then when he was told by various people that she was keeping very steady and investing money in government securities, that she was no gadabout, but was maintained by a Monsieur Dubois, who was a judge of the Tribunal of Commerce, the father was appeased.

He even showed some anxiety as to how she was faring, asked some of her old friends who had

been to see her how she was getting on; and
when told that she had her own furniture, and that
her mantelpiece was covered with vases and the
walls with pictures, that there were clocks and car-
pets everywhere, he gave a broad, contented smile.
He had been working for thirty years to get together
a wretched five or six thousand francs. This girl
was evidently no fool.

One fine morning the son of Touchard, the cooper
at the other end of the street, came and asked him
for the hand of Rose, the second girl. The old man's
heart began to beat, for the Touchards were rich and
in a good position. He was decidedly lucky with
his girls.

The marriage was agreed upon. It was settled
that it should be a grand affair, and the wedding
dinner was to be held at Sainte-Adresse, at Mother
Lusa's restaurant. It would cost a lot certainly; but
never mind, it did not matter just for once in a way.

But one morning, just as the old man was going
home to breakfast with his two daughters, the door
opened suddenly and Anna appeared. She was ele-
gantly dressed, wore rings and an expensive bonnet,
and looked undeniably pretty and nice. She threw
her arms round her father's neck before he could say
a word, then fell into her sisters' arms with many
tears, and then asked for a plate, so that she might
share the family soup. Taille was moved to tears in
his turn and said several times:

"That is right, dear; that is right."

Then she told them about herself. She did not
wish Rose's wedding to take place at Sainte-Adresse,
—certainly not. It should take place at her house,

and would cost her father nothing. She had settled
everything and arranged everything, so it was "no
good to say any more about it,—there!"

"Very well, my dear! very well!" the old man
said, "we will leave it so." But then he felt some
doubt. Would the Touchards consent? But Rose,
the bride-elect, was surprised, and asked, "Why
should they object, I should like to know? Just leave
that to me, I will talk to Philip about it."

She mentioned it to her lover the very same day,
and he declared that it would suit him exactly.
Father and Mother Touchard were naturally delighted
at the idea of a good dinner which would cost them
nothing and said:

"You may be quite sure that everything will be
in first-rate style, as M. Dubois is made of money."

They asked to be allowed to bring a friend, Mme.
Florence, the cook on the first floor, and Anna agreed
to everything. The wedding was fixed for the last
Tuesday of the month.

II.

After the civil formalities and the religious cere-
mony the wedding party went to Anna's house.
Among those whom the Tailles had brought was a
cousin of a certain age, a M. Sauvetanin, a man given
to philosophical reflections, serious, and always very
self-possessed, and Mme. Lamonoois, an old aunt.

M. Sauvetanin had been told off to give Anna his
arm, as they were looked upon as the two most important persons in the company.

As soon as they had arrived at the door of An-na's house she let go her companion's arm, and ran on ahead, saying, "I will show you the way," while the invited guests followed more slowly. When they got upstairs, she stood on one side to let them pass, and they rolled their eyes and turned their heads in all directions to admire this mysterious and luxu-rious dwelling.

The table was laid in the drawing-room as the dining-room had been thought too small. Extra knives, forks, and spoons had been hired from a neighboring restaurant, and decanters full of wine glittered under the rays of the sun, which shone in through the window.

The ladies went into the bedroom to take off their shawls and bonnets, and Father Touchard, who was standing at the door, squinted at the low, wide bed, and made funny signs to the men, with many a wink and nod. Daddy Taille, who thought a great deal of himself, looked with fatherly pride at his child's well-furnished rooms, and went from one to the other holding his hat in his hand, making a men-tal inventory of everything, and walking like a verger in a church.

Anna went backward and forward, and ran about giving orders and hurrying on the wedding feast. Soon she appeared at the door of the dining-room, and cried: "Come here, all of you, for a moment," and when the twelve guests did as they were asked they saw twelve glasses of Madeira on a small table.

Rose and her husband had their arms round each other's waists, and were kissing each other in every corner. M. Sauvetanin never took his eyes off Anna;

he no doubt felt that ardor, that sort of expectation which all men, even if they are old and ugly, feel for women of a certain stamp.

They sat down, and the wedding breakfast began; the relatives sitting at one end of the table and the young people at the other. Mme. Touchard, the mother, presided on the right and the bride on the left. Anna looked after everybody, saw that the glasses were kept filled and the plates well supplied. The guests evidently felt a certain respectful embarrassment at the sight of the sumptuousness of the rooms and at the lavish manner in which they were treated. They all ate heartily of the good things provided, but there were no jokes such as are prevalent at weddings of that sort; it was all too grand, and it made them feel uncomfortable. Old Madame Touchard, who was fond of a bit of fun, tried to enliven matters a little, and at the beginning of the dessert she exclaimed: "I say, Philip, do sing us something." The neighbors in their street considered that he had the finest voice in all Havre.

The bridegroom got up, smiled, and turning to his sister-in-law, from politeness and gallantry, tried to think of something suitable for the occasion, something serious and correct, to harmonize with the seriousness of the repast.

Anna had a satisfied look on her face, and leaned back in her chair to listen, and all assumed looks of attention, though prepared to smile should smiles be called for.

The singer announced, "The Accursed Bread," and extending his right arm, which made his coat ruck up into his neck, he began.

It was decidedly long, three verses of eight lines each, with the last line and the last line but one repeated twice.

All went well for the first two verses; they were the usual commonplaces about bread gained by honest labor and by dishonesty. The aunt and the bride wept outright. The cook, who was present, at the end of the first verse looked at a roll which she held in her hand with moist eyes, as if they applied to her, while all applauded vigorously. At the end of the second verse the two servants, who were standing with their backs to the wall, joined loudly in the chorus, and the aunt and the bride wept outright. Daddy Taille blew his nose with the noise of a trombone, old Touchard brandished a whole loaf half over the table, and the cook shed silent tears on to the crust which she was still holding.

Amid the general emotion M. Sauvetanin said:

"That is the right sort of song; very different to the pointed things one generally hears at weddings."

Anna, who was visibly affected, kissed her hand to her sister and pointed to her husband with an affectionate nod, as if to congratulate her.

Intoxicated by his success, the young man continued, and unfortunately the last verse contained words about the bread of dishonor gained by young girls who had been led astray from the paths of virtue. No one took up the refrain about this bread, supposed to be eaten with tears, except old Touchard and the two servants. Anna had grown deadly pale and cast down her eyes, while the bridegroom looked from one to the other without understanding the reason for this sudden coldness, and the cook hastily dropped the crust as if it were poisoned.

M. Sauvetanin said solemnly, in order to save the situation: "That last couplet is not at all necessary"; and Daddy Taille, who had got red up to his ears, looked round the table fiercely.

Then Anna, with her eyes swimming in tears, told the servants, in the faltering voice of a woman trying to stifle her sobs, to bring the champagne.

All the guests were suddenly seized with exuberant joy, and their faces became radiant again. And when old Touchard, who had seen, felt, and understood nothing of what was going on, and, pointing to the guests so as to emphasize his words, sang the last words of the refrain: "Children, I warn you all to eat not of that bread," the whole company, when they saw the champagne bottles with their necks covered with gold foil appear, burst out singing, as if electrified by the sight:

"Children, I warn you all to eat not of that bread."

MY TWENTY-FIVE DAYS

I HAD just taken possession of my room in the hotel, a narrow apartment between two papered partitions, so that I could hear all the sounds made by my neighbors. I was beginning to arrange in the glass cupboard my clothes and my linen, when I opened the drawer which was in the middle of this piece of furniture, I immediately noticed a manuscript of rolled paper. Having unrolled it, I spread it open before me, and read this title:

"MY TWENTY-FIVE DAYS."

It was the diary of a bather, of the last occupant of my room, and had been left behind there in forgetfulness at the hour of departure.

These notes may be of some interest to sensible and healthy persons who never leave their own homes. It is for their benefit that I here transcribe them without altering a letter.

"CHÂTEL-GUYON, July 15.

"At the first glance, it is not gay, this country. So, I am going to spend twenty-five days here to have my liver and my stomach treated, and to get rid of flesh. The twenty-five days of a bather are very like the twenty-eight days of a *reserviste*; they are all devoted to fatigue-duty, severe fatigue-duty. To-day, nothing as yet; I am installed; I have made the acquaintance of locality and the doctors. Châtel-Guyon is composed of a stream in which flows yellow water, in the midst of several mountain-peaks, where are erected a Casino, houses, and stone-crosses. At the side of the stream, in the depths of the valley, may be seen a square building surrounded by a little garden: this is the establishment of the baths. Sad people wander around this building — the invalids. A great silence reigns in these walks shaded by trees, for this is not a pleasure-station but a true health-station: you take care of your health here through conviction, but you cannot get cured, it seems.

"Competent people declare that the mineral springs perform true miracles here. However, no votive offering is hung around the cashier's office.

"From time to time, a gentleman or a lady comes over to a kiosk with a slate roof, which shelters a woman of smiling and gentle aspect and a spring boiling in a basin of cement. Not a word is exchanged between the invalid and the female custodian of the healing water. She hands to the newcomer a little glass in which air-bubbles quiver in the transparent liquid. The other drinks and goes off with a grave step in order to resume his interrupted walk under the trees.

"No noise in the little park, no breath of air in the leaves, no voice breaks through this silence. Inscribed over the entrance to this district should be: 'Here you no longer laugh; you nurse yourself.'

"The people who chat resemble mutes who open their mouths in order to simulate sounds, so much are they afraid of letting their voices escape.

"In the hotel, the same silence. It is a big hotel where you dine solemnly with people of good position, who have nothing to say to each other. Their manners bespeak good-breeding and their faces reflect the conviction of a superiority of which it would be difficult to give actual proof.

"At two o'clock, I make my way up to the Casino, a little wooden hut perched on a hillock to which one climbs by paths frequented by goats. But the view from that height is admirable. Châtel-Guyon is situated in a very narrow valley, exactly between the plain and the mountain. At the left I see the first great waves of the mountains of Auvergne covered with woods, exhibiting here and there big gray spots, their hard lava-bones, for we are at the foot of the extinct volcanoes. At the right, through the narrow slope of the valley, I discover a plain infinite as the sea, steeped in a bluish fog which lets one only dimly discern the villages, the towns, the yellow fields of ripe corn, and the green squares of meadow-land shaded with apple-trees. It is the Limagne, immense and flat, always enveloped in a light veil of vapor.

"The night has come. And now, after having dined alone, I write these lines beside my open window. I hear, over there, in front of me, the little orchestra of the Casino, which plays airs just as a wild bird sings all alone in the desert.

"From time to time a dog barks. This great calm does me good. Good night.

"*July 16.* Nothing. I have taken a bath, or rather a douche. I have swallowed three glasses of water and I have walked in the pathways of the park for a quarter of an hour between each glass, then half-an-hour after the last. I have begun my twenty-five days.

"*July 17.* Remarked two mysterious pretty women who are taking their baths and their meals after everyone else.

"*July 18.* Nothing.

"*July 19.* Saw the two pretty women again. They have style and a little indescribable air which I like very much.

"*July 20.* Long walk in a charming wooded valley as far as the Hermitage of Sans-Souci. This country is delightful though sad; it is so calm, so sweet, so green. Along the mountain-roads you meet the long wagons loaded with hay drawn by two cows at a slow pace or held back in descending the slopes by their straining heads, which are tied together. A man with a big black hat on his head is driving them with a slight switch, tipping them on the side or on the forehead; and often with an simple gesture, a gesture energetic and grave, he suddenly draws them up when the excessive load hastens their journey down the rougher descents.

"The air is good in these valleys. And, if it is very warm, the dust bears with it a light odor of vanilla and of the stable, for so many cows pass over these routes that they leave a little scent everywhere. And the odor is a perfume, whereas it would be a stench if it came from other animals.

"*July 21.* Excursion to the valley of the Enval. It

is a narrow gorge inclosed in superb rocks at the very foot of the mountain. A stream flows through the space between the heaped-up bowlders.

"As I reached the bottom of this ravine, I heard women's voices, and I soon perceived the two mysterious ladies of my hotel, who were chatting seated on a stone.

"The occasion appeared to me a good one, and without hesitation I presented myself. My overtures were received without embarrassment. We walked back together to the hotel. And we talked about Paris. They knew, it seemed, many people whom I knew too. Who can they be?

"I shall see them to-morrow. There is nothing more amusing than such meetings as this.

"*July 22.* Day almost entirely passed with the two unknown ladies. They are very pretty, by Jove, one a brunette and the other a blonde. They say they are widows. Hum!

"I offered to accompany them in a visit to Royat to-morrow, and they accepted my offer.

"Châtel-Guyon is less sad than I thought on my arrival.

"*July 23.* Day spent at Royat. Royat is a little cluster of hotels at the bottom of a valley, at the gate of Clermont-Ferrand. A great deal of society there. A great park full of movement. Superb view of the Puy-de-Dôme, seen at the end of a perspective of vales.

"I am greatly occupied with my fair companions, which is flattering to myself. The man who escorts a pretty woman always believes himself crowned with an aureole,—with much more reason, therefore, the man who goes along with one on each side of him. Nothing is so pleasant as to dine in a restaurant well frequented, with a female companion at whom everybody stares, and besides there is nothing better calculated to set a man up in the estimation of his neighbors.

"To go to the Bois in a trap drawn by a sorry nag, or to go out into the boulevard escorted by a plain woman, are the two most humiliating accidents which could strike a delicate heart preoccupied with the opinions of others. Of all luxuries woman is the rarest and the most distinguished; she is the one that costs most, and which we desire most; she is, therefore, the one that we like best to exhibit under the jealous eyes of the public.

"To show the world a pretty woman leaning on your arm is to excite, all at once, every kind of jealousy. It is as much as to say: Look here! I am rich, since I possess this rare and costly object; I have taste, since I have known how to discover this pearl; perhaps even I am loved, unless I am deceived by her, which would still prove that others, too, consider her charming.

"But what a disgraceful thing it is to bring an ugly woman with you through the city! And how many humiliating things this gives people to understand!

"In the first place, they assume she must be your wife, for how could it be supposed that you would have an unattractive mistress? A real wife might be ungraceful; but then her ugliness suggests a thousand things disagreeable to you. One supposes you must be a notary or a magistrate, as these two professions have a monopoly of grotesque and well-dowered spouses. Now, is this not painful for a man? And then it seems to proclaim to the public that you have the odious courage, and are even under a legal obligation, to caress that ridiculous face and that ill-shaped body, and that you will, without doubt, be shameless enough to make a mother of this by no means desirable being,—which is the very height of ridicule.

"*July 24.* I never leave the side of the two unknown widows, whom I am beginning to know well. This country is delightful and our hotel is excellent. Good season. The treatment has done me an immense amount of good.

"*July 25.* Drive in a landau to the lake of Tazenat. An exquisite and unexpected party, decided on at lunch. Abrupt departure after getting up from the table. After a long journey through the mountains, we suddenly perceived an admirable little lake, quite round, quite blue, clear as glass, and situated at the bottom of a dead crater. One edge of this immense basin is barren, the other is wooded. In the midst of the trees is a small house, where sleeps a good-natured, intellectual man, a sage who passes his days in this Virgilian region. He opens his dwelling for us. An idea comes into my head. I exclaim: 'Suppose we bathe?'

"'Yes,' they said, 'but—costumes?'

"'Bah! we are in the desert.'

"And we did bathe!

"If I were a poet, how I would describe this unforgettable vision of bodies young and naked in the transparency of the water! The sloping high sides shut in the lake, motionless, glittering, and round, like a piece of silver; the sun pours into it its warm light in a flood; and along the rocks the fair flesh slips into the almost invisible wave in which the swimmers seemed suspended. On the sand at the bottom of the lake we saw the shadows of the light movements passing and repassing!

"*July 26.* Some persons seemed to look with shocked and disapproving eyes at my rapid intimacy with the two fair widows! Persons so constituted imagine that life is made for worrying oneself. Everything that appears to be amusing becomes immediately a breach of good-breeding or morality. For them duty has inflexible and mortally sad rules.

"I would draw their attention with all respect to the fact that duty is not the same for Mormons, Arabs, Zulus, Turks, Englishmen, and Frenchmen; and that one will find very virtuous people among all these nations. As for me, I take a little of each people's notion of duty, and of the whole I make a result comparable to the morality of holy King Solomon.

"*July 27.* Good news. I have grown 620 grams thinner. Excellent, this water of Châtel-Guyon! I am bringing the widows to dine at Riom. Sad town! Its anagram constitutes an offense in the vicinity of healing springs: Riom, Mori.

"*July 28.* Hoity-toity! My two widows have been visited by two gentlemen who came to look for them. Two widows, without doubt. They are leaving this evening. They have written to me on fancy note-paper.

"*July 29.* Alone! Long excursion on foot to the extinct crater of Nackère. Splendid view.

"*July 30.* Nothing. I am taking the treatm⟩nt.

"*July 31.* Ditto. Ditto. This pretty country is full of polluted streams. I am drawing the notice of the municipality to the abominable sink which poisons the road in front of the hotel. All the remains of the kitchen of the establishment are thrown into it. This is a good way to breed cholera.

"*August 1.* Nothing. The treatment.

"*August 2.* Admirable walk to Châteauneuf, a station for rheumatic patients where everybody is lame. Nothing can be queerer than this population of cripples!

"*August 3.* Nothing. The treatment.

"*August 4.* Ditto. Ditto.

"*August 5.* Ditto. Ditto.

"*August 6.* Despair! I have just weighed myself. I have got fatter by 310 grams. But what then?

"*August 7.* 66 kilometers in a carriage in the mountain. I will not mention the name of the country through respect for its women.

"This excursion had been pointed out to me as a beautiful one, and one that was rarely made. After four hours on the road I arrived at a rather pretty village, on the border of a river in the midst of an admirable wood of walnut-trees. I had not yet seen a forest of walnut-trees of such dimensions in Auvergne. It constitutes, moreover, all the wealth of the district, for it is planted on the common. This common was formerly only a hillside covered with brushwood. The authorities had tried in vain to get it cultivated. It was scarcely enough to feed a few sheep.

"To-day it is a superb wood, thanks to the women, and it has a curious name: it is called — 'the Sins of the Curé.'

"Now it is right to say that the women of the mountain district have the reputation of being light, lighter than in the plain. A bachelor who meets them owes them at least a kiss; and if he does not take more, he is only a blockhead. If we think rightly on it, this way of looking at the matter is the only one that is logical and reasonable. As woman, whether she be of the town or the country, has for her natural mission to please man, man should always prove that she pleases him. If he abstains from every sort of demonstration, this means that he has found her ugly; it is almost an insult to her. If I were a woman, I would not receive a second time a man who failed to show me respect at our first meeting, for I would consider that he had failed to appreciate my beauty, my charm, and my feminine qualities.

"So the bachelors of the village X —— often proved to the women of the district that they found them to their taste, and, as the curé was unable to prevent these demonstrations as gallant as they were natural, he resolved to utilize them for the profit of the natural prosperity. So he imposed as a penance on every woman who had gone wrong a walnut to be planted on the common. And every night lanterns were seen moving about like will-o'-the-wisps on the hillock, for the erring ones scarcely liked to perform their penances in broad daylight.

"In two years there was no room any longer on the lands belonging to the village; and to-day they calculate that there are more than three thousand trees around the belfry which rings for the offices through their foliage. These are 'the Sins of the Curé.'

''Since we have been seeking for so many plans for rewooding in France, the Administration of Forests might surely enter into some arrangement with the clergy to employ a method so simple as that employed by this humble curé.

"*August 8*. Treatment.

"*August 9*. I am packing up my trunks, and saying good-bye to the charming little district so calm and silent, to the green mountain, to the quiet valleys, to the deserted Casino from which you can see, almost veiled by its light, bluish mist, the immense plain of the Limagne.

"I shall leave to-morrow."

*   *   *   *   *   *   *

Here the manuscript stopped. I wish to add nothing to it, my impressions of the country not having been exactly the same as those of my predecessor. For I did not find the two widows!

A LUCKY BURGLAR

THEY were seated in the dining-room of a hotel in Barbizon.

"I tell you, you will not believe it."

"Well, tell it anyhow."

"All right, here goes. But first I must tell you that my story is absolutely true in every respect; even if it does sound improbable." And the old artist commenced:

"We had dined at Soriel's that night. When I say dined, that means that we were all pretty well tipsy. We were three young madcaps. Soriel (poor fellow! he is dead now), Le Poittevin, the marine painter, and myself. Le Poittevin is dead, also.

"We had stretched ourselves on the floor of the little room adjoining the studio and the only one in the crowd who was rational was Le Poittevin. Soriel, who was always the maddest, lay flat on his back, with his feet propped up on a chair, discussing war and the uniforms of the Empire, when, suddenly, he got up, took out of the big wardrobe where he kept his accessories a complete hussar's uniform and put it on. He then took out a grenadier's uniform and told Le Poittevin to put it on; but he objected, so we forced him into it. It was so big for him that he was completely lost in it. I arrayed myself as a cuirassier. After we were ready, Soriel made us go through a complicated drill. Then he exclaimed: 'As long as we are troopers let us drink like troopers.'

"The punch-bowl had been brought out and filled for the second time. We were bawling some old camp songs at the top of our voice, when Le Poittevin, who in spite of all the punch had retained his self-control, held up his hand and said: 'Hush! I am sure I heard some one walking in the studio.'

"'A burglar!' said Soriel, staggering to his feet. 'Good luck!' And he began the 'Marseillaise':

"'To arms, citizens!'

"Then he seized several weapons from the wall and equipped us according to our uniforms. I received a musket and a saber. Le Poittevin was handed an enormous gun with a bayonet attached. Soriel, not finding just what he wanted, seized a pistol, stuck it in his belt, and brandishing a battle-axe in one hand, he opened the studio door cautiously. The army advanced. Having reached the middle of the room Soriel said:

"'I am general. You [pointing to me], the cuirassiers, will keep the enemy from retreating—that is, lock the door. You [pointing to Le Poittevin], the grenadiers, will be my escort.'

"I executed my orders and rejoined the troops, who were behind a large screen reconnoitering. Just as I reached it I heard a terrible noise. I rushed up with the candle to investigate the cause of it and this is what I saw. Le Poittevin was piercing the dummy's breast with his bayonet and Soriel was splitting his head open with his axe! When the mistake had been discovered the General commanded: 'Be cautious!'

"We had explored every nook and corner of the studio for the past twenty minutes without success, when Le Poittevin thought he would look in the cupboard. As it was quite deep and very dark, I advanced with the candle and looked in. I drew back stupefied. A man, a real live man this time, stood there looking at me! I quickly recovered myself, however, and locked the cupboard door. We then retired a few paces to hold a council.

"Opinions were divided. Soriel wanted to smoke the burglar out; Le Poittevin suggested starvation, and I proposed to blow him up with dynamite. Le Poittevin's idea being finally accepted as the best, we proceed to bring the punch and pipes into the studio, while Le Poittevin kept guard with his big gun on his shoulder, and settling ourselves in front of the cupboard we drank the prisoner's health. We had done this repeatedly, when Soriel suggested that we bring out the prisoner and take a look at him.

"'Hooray!' cried I. We picked up our weapons and made a mad rush for the cupboard door. It was finally opened, and Soriel, cocking his pistol which was not loaded, rushed in first. Le Poittevin and I followed yelling like lunatics and, after a mad scramble in the dark, we at last brought out the burglar. He was a haggard-looking, white-haired old bandit, with shabby, ragged clothes. We bound him hand and foot and dropped him in an armchair. He said nothing.

"'We will try this wretch' said Soriel, whom the punch had made very solemn. I was so far gone that it seemed to me quite a natural thing. Le Poittevin was named for the defense and I for the prosecution. The prisoner was condemned to death by all except his counsel.

"'We will now execute him,' said Soriel. 'Still, this man cannot die without repenting,' he added, feeling somewhat scrupulous. 'Let us send for a priest.'

"I objected that it was too late, so he proposed that I officiate and forthwith told the prisoner to confess his sins to me. The old man was terrified. He wondered what kind of wretches we were and for the first time he spoke. His voice was hollow and cracked:

"'Say, you don't mean it, do you?'

"Soriel forced him to his knees, and for fear he had not been baptized, poured a glass of rum over his head, saying: 'Confess your sins; your last hour has come!'

"'Help! Help!' screamed the old man rolling himself on the floor and kicking everything that came his way. For fear he should wake the neighbors we gagged him.

"'Come, let us end this'; said Soriel impatiently. He pointed his pistol at the old man and pressed the trigger. I followed his example, but as neither of our guns were loaded we made very little noise. Le Poittevin, who had been looking on said:

"'Have we really the right to kill this man?'

"'We have condemned him to death!' said Soriel.

"'Yes, but we have no right to shoot a civilian. Let us take him to the station-house.'

"We agreed with him, and as the old man could not walk we tied him to a board, and Le Poittevin and I carried him, while Soriel kept guard in the rear. We arrived at the station-house. The chief, who knew us and was well acquainted with our manner of joking, thought it was a great lark and laughingly refused to take our prisoner in. Soriel insisted, but the chief told us very sternly to quit our fooling and go home and be quiet. There was nothing else to do but to take him back to Soriel's.

"'What are we going to do with him?' I asked.

"'The poor man must be awfully tired!' said Le Poittevin, sympathizingly.

"He did look half dead, and in my turn I felt a sudden pity for him (the punch, no doubt), and I relieved him of his gag.

"'How do you feel old man?' I asked.

"'By Jingo! I have enough of this,' he groaned.

"Then Soriel softened. He unbound him and treated him as a long-lost friend. The three of us immediately brewed a fresh bowl of punch. As soon as it was ready we handed a glass to the prisoner, who quaffed it without flinching. Toast followed toast. The old man could drink more than the three of us put together; but as daylight appeared, he got up and calmly said: 'I shall be obliged to leave you; I must get home now.'

"We begged him not to go, but he positively refused to stay any longer. We were awfully sorry and took him to the door, while Soriel held the candle above his head saying: 'Look out for the last step.'"

AN ODD FEAST

I T WAS in the winter of—I do not remember what year, that I went to Normandy to visit my bachelor cousin, Jules de Banneville, who lived alone in the old manor, with a cook, a valet, and a keeper. I had the hunting fever and for a month did nothing else from morning until night.

The castle, an old, gray building surrounded with pines and avenues of tall oaktrees, looked as if it had been deserted for centuries. The antique furniture and the portraits of Jules's ancestors were the only inhabitants of the spacious rooms and halls now closed. We had taken shelter in the only habitable room, an immense kitchen, which had been plastered all over to keep the rats out. The big, white walls were covered with whips, guns, horns, etc., and in the large fireplace a brushwood fire was burning, throwing strange lights around the corners of the dismal room. We would sit in front of the fire every night, our hounds stretched in every available space between our feet, dreaming and barking in their sleep, until, getting drowsy, we would climb to our rooms and slip into our beds shivering.

It had been freezing hard that day and we were sitting as usual in front of the fire, watching a hare and two partridges being roasted for dinner, and the savory smell sharpened our appetites.

"It will be awfully cold going to bed to-night," said Jules.

"Yes, but there will be plenty of ducks to-morrow morning," I replied indifferently.

The servant had set our plates at one end of the table and those of the servants at the other.

"Gentlemen, do you know it is Christmas eve?" she asked.

We certainly did not; we never looked at the calendar.

"That accounts for the bells ringing all day," said Jules. "There is midnight service to-night."

"Yes, sir; but they also rang because old Fournel is dead."

Fournel was an old shepherd, well known in the country. He was ninety-six years old and had never known a day's sickness until a month ago, when he had taken cold by falling into a pool on a dark night and had died of the consequences.

"If you like," said Jules, "we will go and see these poor people after dinner."

The old man's family consisted of his grandson, fifty-eight years old and the latter's wife, one year younger. His children had died years ago. They lived in a miserable hut at the entrance of the village.

Perhaps Christmas eve in a lonely castle was an incentive, at all events we were very talkative that night. Our dinner had lasted way into the night and long after the servant had left us, we sat there smoking pipe after pipe, narrating old experiences, telling of past revels and the surprises of the morrow which followed our adventures. Our solitude had brought us closer together and we exchanged those confidences which only intimate friends can.

"I am going to church, sir," said the servant, re-appearing.

"What, so soon!" exclaimed Jules.

"It lacks only a quarter of twelve, sir."

"Let us go to church too," said Jules. "The midnight service is very attractive in the country."

I assented and having wrapped ourselves up we started for the village. It was bitterly cold, but a clear, beautiful night. We could hear the peasants' wooden shoes on the crisp, frozen earth and the church bell ringing in the distance. The road was dotted here and there with dancing lights. It was the peasants carrying lanterns, lighting the way for their wives and children. As we approached the village, Jules said:

"Here is where the Fournels live, let us go in."

We knocked repeatedly, but in vain. A neighboring peasant informed us that they had gone to church to pray for their father.

"We will see them on our way back," said Jules.

The service had begun when we entered the church. It was profusely decorated with small candles, and to the left, in a small chapel, the birth of

Christ was represented by wax figures, pine brush forming a background. The men stood with bowed heads, and the women, kneeling, clasped their hands in deep devotion. After a few minutes Jules said:

"It is stifling in here, let us go outside."

We left the shivering peasants to their devotions and regaining the deserted road, we resumed our conversation. We had talked so long that the service was over when we came back to the village. A small ray of light filtered through the Fournels' door.

"They are watching their dead," said Jules. "They will be pleased to see us."

We went in. The low, dark room was lighted only by a smoking candle, placed in the middle of the large, coarse table, under which a bread bin had been built, taking up the whole length of it. A suffocating odor of roasted blood pudding pervaded every corner of the room. Seated face to face, were Fournel and his wife, a gloomy and brutish expression on their faces. Between the two, a single plate of the pudding, the popular dish on Christmas eve, out of which they would take turns in cutting a piece off, spread it on their bread and munch in silence. When the man's glass was empty, the woman would fill it out of an earthen jar containing cider.

They asked us to be seated and to "join them," but at our refusal they continued to munch. After a few minutes' silence Jules said:

"Well, Anthime, so your grandfather is dead!"

"Yes, sir, he died this afternoon."

The woman snuffed the candle in silence and I, for the want of something to say, added:

"He was quite old, was he not?"

"Oh, his time was up," she answered; "he was no earthly use here."

An invincible desire to see the old man took possession of me and I asked to see him. The two peasants suddenly became agitated and exchanged questioning glances. Jules noticed this and insisted. Then the man with a sly, suspicious look, asked:

"What good would it do you?"

"No good," said Jules; "but why will you not let us see him?"

"I am willing," said the man, shrugging his shoulders, "but it is kind of unhandy just now."

We conjectured all sorts of things. Neither of them stirred. They sat there with eyes lowered, a sullen expression on their faces seeming to say: "Go away."

"Come, Anthime, take us to his room," said Jules with authority.

"It's no use, my good sir, he isn't there any more," said the man resolutely.

"Where is he?" said Jules.

The woman interrupted, saying:

"You see, sir, we had no other place to put him so we put him in the bin until morning." And having taken the top of the table off, she held the candle near the opening. We looked in and sure enough, there he was, a shriveled gray mass, his gray hair matted about his face, barefooted and rolled up in his shepherd's cloak, sleeping his last sleep among crusts of bread as ancient as himself.

His grandchildren had used as a table the bin which held his body!

Jules was indignant, and pale with anger, said:

"You villians! Why did you not leave him in his bed?"

The woman burst into tears and speaking rapidly:

"You see, my good gentlemen, it's just this way. We have but one bed, and being only three we slept together; but since he's been so sick we slept on the floor. The floor is awful hard and cold these days, my good gentlemen, so when he died this afternoon we said to ourselves: 'As long as he is dead he doesn't feel anything and what's the use of leaving him in bed? He'll be just as comfortable in the bin.' We can't sleep with a dead man, my good gentlemen!—now can we?"

Jules was exasperated and went out banging the door, and I after him, laughing myself sick.

SYMPATHY

E WAS going up the Rue des Martyrs in a melancholy frame of mind, and in a melancholy frame of mind she also was going up the Rue des Martyrs. He was already old, nearly sixty, with a bald head under his seedy tall hat, a gray beard, half buried in a high shirt collar, with dull eyes, an unpleasant mouth, and yellow teeth.

She was past forty, with thin hair over her puffs, and with a false plait; her linen was doubtful in color, and she had evidently bought her unfashionable dress at a hand-me-down shop. He was thin, while she was chubby. He had been handsome, proud, ardent, full of self-confidence, certain of his future, and seeming to hold in his hands all the trumps with which to win the game on the green table of Parisian life, while she had been pretty, sought after, fast, and in a fair way to have horses and carriages, and to win the first prize on the turf of gallantry among the favorites of fortune.

At times, in his dark moments, he remembered the time when he had come to Paris from the country, with a volume of poetry and plays in his portmanteau, feeling a supreme contempt for all the writers who were then in vogue, and sure of supplanting them. She often, when she awoke in the morning to another day's unhappiness, remembered that happy time when she had been launched on to the world, when she already saw that she was more sought after than Marie G. or Sophie N. or any other woman of that class, who had been her companions in vice, and whose lovers she had stolen from them.

He had had a splendid start. Not, indeed, as a poet and dramatist, as he had hoped at first, but by a series of scandalous stories which had made a sensation on the boulevards, so that after an action for damages and several duels, he had become "our witty and brilliant colleague who, etc., etc."

She had had her moments of extraordinary good luck, though she certainly did not eclipse Marie P. or Camille L., whom men compared to Zenobia or Ninon de l'Enclos. Still her fortune caused her to be talked about in the newspapers, and brought about a revolution at certain *tables d'hôte* in Montmartre. But one fine day, the newspaper in which our brilliant and witty colleague used to write became defunct, having been killed by a much more cynical rival, thanks to the venomous pen of a much more brilliant and witty colleague. Then, the insults of the former having become pure and simple mud-pelting, his style soon became worn out, to the disgust of the public, and the celebrated "Mr. What's-his-name" had great difficulty in getting on to some minor paper, where he was transformed into the obscure penny-a-liner "Machin."

Now one evening the quasi-rival of Marie P. and Camille L. had fallen ill, and consequently into pecuniary difficulties, and the prostitute "No-matter-who" was now on the lookout for a dinner, and would have been only too happy to get it at some *table d'hôte* in Montmartre. Machin had had a return of ambition with regard to his poetry and his dramas, but then, his verses of former days had lost their freshness, and his youthful dramas appeared to him to be childish. He would have to write others, and, by Jove! he felt himself capable of doing it, for he had plenty of ideas and plans in his head, and he could easily demolish many successful writers if he chose to try! But then, the difficulty was, how to set about it, and to find the necessary leisure and time for thought. He had his daily bread to gain, and something besides; his coffee, his game of cards and other little requirements, and the incessant writing article upon article barely sufficed for that, and so days and years went by, and Machin was Machin still.

She also longed for former years, and surely it could not be so very hard to find a lover to start her on her career once more, for many of her female friends, who were not nearly so nice as she, had unearthed one, so why should not she be equally fortunate? But there, her youth had gone and she had lost all her chances; other women had their fancy men, and she had to take men on every day at reduced prices, and so day after day and months and years passed, and the prostitute No-matter-who had remained the prostitute No-matter-who.

Often, in a fit of despondency, he used to say to himself, thinking of some one who had succeeded in life: "But, after all, I am cleverer than that fellow."

And she always said to herself, when she got up to her miserable, daily round, when she thought of such and such a woman, who was now settled in life: "In what respect is that slut better than I am?"

And Machin, who was nearly sixty, and whose head was bald under his shabby tall hat, and whose gray beard was half buried in a high shirt collar, who had dull eyes, an unpleasant mouth, and yellow teeth, was mad with his fellow-men, while the prostitute No-matter-who, with thin hair over her puffs, and with a false plait, with linen of a doubtful color, and with her unfashionable dress, which she had evidently bought at a *hand-me-down* shop, was enraged with society.

Ah! Those miserable, dark hours, and the wretched awakenings! That evening he was more than usually wretched, as he had just lost all his pay for the next month, that miserable stipend which he earned so hardly by almost editing the newspaper, for three hundred francs* a month, in a brothel.

And she, too, that evening, was in a state of semi-stupidity, as she had had too many glasses of beer, which a charitable female friend had given her. She was almost afraid to go back to her room, as her landlord had told her in the morning that unless she paid the fortnight's back rent that she owed at the rate of a franc a day, he would turn her out of doors and keep her things.

---

* $60.

This was the reason why they were both going up the Rue des Martyrs in a melancholy frame of mind. There was scarcely a soul in the muddy streets; it was getting dark and beginning to rain, and the drains smelt horribly.

He passed her, and in a mechanical voice she said: "Will you not come home with me, you handsome, dark man?"

"I have no money," he replied.

But she ran after him, and catching hold of his arm, she said: "Only a franc; that is nothing."

And he turned round, looked at her, and seeing that she must have been pretty, and that she was still stout (and he was fond of fat women), he said: "Where do you live? Near here?"

"In the Rue Lepic."

"Why! So do I."

"Then that is all right, eh? Come along, old fellow."

He felt in his pockets and pulled out all the money he found there, which amounted to thirteen sous,* and said: "That is all I have, upon my honor!"

"All right," she said; "come along."

And they continued their melancholy walk along the Rue des Martyrs, side by side now, but without speaking, and without guessing that their two existences harmonized and corresponded with each other, and that by huddling up together, they would be merely accomplishing the acme of their twin destinies.

---

* Thirteen cents.

JULOT'S OPINION

THE Duchess Huguette de Lionzac was very much infatuated with herself, but then she had a perfect right to be, for who, in her place, would not have shown a spice of conceit? There was no success she had wished for that she had not attained. She had received a medal for sculpture at the Salon, and at the Exhibition des Excessives, she had shown a water-color which looked eccentric even there.

She had published a collection of poems which was crowned by the French Academy, and a small volume of "Rhythmic Prose" of which the "Revue de Demain" said that it showed "a most subtle and evanescent execution of fugitive pieces and was sure to descend to posterity." When she acted in private theatricals, some exclaimed: "It is better than the 'Comédie Française,'" while others, who were more refined, went so far as to utter the supreme praise: "Better than the 'Théâtre Libre.'"

At one time there had been a report, which had been propagated by the newspapers, that she was

going to come out at the "Opéra Comique," in a part
that had been written especially for her extraordinary
voice, for it appeared that Massenet would not hear
of anybody else for the part.

She was the circus-rider, Miss Edith, who, under
that assumed name, gave a unique and never-to-be-
forgotten exhibition of horsemanship. What cheers
there were, and what quantities of flowers covered
the arena! And one must not forget that this was
before a *paying public!*

Then, it was notorious that she had carried off
the lovers of several celebrated courtesans, which
was not one of the smallest of her triumphs, for she
had chosen as her rivals some of those terrible and
hitherto unconquered women, of whom it was said:

"Oh! When she has got hold of a man, she does
not let him go again. She has some secrets that
attach them to her."

There was, therefore, nothing surprising in the
fact, that the Duchess Huguette should have been so
proud of so many victories, and in such various
sports; but now, for the first time, a doubt had entered her mind. In turning over the "Notules Psy-
chologiques" * of her favorite novel-writer, she had
just read these two sentences, which disturbed her:

"If anyone wishes to excel in an art, he must have
gained a living by it."

"What pleases us in a woman of the world who
gives herself up to debauchery, is the contrast between what she is and what she would like to be."

And she asked herself, whether she could really

---

* Psychological Notes.

have lived by those arts in which she excelled, and whether the successes that she had obtained did not chiefly depend on her charm of a woman of the world, who wished to be what she was not. The last *whether*, especially, made her anxious. For was not it precisely that special charm which had given her an advantage over courtesans who employed secrets.

Would she have been victorious if she had been deprived of that weapon? How could she find out?

"And yet," she said to herself, "I must know, for everything depends on this point. If I can win the game without playing that card, I am sure of all my other triumphs, my mind will be easy then, whatever it may cost."

She consulted her old godfather, Viscount Hugues de Pierras, on the subject, and, after a few complimentary words, as she had begged him to be sincere, he said:

"Good heavens! my dear child, I must confess that your psychologist is not altogether wrong, nor your apprehensions either. I have before now left many learned mistresses for women who were not in the least learned, and who pleased me all the better on that account. But that did not prevent the mistresses I had sacrificed from being women of incomprehensible talents in spite of their defeat. But what does that matter? It ought to be enough for you that you conquer, without troubling yourself about the means by which you obtain your victory. I do not suppose that you have any pretensions to being a *virtuosa* in—"

"In everything, yes. Excuse me godfather, I

have such pretensions. And what I ask of you, is the means of obtaining absolute proof that my pretensions are justified."

"Hum! Hum!" the Viscount said, in some embarrassment, "I do not know of any means, my dear child, unless we get together a jury."

"Please do not joke about it!" Huguette exclaimed.

"I am perfectly serious."

"I am very serious also, I assure you, I think that a jury—"

"Composed of whom? Of men of the world, I suppose? commonly called *Fine Gueule*." *

"And what does this Julot do?"

"Oh! really, Duchess, you force me to speak of persons and things, which—"

"Yes, yes, I force you to; we understand that. But tell me! Bluntly, without mincing matters, if necessary. You know that I have no objection to that sort of thing, so go on. Do not keep me in suspense like this. I am burning with curiosity. What does Julot do?"

"Very well, little volunteer, if you insist on knowing, I will tell you. Julot, generally called *Fine Gueule*, is a trier of women."

"I beg your pardon?"

"I will explain it to you. There are a few of us old amateurs in Paris, who are too old and impatient to hunt for truffles, but who want them of such and such a flavor, exactly to our taste. Now Julot knows our tastes, our various fancies, and he undertakes—"

"Capital! capital!"

---

* Epicure. *Gueule* is a vulgarism.